Jasper knelt before her and put his hand over her now tightly clasped hands. "If there's something  **don't keep it from**

Sadie only met his eyes

"You can trust me," he s

After long seconds where she blinked some more and bit her lower lip, he thought she'd relent and start talking. But then she brushed his hand off hers and stood, forcing him to move back.

Moving away, she turned to face Jasper, a guarded mask now, hands at her sides, chin lifted, eyes fierce with determination. "I hired you to solve a murder. Beyond that, nothing else about me is any of your business."

He half admired and half cursed her. She stuck to her objective and didn't trust easily. She didn't know him very well and had only hired him to help with the murder investigation. She didn't argue that the attack could be unrelated. She didn't deny there might be more she wasn't saying.

He wouldn't rest until he had the whole truth.

* * *

Be sure to check out the next books in this miniseries.

Cold Case Detectives: Powerful investigations, unexpected passion...

* * *

If you're on Twitter, tell us what you think of Harlequin Romantic Suspense! #harlequinromsuspense

Dear Reader,

I'm excited about the next release in my Cold Case Detectives series! I was thrilled to start with *A Wanted Man*, where Kadin Tandy spearheads an organization dedicated to catching killers. Writing murder mysteries is a new venture for me, much different than my military-hero All McQueen's Men series. But equally suspenseful and full of romance and the happy endings we all crave.

I love something special about each of my stories, and in *Runaway Heiress* (aside from the catchy title!), I grew quite attached to the heroine's strength. She's on the run from a dangerous man and offers trust sparingly. The hero has to prove himself worthy before she gives her heart. Their growth together is rewarding and they make a lovely couple. So get cozy and enjoy reading my latest story.

Happy reading!

Jennie

RUNAWAY HEIRESS

Jennifer Morey

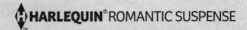
HARLEQUIN® ROMANTIC SUSPENSE

Recycling programs
for this product may
not exist in your area.

ISBN-13: 978-1-335-47454-4

Runaway Heiress

Printed in U.S.A.

Two-time RITA® Award nominee and Golden Quill Award winner **Jennifer Morey** writes single-title contemporary romance and page-turning romantic suspense. She has a geology degree and has managed export programs in compliance with the International Traffic in Arms Regulations (ITAR) for the aerospace industry. She lives at the foot of the Rocky Mountains in Denver, Colorado, and loves to hear from readers through her website, jennifermorey.com, or Facebook.

Books by Jennifer Morey

Harlequin Romantic Suspense

Cold Case Detectives
A Wanted Man
Justice Hunter
Cold Case Recruit
Taming Deputy Harlow
Runaway Heiress

The Coltons of Texas
A Baby for Agent Colton

Ivy Avengers
Front Page Affair
Armed and Famous
One Secret Night
The Eligible Suspect

All McQueen's Men
The Secret Soldier
Heiress Under Fire
Unmasking the Mercenary
Special Ops Affair
Seducing the Accomplice
Seducing the Colonel's Daughter

Visit Jennifer's Author Profile page at Harlequin.com, or jennifermorey.com, for more titles.

For Mom

Prologue

Sadie Moreno sat across from Steven Truscott at a downtown Jackson Hole twenty-four-hour diner. In his sleek black suit and tie with pristine white dress shirt and medium brown hair brushed back to hide signs of recession, he made a handsome picture. Once upon a time she might have attempted to break through his staunch wall of professionalism for a more personal relationship. Life had intervened.

"Do you have news for me?" He usually didn't come to see her unless he did.

In the next instant, her spirits dimmed along with his grim mouth line.

"The last lead didn't produce anything, Sadie. Bernie's case has gone cold."

He'd been keeping tabs on the progress of the investigation so she wouldn't have to. So that was why he'd come all this way. He knew how this would devastate her. "But it was so promising."

"I'm sorry. They've got nothing now. No evidence. No witnesses. Not a single shred of anything."

Disappointment crushed her. "What are they going to do now?" There had to be something they could do.

"We'll just have to wait for something new to come up."

The injustice soured and rotted hope.

She tapped her sunglasses on the table. Turning away from Steven's sympathetic, silver gaze, she saw nothing as she thought of Bernie King. He didn't deserve to die the way he had. The first homeless person she'd helped, he had become her close friend. He'd spent the longest in her program, but only because she wanted to help him as much as she could, giving him a place to live while he got back on his feet.

She bobbed her crossed leg, jeans tucked into a pair of calf-high leather boots. How could she endure yet another tragedy she was powerless to avenge?

A waitress came with water and Steven's coffee.

She was too upset to ingest anything.

"The case has gone cold, that's all." He sipped his coffee. "The police won't give up. We will just have to be patient."

Sadie didn't do patience very well, especially when someone close to her had been brutally killed. It could be years—or never—before any more leads emerged.

"I can't sit around and wait." She had to do something. "The location of the body should tell them something, shouldn't it?"

Bernie had been shot and his body moved to Warren Park, far from downtown San Francisco. Too far to walk anyway. Bernie had recently moved to the new facility she'd constructed, well on his way to rebuilding his life, transitioning from homeless to home. He had planned to buy a car the next day, and had been within weeks of moving to his own apartment. She couldn't stand it that he'd been ambushed, that his life had been stolen, his new life. Slaughtered dreams.

Steven sipped his coffee again. She sensed his doubt in police finding new leads anytime soon. That was why he'd come all this way. He had to meet her in person to deliver the bad news.

"Just because he was homeless doesn't mean his life mattered less." She almost spoke to herself. So many people lacked awareness about the homeless. The homeless weren't parasites to be cleansed from the community. They were live, breathing human beings who once had a life not much different than those who passed them on the streets with barely a glance. Out of sight out of mind, right?

"Don't forget about him, Steven," she said.

With a resigned look, he put down his cup. "His case isn't being treated any differently than someone who had a home. The killer did a good job of hiding evidence. It's going to take some smart detective work to catch him."

She knew that. Bernie's killer hadn't left any evidence, no trace evidence. While she debated whether his case was treated any differently than if he'd been a contributing figure in his community, she had to acknowledge the prowess of his killer. But damn it, why did he have to die on the brink of getting his life back on track? The injustice choked her up.

"Bernie was like family to me." Many of her clients were, but Bernie was special. He was the reason she started the Revive Center. When she met him on the street, she had taken him to the hotel where she was staying, not knowing then what she'd do. Give him money, but he needed more than money. He needed help.

Born, the Revive Center.

She and Bernie had become very close since then. After a long rehabilitation, he'd gone to college and got a job. Success. She wouldn't say he was as happy as he could be. He still felt his tragic losses, but he'd been well on his way to a good life.

"What you do is an inspiration to humanity, Sadie. You put your whole heart into your organization. You've come a long way in rebuilding your own life, too. Hell, no wonder why you gravitated to them. Even with all your money, you're not much different than them."

She laughed despite her sadness. Sometimes she forgot how well Steven knew her.

"Don't jeopardize your new beginning by involving yourself in Bernie's case," Steven said. "That's my job."

"I have to do something." She could not stand by and let him do all the work, especially now.

"Sadie…" His voice trailed off on a warning tone.

"Don't try to talk me out of it. You always do that. You're too cautious. No one will recognize me."

He cocked his head that gave his eyes a sardonic look. "The car?"

"It's a gray sedan." But she knew he had her there. "Money is the one thing I have in common with my father," she said ruefully. "I kept the car because if I need money, I can sell it."

"Fine, leave it in the garage."

She felt safe here. No one knew her. Aside from the fun of it—and the defiance of her situation, she drove the car to keep the oil from pooling in the engine, but she could have her staff do that. "I don't drive it that much, Steven. I'm careful with that. But for you I won't drive it until my ex is either dead or in jail." Small chance of that happening. He'd evaded both Steven's secret investigating and the police. He'd likely be killed by one of his own enemies before law enforcement caught him, given the type of activities he practiced.

Steven smiled softly, fondly at her easy obedience. She always listened to him.

"You enjoy money for much different reasons than your father. Don't compare yourself to him." He'd always been sympathetic to her plight. She was lucky to have him as a friend. "I do have to say, though, he'd implode if he saw you in flannel."

She returned his fond smile. "I spent a lot of years repressing who I really was just to please him." She'd been a peacekeeper, allowing her father to mold her into his corporate minion, his clone—at great expense to her soul. She looked down at her flannel shirt. "This is my rebellion."

His regard warmed. "You wear it well."

"I wear little black dresses better."

He didn't even falter with the image she must have given him. "He'd implode seeing you in that, too."

"Then it's good for my rebellion. It took a lot of therapy to break out of my old pattern. I'm enjoying the fruit of my labor." Her father had expected her to dress business at all times. And for social engage-

ments, nothing sexy had been permitted. Ultra con-
servative attire all the way down the line. No lingerie,
no short skirts, no makeup and no jeans. It felt like
breaking out of prison getting away from that.

"Are you running from your ex or your father?"
he asked.

"Both." Her ex had given her a reason to run, not
one she welcomed but having to escape him had
opened her eyes to a lot of things—namely her father's control over her.

"Then continue to enjoy it. Just stay out of the investigation and keep the car in your garage. Please. I
know it's been a long time and you feel safe here, but
don't forget the kind of man your ex is."

She stared at him, unable to deny anything he said.
Maybe she had been a little careless driving her car,
but how could she stand idly by? But he was right. She
had to be careful not to risk all she'd worked so hard
to build. She'd escaped her ex—and in the process her
father. Ever since then she'd managed to stay hidden.
Five years had passed. She'd like to stay hidden. And
Steven had experience where she did not.

"All right. I won't intervene." Steven felt like a
brother to her. And he'd helped her so much. Faith-
fully and consistently. She could count on him no matter what. But he had to understand that she had to do
something.

She looked at him in a way to convey that without words.

As she anticipated, he read her. "Sadie…?"

"I won't intervene," she reiterated. "I'll be cautious.
But I've been thinking maybe I should hire a private
investigations agency."

To her delight he didn't reject the suggestion. His brow rose a bit as though he liked the idea. "Good thinking. I'll check into a few."

"I already found one." She put her hand on the overturned printout she'd put on the table when they'd first arrived and slid it toward him. "Dark Alley Investigations specializes in cases like Bernie's."

Steven turned the page over and with a glance at her first, read the printout of the About page of the agency's website. After a few moments, his gaze returned to her. "This would draw too much attention to you. The guy who runs this is an international celebrity."

"That's exaggerating a bit much, Steven. International?"

"National, international, it doesn't matter. He's growing in popularity. Even I've heard of him. You could be caught on camera. It's too dangerous."

"They're the best. They could solve Bernie's case quickly."

Seeing he wasn't convinced, Sadie had to reassure him. "Safety is one of their number one protocols. They just hired a new head of security. Jamie Knox. There's a paragraph about him on the printout."

Steven didn't move to read.

"I'd be safer with them than I am now," she said.

"Are you questioning the qualifications of the team I sent you?"

"No." She shook her head. "Not at all. Don't think that way. This is murder we're talking about. It goes beyond security." She needed an expert detective *and* security. She saw him digest that and begin to understand.

"It sounds like you've made up your mind," he finally said.

She realized just then that she had. "Yes. I wasn't sure before, but now that you've told me Bernie's case has gone cold, I am."

"If you're looking for my approval, you don't need it. I trust your instinct. Just keep me informed and don't shut out my team. They communicate with me. I don't want anything to happen to you, Sadie."

He was so sweet. "Your girlfriend is a lucky lady."

"I'm the lucky one. How'd you know I was seeing someone? I just met her."

"I didn't." Sadie hadn't thought a man like him would be single long.

Taking another drink of his coffee, Steven took out his wallet. "I should get going. I have a late flight."

"No, no. I'll get this," she said, letting go of her sunglasses to dig for her wallet in her diamond-studded clutch. She didn't care how much it clashed with her flannel.

"I can afford my own coffee." He shook his head, putting down a bill and then standing. "I pity the man who falls in love with you."

She dropped her wallet. Her ability to pay threatened his ego? He must be teasing. She could be pushy when she wanted something, but she let him get away with paying.

Standing as well, she picked up her sunglasses and clutch, then stepped to him and touched a friendly kiss on his cheek. "Thank you. I know you mean that as a compliment."

He put his hand on her upper arm and returned her

kiss with one of his own on her cheek. "You're one of a kind, Sadie Moreno. Stay safe."

That's what he always said. *Stay safe.*

She watched him walk away, hoping she could do as he wished.

The next morning, Sadie drove toward a parking space in front of Dark Alley Investigations. It was an elegant, historical but unassuming building. She wasn't sure what she expected but this wasn't it. Something bigger. Taller. And more corporate. The white stone and trimmed, tinted windows gave no hint of the grisly crimes this agency solved. It could be a department store or an upscale boutique.

Two men walked out of the front as she parked, both stopping when they saw her car. She climbed out, her spiky boots giving her even more height as she straightened and started walking to the sidewalk. She'd forgone her flannel for this meeting. Maybe her meeting with Steven had inspired her to dress in a way that would make her father cringe. Sexy. He'd call it something else, but Sadie didn't dress inappropriately. She just looked good.

The big Swiss-looking man stared without blinking, giving her an unexpected spark. He liked what he saw, apparently. It had been a long time since a man made her feel this way, and with only a look. She found herself also compelled to stare, taken in by his Viking good looks. His thick blond hair waved slightly in a breeze and she could see the brilliance of his blue eyes from here. She barely noticed the other man, who put on sunglasses, his military short black hair and a dark suit made him look like a star in *Men in Black*.

Is this what all the Dark Alley detectives looked like? My-oh-my, was she in for a treat. Before she let her excitement get too carried away, she scanned the area as she always did when she went out in public, checking for anything suspicious. She saw nothing unusual. A few people walked along the street and didn't pay her any attention. A man glanced over at her car but after a few seconds moved on. A few cars passed on the street.

She started walking around the front of the car when she noticed an approaching car slow. Both the driver and the passenger were watching her. That caused her some alarm. Had they recognized her? She stopped, wondering if she should get back into her car. She looked for a place to get out of sight. Only the Dark Alley Investigations building would give her that.

She started to turn when she saw the man in the passenger seat of the dark sedan draw a gun.

She screamed and tried to duck for cover, but the man fired and a bullet slammed through her. The impact sent her jolting backward. She hit the ground hard, vaguely aware of the Viking rushing to her and his partner firing back at the passing car before everything went black.

Chapter 1

Sitting on an uncomfortable hospital room chair with his legs outstretched, elbows on the armrests and fingers teepeed together, Jasper Roesch watched Sadie Moreno sleep. Rest in unconsciousness, more like. She'd gone through twelve hours of surgery and a day of intensive care before the doctors rolled her into a recovery room. She'd survive her gunshot wound, which had narrowly missed her heart.

The tall, slender Spanish-looking woman had long manicured nails. The nursing staff had put her ample head of jet-black hair up. Her Angelina Jolie lips were pale and dark circles shadowed the skin beneath her eyes. But even the signs of her close brush with death didn't diminish her beauty.

Three knocks on the door brought him turning to see a well-dressed man with neatly trimmed and combed brown hair and nickel-gray eyes.

"Jasper Roesch from Dark Alley Investigations?" the man queried.

Jasper stood and faced the man. "That's me. And you are?"

"Steven Truscott." He stepped forward. "Sadie's security officer." After a brief shake of hands, the man looked over at Sadie. "She said she was going to hire one of you."

"I figured she had a reason for showing up at DAI." And that reason ended up shooting her. "How did you find out she was here?"

"The doctor called her home and her estate manager notified me." Steven said. "Your agency called before the hospital. The estate manager passed the number on to me. Kadin Tandy said you were here watching over Sadie until I arrived."

The founder of DAI had let Jasper know Sadie's security officer would be coming to the hospital to explain a homeless man's murder case. He'd thought it odd someone like that would show up rather than a family member.

"I was assured her safety would be your top priority," Steven said. "I can't be with her all the time."

"Where did you come from?"

"Sadie runs an organization for the homeless. She has three facilities, one in New York, one in Dallas and headquarters in San Francisco. I work intermittently at her headquarters."

"Her address is in Wyoming."

"She works remotely."

He did, too, if he only worked *intermittently*. Many people worked from their homes, but something about this didn't add up. Sadie worked from her home but the one person who came to see her at the hospital is her head of security who works remotely as she did.

"She prefers reclusiveness," Steven added, as though he felt he needed an excuse. Jasper would have questioned him further if he hadn't turned a grave face to Sadie.

"I worried something like this would happen," Steven said. "She's been after the police to catch Bernie's killer. I kept telling her to stay out of the investigation. A woman like her stands out in a crowd."

Who *wouldn't* be after police to catch the criminal who'd killed someone close to them? Bernie, he presumed, was one of her homeless men and the victim of murder that had brought her to DAI's door.

"Is there a reason she should stay out of the investigation?" Did she just want to avoid the public? Jasper hadn't heard of her so she couldn't be so famous for that to be a threat.

"As I said, she prefers to remain reclusive."

The more he talked with this man, the more suspicious he became. He questioned a lot of criminals, many of them experts at lying. Steven was no expert, at least not when it came to Sadie. Maybe her being shot had caught him off guard.

"Has anyone notified her family?" he asked.

"I'm the closest she has to family. Her father passed several years ago. She was his sole heir." He eyed Jasper as though sharing a piece of gossip. "Holdings in an oil and refining corporation." So, Sadie had inherited her wealth, but hid herself from the rest of civilization in Wyoming. Why?

"What about Bernie King?" Jasper asked. "Who is he to her?" For Sadie to hire DAI to investigate his murder meant she cared more than she might if Bernie was just another one of her homeless people.

"Bernie is a special friend."

Movement from the hospital bed shifted Jasper's concentration. Sadie began to open her eyes. He went to stand beside her, Steven going to the opposite side of the bed.

"Steven?"

"Yes, Sadie, I'm here."

Steven took her hand and held it while Sadie groggily smiled up at him. "I thought you went home."

"I did. But then someone from Dark Alley Investigations called and told me what happened."

Steven had been here recently? Jasper wondered if that was how the shooters had found her. He also noticed she had no accent. She looked Spanish but she must have been raised in the United States. He hadn't had time to dig into her background yet.

Sadie's brow twitched in confusion. Memory must elude her after enduring the trauma she had. She slowly turned her head and soft chocolate-brown eyes fringed with thick dark lashes found him. Their clear, dramatic beauty struck him. The unexpectedness made him clamp down on the attraction. She stared at him for endless seconds, confusion going to recollection and then purely personal observation.

"This is Jasper Roesch," Steven said. "The founder of DAI put him on Bernie's case."

"Oh." She stared at him awhile longer and then her brow twitched again. "Where am I?" She looked around the room.

"You were shot outside Dark Alley Investigations," Jasper said.

She stared at the ceiling awhile and then seemed to connect more dots. Driving up to DAI, getting out…

"I remember going there, but I don't remember what happened after I got out of my car."

"Someone drove by in a stolen car and shot at you," Jasper said. "There were two, a driver and a passenger. They both wore hats and sunglasses." Kadin had run the plates. The car had been found outside town.

"She was coming to see you about the murder of Bernie King," Steven said to Jasper. "He was a homeless man going through Sadie's reestablishment program at the Revive Center. There are no leads."

Jasper nodded a couple of times. "I've got a call in to the lead investigator. I'll meet with him and get all the details."

"I saw you in front of Dark Alley Investigations," Sadie said to Jasper.

"Yes. I saw you, too. You were a little hard to miss." While he meant because of the men who'd shot at her, she was hard to miss for an entirely different reason. He wondered if he revealed too much about how seeing her had impacted him. A moment of awareness of the effect of that first sight passed between them.

Jasper shook off the distraction. "The doctor said you'd be released by the end of the week, but you're going to need time to recover. I've got some security guards ready to accompany us to your house."

"I don't need security. I have my own." She looked up at Steven with a soft, exhausted smile that revealed how much she valued the man, maybe as a family member but probably more as her head of security. She valued his protection.

Jasper began to have a lot of questions. Sadie had

her own security, worked remotely and liked reclusiveness, although he didn't quite believe that. Steven had seemed to throw that out for Jasper.

What were the two of them hiding?

"Don't argue with the man, Sadie," Steven said. "You said it—this about more than murder."

"I'm only talking about getting us there safely. I'll evaluate what you've got on your property and decide if it's enough," Jasper said. "How's that?"

"Thank you," Sadie said tiredly. "I don't want to tell anyone they're out of a job."

He didn't care where the security came from, as long as it was solid. If hers met DAI requirements, they'd be fine. And they'd spare DAI the resources.

Sadie's head rolled to the side and she stared across the hospital room.

Steven put a reassuring hand on her arm, above the IV.

"Why would the killer come after me like that?" she asked. "I thought I was safe here."

"Shh," Steven said. "Get some rest."

Jasper had to agree the killer going after her seemed extreme. And why would more than one? There had been two in that car.

Jasper refrained from asking why she had to be safe. He'd like to question Sadie without her esteemed security head in the room.

"We'll discuss the case in detail once I've had a chance to review the file," he said.

"I hope you have better luck than the San Francisco police," Sadie said.

"If I relied on luck I wouldn't be working for DAI," Jasper said.

Her exhausted eyes found his and he felt her appreciation. "That's nice to hear, Mr. Roesch. It's upsetting to think Bernie's murder will go unsolved. He was so dear to me." Sadie paused, seeming to fall into thoughts of the dead man, who clearly was someone close to her. Did she get close to all of her homeless people or did only a few stand out?

"He had so much going for him," she gave him a hint by saying. "Not every homeless person is as successful as he would have been. He was so close to starting a new life."

And now whoever had killed him may have a reason to stop her from hiring an agency like DAI to investigate his murder.

"Who knew you were going to hire DAI services?" he asked.

"Just Steven. He talks to the police in San Francisco for me and comes to meet me occasionally."

For her? "Do you mean he's taken over keeping in contact with the police?"

"Yes."

"That's true now," Steven interjected, "But at first Sadie badgered the police to work harder on his case."

"And you think they didn't like the badgering?" Why had she withdrawn from her badgering? Why hand that task over to Steven? Was it a rich woman thing or would the answer tell him more about her reclusiveness?

"No. We thought she'd be safer if she let me look into things."

There was that hypersensitivity to safety again. He'd table that for a while. "Have you told anyone? Talked to anyone about the murder? Friends? Family?"

She stared at him as though thinking it an unusual question. "No."

"You don't talk to anyone other than Steven?" No one?

She looked up at the ceiling in thought and then back at him when something must have come to her. "I did tell my friends at The University Club. And my household staff all know."

He'd check all of them out when he arrived at her house. "University Club? What is that?"

"It's a women-only club in London," Steven said. "She flies there almost every month."

"What about closer to home?"

"I live in a very remote area near Jackson Hole. I do go to the golf club, but I'm not close to anyone there. I belong to an online social club and have gotten a little chatty with one of the other members."

As wealthy as she was, he wasn't surprised she belonged to elite groups, but an online social club sounded more mainstream.

"What kind of social club?"

"Dating. It's a special interest group, not only for the purpose of dating. I meet people who like to hike, that sort of thing."

"And you've met a man on this site?"

She nodded.

"Would that person have any reason to stop you from investigating Bernie's murder?"

She breathed a laugh and then winced, digging her head back into the pillow in pain.

"Easy, Sadie." Steven put his hand on her arm again, catching the edge of her hospital gown and moving it down her shoulder a fraction, revealing part of the bandage on her chest.

"No," she said to Jasper. "I haven't even met him yet."

"Would he have any other reason to go after you?"

She rolled her head from side to side, a silent response.

"What about events? Dates? Anything like that?"

"I attend all of my fund-raiser events. That keeps me very busy."

"Anyone come to mind at any of those who might be worth checking out?"

She thought awhile. "I don't know. I don't think so."

"We'll look into that more later. Right now, you should get some rest like your friend here suggested. You have a long road ahead of you for recovery. We'll head to your place as soon as you're released."

Sadie's brow creased slightly. *"We?"*

"I'll require a room close to where you sleep." He wouldn't negotiate this part. DAI had a strong policy on client safety.

"Where...what are you saying? You're going *home* with me?"

"Somebody almost succeeded in killing you, Ms. Moreno. Long-distance comms aren't going to work." Something much more up close and personal was her only option. "That's nonnegotiable."

As her incredible eyes softened into acquiescence, he almost dreaded what would happen when she regained her strength.

Sadie lived in the Tetons, soaring rocky peaks and steep forested slopes her view from every window of her English fairy-tale home. Landscaping painted the property near the house. The manicured lawns and gardens would be spectacular in the warmer months ahead. A ten-foot stone fence looked to surround the estate and a heavy iron gate prevented entry until the guard on duty recognized Sadie and let them onto the property. So far so good. He liked what he saw. No one had followed them, either.

He drove Sadie's Ferrari up the gravel driveway to a turning circle and gawked at the oolitic limestone mansion. He sat in the car and stared. With sash windows running the length of two stories and two turrets, he could have traveled through time to the old English countryside of Cotswold. Still transfixed with the Ferrari engine purring, he heard Sadie stir on the seat beside him. Weak as a kitten, the trip home had taxed her.

He climbed out from the low seat and went around to Sadie's side. She'd managed to get the door open but now cringed in pain.

"Let me help you." Jasper slipped his arms beneath her and alighted her from the car. She winced and put her forehead against his shoulder. He could imagine the kind of pain she was in.

As he approached the wood double doors, one of them opened and a man stepped out onto a stone porch that extended to the driveway with gardens surrounding it. Not a tall man, or large, he had a butler look to him with expressionless eyes, neatly combed-back thick brown hair and an unsmiling mouth. He wore tan slacks and a white dress shirt and had a radio clipped to his belt. He allowed Jasper to enter.

Inside, Jasper stepped onto a marble-floored entry with a waiting room off to one side.

"Right this way, Mr. Roesch," the man said. "I'm the estate manager, Finley."

No introductions necessary, Jasper mused. "Hello, Finley."

They entered the main living area, a large walnut-paneled room partially open to the second floor. The coffered ceiling contained ornate insets and the trim held equal detail. A curvy ivory sofa and chairs around a large square cocktail ottoman brightened up the room.

"What kind of electronic security does she have here?" he asked as he followed the man up a turreted stone stairway worthy of a princess.

"The property is surrounded by a ten-foot stone fence topped with barbed wire, cameras and move-ment detection devices. A single guard is stationed in the gatehouse and several others stay in one of the guesthouses. There's a small ops center there."

Impressive, but…why?

"Don't even think about making changes," Sadie said against his shoulder and neck.

He chuckled. "I wasn't…" Just the opposite.

"I don't want intrusive security. This is my home. My sanctuary. It's bad enough that the perimeter wall makes me feel like I'm in prison."

Didn't she think she already had intrusive secu-rity? "Noted." He wouldn't reveal his thoughts, not yet.

He took in the railing with a view of downstairs and then stepped into a wide arching stone hallway with nineteenth-century mirror, lantern-style lighting and floral crewel drapes. He passed a walnut-paneled library with vaulted ceiling and early evening light bringing out the colors of books. A Persian rug and old-fashioned seating were arranged before a fireplace. "Were you into castles and princesses as a kid?"

"What girl isn't?" she asked sleepily. She'd taken a painkiller a couple of hours ago.

Finley entered a room at the end of the hall. Rose, soft green and cream colors hit the eye first. Then the rich detail came out. The bed looked French, probably hand carved, and a toile fabric chair and ottoman were angled before six sash windows. An etched glass closet door was open to reveal a large walk-in closet with organized walnut shelves and more seating.

Finley pulled back the soft, downy covers. Jasper laid her down and her arms stayed around him as their gazes met. He couldn't look away and watched her eyes slide closed once, twice, three times, and then they didn't open. It had to be one of the sweetest sights he'd ever experienced.

"Your quarters are across the hall from the miss," Finley said. "Cook has prepared dinner. Where would you like it served?"

"Right in here." Jasper went to one of the pretty chairs and sat.

"Excuse me?"

Noticing Finley's alarm, he explained. "My first concern is for Sadie's safety. Best if you tell everyone that's nonnegotiable." He nodded toward his charge. "She's as vulnerable as she'll ever be in this condition. I won't take a single chance." He adjusted his seat. "In fact, why don't you bring a cot or something in here? I'll be sensitive to her need of privacy."

Finley seemed to smother a pleased smile. "Yes, sir."

"Where did she find you?" Jasper asked before the estate manager could turn to leave.

"I had to take classes on how to manage property like this," Finley said. "She sent our cook to culinary school."

"You didn't answer my question," Jasper said.

"No, sir, I didn't. I'll let the miss tell you."

"Why does she have such robust security?" Jasper asked. He got that protection was necessary when you were as wealthy as Sadie, but her fence seemed overboard. Was there a reason or was she just paranoid? She did not strike him as the paranoid type.

"It's remote country out here," Finley said.

"How many guards?"

"Eight."

Eight guards for a residential home. "I'd like to talk to the one in charge."

"That's Dwight Mitchel. Former Special Forces. Had a bit of financial trouble during his divorce. You wouldn't know it but Sadie has more heart than most in this world. When most first meet her they might get the wrong impression."

Jasper's impression had been based on attraction. Her car would stamp her as rich. Is that what Finley meant?

"She likes her money but she spends most of it on her charities." Finley looked up and around the no-expense-spared bedroom. "A first look at her doesn't reveal much about her other than appearances, but inside she's a well of humanity. You have to see her as she lives here to truly know her."

Comparing the Sadie he'd seen step out of a Ferrari to the one he met in the hospital, he had to agree. She was more than a rich, beautiful woman to Jasper, and just how much had him putting himself in check. Not only would living so remotely bore him to death, the idea of domesticating gave him hives.

Sometime later, Sadie roused. Jasper heard her and came awake, something he'd learned to do long ago. She moaned in pain. He rose up from the cot Finley had provided along with some bedding. Going to the bedside table, he helped her sit up against several pillows. While she overcame a wave of agony, he took a pain pill from its container and handed that to her along with a bottle of water.

After she swallowed and sat with her eyes closed awhile, she blinked and met his. "What are you doing up?"

"Watching over you."

At first a warm and content look drooped her eyes, but then she saw the cot. Her eyes opened more. "What is that?"

"I asked Finley to put it in here. I'm going to guard you until you can move around on your own."

"That isn't necessary. In fact, it's…it's improper and…presumptuous on your part!"

"I can see how you'd look at it that way. I can assure you my only motive is to protect you." And get to the bottom of her mystery—which included far more than Bernie King's murder.

"There's plenty of other rooms. Go stay in one of them."

"I will—when you're better and not this defenseless."

Her mouth opened and a few audible breaths stammered out. "Are you always this bullheaded?"

He grinned, a natural thing her petulant face and direct question brought on. "Yes. I have a reputation of solving cases faster than most. No one's ever been harmed under my watch, either."

"You've done this before?"

"Many times."

"What are you? A detective or a bodyguard?"

"I was a cop and a detective before I joined DAI. I often stayed with family of victims until I caught the killer."

She studied him thoughtfully. "That sounds unconventional."

"It is, which is why I like working for Kadin Tandy."

Her questions seemingly satisfied for now, she glanced down at herself, smoothing covers and patting the demure neckline of her nightgown. Then her hand stilled.

"How did I get into this?" she asked.

"One of your maids changed you. I waited outside the door. She said you woke but barely."

She blinked once, and again. Then her gaze traveled down his body and back up to his face, noticing him differently than before, less combative, much warmer. Even under the influence of painkillers she seemed rested, and as long as she didn't move, relatively pain free.

"Do you feel up to talking?" he asked.

"Sure. About what?"

He moved around the bed and went to the chairs,

sitting down. "Why don't we start with Bernie? Who was he to you and when is the last time you saw him?"

She rolled her head and looked up at the ceiling, obviously upset. "He's what made me start the Revive Center. I met him on a trip to San Francisco, one of my few and far between getaways. He was sitting against a building, holding a cup and nodding off. He'd been drinking. A policeman approached him and tried to order him to leave." She rolled her head to look at him. "Bernie chose an upscale spa to take his nap." She smiled fondly and looked back up at the ceiling. "I intervened. I don't know what made me. I took Bernie to my hotel, sat him down in the restaurant and gave him coffee and food. When the alcohol wore off, he told me his story. He lost his wife to cancer a few months ago, and then his daughter committed suicide, leaving him alone and facing a crisis he didn't have enough strength to handle."

Jasper let her have a few moments to her thoughts, feeling how deeply moved she'd been with Bernie. She showed him a glimpse of her true self, not the one hiding in Wyoming.

"On that particular trip I was scouting for a location for a business. I hadn't decided what kind of business yet, I only knew I wanted to be involved in some kind of charity. Animal rescue. Health. I hadn't thought of the homeless, but meeting Bernie made me realize how passionate I felt about them." She looked at Jasper again. "People will shove the homeless aside before they'll do anything to fix the problem. Where do people expect them to go? They wouldn't be in the street if they had somewhere else to go. Bernie had nowhere to go. He made me want to do something."

"Bernie stayed with you while you started the Revive Center?"

"I put him in rehab first. He had to quit drinking. Once he completed that, then I set him up in an apartment. He needed psychiatric care because of his losses. He did that pretty extensively for a few months. By then I had some space lined up and the apartment building under construction. I kept Bernie in his own apartment. We'd meet once a week so I could check on his progress. He slowly improved. We got to know each other very well."

She drifted off and Jasper would love to know what her last sentence had made her remember. How much had she told Bernie? Maybe Bernie—other than Steven—was the only other living soul who really knew Sadie Moreno from a remote area of Wyoming who seemed to have carried at least some of her past with her to her new life, namely, the Ferrari.

"Why did you move to Wyoming?" he asked.

Her rumination on the past ended and Jasper watched her eyes grow guarded as she looked at him. "I wanted to get away from the life my father had."

"What kind of life was that?"

"Rich." She looked away.

"Why do you have such tight security here?" he asked.

"I like to feel safe."

"Locking your doors doesn't do that?"

After a few seconds she met his eyes across the distance between the bed and the seating area. "What are your plans for the investigation? What will you do to start?"

Okay, that was all he'd get out of her for now. "I have a message in to the lead investigator. I'll talk to him first and ask for a copy of the file. Then I'll spend a fair amount of time researching that."

She nodded and then closed her eyes, the painkillers apparently taking effect.

Jasper stood. "I'll let you get some rest. I won't be far." He put a small, round device with a green call button down on the table, within her reach. "Press that and I'll be here."

"What is this?"

"A pager." He showed her the pager clipped to his belt.

Her eyes rose up to his and he felt her admiration along with her wryness. "A little over the top, isn't it?"

"For your security?" He grinned with his teasing. "Maybe."

She smiled slightly in return.

He left her, hoping he could get more information out of her security officer.

Dwight Mitchel met him in the drawing room, another princess caliber work of architecture and interior design. Incredible crown molding bordered a recessed white painted ceiling with a huge round and tan light fixture. Pretty, ivory diamond tufted back sofas and an armless settee with throw pillows in purple, green and orange surrounded an oval glass table on an irregularly striped area rug. Although more modern than other rooms in Sadie's home, the decor still held a decided English flair.

The guard wore jeans, combat boots and a gun harness over a black henley and stood near a drinks trolley, holding a bottle of sparkling water. A big Colonel Miles Quaritch from *Avatar*, he even had a scar on his right temple.

Jasper went to him and shook his hand.

"We've heard all about you," Dwight said with an unsmiling face.

"I'm not surprised."

"How can I help you?" It wasn't a cordial question. Jasper looked past this man's impassiveness and saw distrust.

"I'd like you to walk me through your procedures. Roles and responsibilities, that sort of thing."

"You don't have to worry, Mr. Roesch. Sadie's security is well covered."

"I need to be familiar with your protocols so I know what everyone will do in the event of an emergency, that's all. I have no issue with the security here. In fact, it seems rather excessive."

The ex-military man didn't falter. "We do regular patrols around the perimeter of the property. I can give you copies of the schedule. There are two guards posted in the mechanical room 24/7. We communicate via radio." He tapped his ear where a clear coiled wire disappeared into his shirt. "One guard at the gate. Cameras have eyes on the gate and the property inside the fenced area."

Jasper hadn't expected to be disappointed with the level of security. He did, however, need everyone on the security team to trust him. Taking out his wallet, he removed a business card.

"In case something happens. I'd like to be informed." He pointed to the radio. "Maybe you could get me one of those."

Dwight eyed him, scrutinizing him as though sizing him up, the most body language he'd seen from the man so far. "Aren't you a detective? You're helping the miss solve Bernie's murder case, isn't that right?"

"That is. But since the attempt on her life, my role has expanded. At Dark Alley Investigations, we take the safety of our clients very seriously."

"All good to know, Mr. Roesch, but we've got her safety taken care of. As long as she's in this house, it's my job to protect her, and I take *that* very seriously."

He could see that Sadie was in good hands, but the lack of trust could pose a problem.

What was it about Sadie that instilled so much loyalty? Everyone called her the miss. And everyone was fiercely protective of her, especially of her past, it appeared. What was going on with that? And did he really want to know? He should be relieved that he wouldn't have to worry about her security. He was here to solve a cold case, not satisfy curiosity over a woman. A beautiful woman. A stunning, warm, intriguing woman who stood apart from any other…

All the more reason to keep his distance. And his hands to himself.

"Why so much security?" Jasper asked.

"You'll have to ask the miss."

"I already did." Jasper left it at that. Dwight didn't seem like an ignorant man. He had to know Jasper was well aware that he and most likely everyone here protected Sadie against anyone learning about her past. And her past had nothing to do with Bernie King's murder.

Or did it?

Chapter 2

Two weeks later, Sadie was ready to step up her physical therapy. The doctor ordered her to rest for two weeks with walking and strength-building exercises and now she had the go-ahead to partially return to normal. Not full steam yet, but on her way.

She put on her suit with help from the maid Finley had hired. He always thought ahead like that. Ever since she'd found him and brought him to her facility, they'd grown close. He joined her program when the Revive Center was still under construction and she'd rented a large older home nearby. He'd been one of her more sensitive cases. He'd lived a normal life up until he lost his job and couldn't find another. The bank kicked him out of his home and he'd found himself homeless. Sadie had spent extra time with him and helped him back onto his feet. Even after he'd been offered a job, he'd turned it down and declared he wanted to serve her for a profession.

Sadie had argued with him. He could do anything he wanted. Why chose servitude?

"I was a waiter before I went to prison for drugs," he'd said.

Finley had a terrible addiction problem. Her center had addressed that first. He'd spent three months in rehabilitation before entering the Revive Program. By then the building had been complete. He had trouble finding a job with the felony on his record, and with the facility complete and pressure from Steven to keep a low profile, she had to return to Wyoming. She'd taken Finley with her and he'd studied how to manage a large house. He'd never given her a reason to regret doing so. And now he was like a brother to her. Of all who worked for her, she trusted him as much as Dwight, who'd been with her the longest.

Dwight had his own story of how he'd come to work for her. He had gone through hell in his divorce. Women could be as abusive as men. His ex was living proof of that. She had been verbally abusive and went after him for as much money as she could drain. She wasn't ambitious and definitely not a productive addition to any community. She just plain did not want to work. She wanted everyone else to pay her way. And Dwight had, up until Sadie had hired him a new lawyer. All that alimony went away real quick. The last Dwight had heard, his ex had found a new victim to bleed dry of heart and soul—and income.

Sadie had accumulated a group of fine individuals who only needed a second chance. Her clan was a lot like the group on *The Walking Dead*. Everyone came from different backgrounds but they were all very close and cared deeply about each other's welfare. While *The Walking Dead* group shared survival from zombies, hers shared survival from real, hard-hitting, life-altering circumstances.

Sadie stepped down the stairs into her indoor pool. Windows took up two walls, framed in pine logs and beams, showing off a panoramic view of the Tetons. Water trickled from a fountain into the pool. Tan-and-beige stone surrounded the pool and stone of differing texture and size made the walls. Dark wicker seating in three corners provided splashes of contrasting color, along with some trees and plants. On warm days the end window opened to an outdoor patio. She didn't spend much time out there. Something about outdoor patios demanded a crowd. She went out there only when she threw barbecues for the household staff.

As soon as she reached deeper water and tried to swim, sharp pain stopped her. She almost went under before regaining her footing.

"Finley said you were in here."

She turned in the water to see Jasper coming down the stairs in swimming trunks. Finley must have hooked him up with those. But it wasn't the swim trunks that tickled her heartstrings. His rippling chest and abdomen. How that had her senses singing. Jasper…wow. Nice.

She'd seen little of him as she recovered, spending much of her time resting in her room or the library. He'd established a rapport with the lead detective working Bernie's case and studied the file. She'd heard him on the phone a couple of times, asking questions, focusing on where the body had been found and what witnesses saw. So far he hadn't progressed any further than the San Francisco police, but he'd asked questions and looked in directions no one else had yet. Something would develop soon. She felt confident of that, and in him.

"Are you sure it's not too soon to start rehab?"

"Doctor said I should get moving as soon as possible."

"Then let me help you ease into it." He stood next to her. "Why don't we start with floating on your back? You can move your arms, stretch your muscles."

"All right." That sounded delightful. She lay back on Jasper's arms. He created a shelf under her mid- and lower back. Her left arm was stiff and sore. She couldn't move it far. She rested her other hand on Jasper's lower back. "This is going to take a while."

"It'll probably be a few months before you're back up to full speed. We'll take baby steps."

She didn't miss how he said *we*, but she wondered if he knew he'd referred to months. Did he expect to be here that long? She didn't comment and floated for a while. He kept her head above water so all she had to do was concentrate on moving her left arm.

"You have an interesting staff," he said after a while.

Was he merely making conversation? Or was he fishing for information? "I'm very attached to them all."

"Your family must be envious."

"I have no family." She stared up at the pine ceiling, a circle of glass in the middle showing a sunny blue sky. "Didn't Steven tell you that at the hospital?"

"Your father passed, but what about your mother?"

More fishing? She always got anxious when people asked her about her past. She had to be careful what she said. "My mother died when I was born." She kept her emotion out of her response. Any talk of her mother usually spurred up some kind of sad thought.

"No other relatives?"

"No. None." She hoped she didn't sound rehearsed. And that he would stop asking personal questions.

"Do you miss him?" he asked.

She found that an odd question. Moving her gaze to him, she tried to see if he had a purpose, an ulterior motive, for doing so. But the detective in him kept his facial expression blank.

"No." She could speak honestly about this part. "My father was not an easy man to please."

"A lot of dads are like that. They want what's best for their kids. They want them to be successful. Sometimes that means pushing them hard."

"Well, then I'm a stereotypical rich kid when it comes to my father's expectations. He gave me everything I wanted as long as it was within his rules. I grew up in a mansion and had lots of toys. He planned for me to take over for him since I was in high school. He planned my career path, made me study business in college. Nothing I did was my choice. The only women he respected were the ones he worked with, and then only those who practically killed themselves for their jobs. Forty hours a week was never enough. And if you didn't work when you were home, you received more black marks. He didn't care about family. He only cared about making money. And if those who worked for him didn't feed his love for it, they didn't last long. He was never faithful in his personal relationships, either. He was the most selfish person I've ever known or even ever heard of."

"You resent him quite a bit," Jasper said.

"Resent?" She thought on that awhile. Resent didn't describe her feelings toward her father. "I might resent the way he dictated my life, but I don't resent him. I feel sorry for him sometimes. But mostly I'm…" She caught herself before she said the wrong thing. "I'm glad he's gone."

"So are a lot of people who worked for him, I bet."

She smiled up at him, floating on the water, slowly paddling one arm. "I did inherit his money. I suppose I like him for that part."

"You do a lot of good with it."

"I do a lot of frivolous things with it, too." She winced as she overextended her arm but continued to work her muscles.

"Are you all right?" Jasper asked.

"Yes." Had she ever been with a man this attentive before?

"Do you want to stop?"

"Not yet." She looked up at him and couldn't look away.

As the seconds ticked by, an attracted sort of awareness sparkled in his blue eyes.

"Where did you grow up?"

She wasn't sure why he asked, maybe because she'd said she grew up in a mansion. "San Francisco."

"Is that where his company was?"

She didn't want to answer that. After a few seconds she finally did, reluctantly. "Yes."

He seemed to notice so she treaded water with her hand, pretending not to notice him, as well.

"Why do you care so much about homeless people?" he asked at last.

No one had ever asked her why. "I didn't until I met Bernie."

The charity held special significance because of the injustice many homeless people endured. Whether they landed on the streets after suffering financial catastrophes or mental illness, they were treated like trash by the rest of civilization. But why did she care so much? She did care. A great deal. She cared about the people and their destitute circumstances.

"I needed something to do with my time and I wanted to run a nonprofit," she said. "Bernie opened my eyes to a lot of things."

"What things?"

She remembered her childhood, going to her father's corporation and witnessing him rule like a bloated king. It used to disgust and embarrass her.

"The way my father treated people he viewed lesser than him. How many people did he drive into that kind of destitution?" She lowered her legs and stood, Jasper aiding her until she found her footing. Then he dropped his arms. She put her hand on his arm to steady herself. The contact sent a river of shivering tickles up her arm and through her core. She met his eyes, impossibly blue, and again couldn't look away.

"You think your father drove people into destitution?" He found his aplomb before her.

She lowered her hand but he kept his on her waist. It was distracting. Then she went back in time. "He was a tyrant to his employees and looked down at the lower-earning personnel. He treated his secretary horribly. He taught me that the underprivileged were beneath us, beneath anyone with money and in positions of power. But the older I grew, the more I realized how wrong that way of thinking is. Lording over people who have less isn't the way to improve society. Encouraging people gives them inspiration and inspiration leads to good, happy productivity. If people thrive the company thrives. People like that are able and willing to contribute more to their community. If you oppress them, they only give what is required because they're afraid to step out of those boundaries. Do as told and that's all. Don't contribute because contributing may lead to more oppression." She ran her hands through the surface of the water. "I believe the key to real success is through positive reinforcement. You don't beat people down by taking away their freedom in the workplace, giving orders and constantly reminding them their place is beneath you. I hated my father for being that kind of man. He obtained his wealth working others like slaves to his dream, not giving a rat about how much they suffered or how unhappy they were, like the privilege of working for him was a gift to be worshipped. I despise supremacists because of him and the example he made. I often wonder if he would have still earned his billions if he'd have been generous and kind and humble, rather than the selfish bully he was."

Not enjoying the memories, she slipped away from his arm and walked through the water to the stairs, taking them slowly and then picking up the towel the maid had left for her. She wrapped it around her and went to the Jacuzzi. The maid had also turned that on. There was no easy way in.

"Let me help you." Jasper climbed in ahead of her

and put his hand on her waist. Gently he helped her
down onto the seat and then the floor of the tub.

She sat, feeling weary but the warmth worked like
a soothing balm. She leaned her head back and closed
her eyes.

"You have very strong feelings about your father,"
Jasper said.

"Let's not talk about him anymore." Thinking about
her father made her feel lousy. "What about you?"

"Me?"

She kept her eyes closed. "Your family. I bet they're
a lot different than mine." They probably hadn't forced
him to do a job he didn't like.

"Both my parents live in Toledo, Michigan. I grew
up there. Me and a brother and three sisters."

She lifted her head in amazement. Such a large
family. What would that have been like? She'd been
an only child. "Are you close to them?"

"We talk on occasion. I see them on the holidays."
He had a fond glint to his eyes that spoke more than
his few words. He was close to them.

"How did you end up becoming a detective?" Had
he dreamed as a boy and followed them in adulthood?
She wished she'd have had the opportunity to explore
her own dreams.

"Video games, books and crime series. I wanted to
be a hero." He grinned, a sexy masculine slide of his
mouth. Then he stretched his muscular arms out along
the edge of the Jacuzzi, momentarily distracting her.

In a way, she'd wanted to be a heroine. She hadn't
been allowed working for her father.

"I was also a hyperactive kid," he said. "Everything
interested me. I had to keep absorbing new things. Ex-

periencing things. Sports. Places. Learning and ana-
lyzing. That's where the crime investigations came in.
I couldn't make a living traveling or rock climbing so
I went to a police academy and worked my way up
to SWAT. That got old, though. I wanted to use my
brain more."

"And now here you are, a detective."

"Yes. I worked in Detroit for several years before
joining DAI."

He seemed to like talking about what he did. He
had pride in his expertise. "Detroit…"

"High crime. Failing economy. Exciting times."
He chuckled a little.

"You need excitement?"

"I can't stand boredom."

Did that translate into relationships? She didn't
know why she wondered. She didn't know him well.
Why would that matter? She took in his bare chest and
no longer had to wonder. How long had it been since
she'd been with a man? A long, long time. That's why
she'd joined the online site.

"How long will it take you to get bored at DAI?"
she asked.

He spent a few seconds contemplating as though
no one else had ever asked him before. Maybe no one
had. "Actually, I think I found my match."

Would he find his match in a woman? She wanted
to ask but didn't. She'd vowed never to put herself in
a situation or relationship where she felt she had to
work at pleasing someone else. Doing nice things out
of happiness didn't count. The key word was *work*.
Slave. She'd grown up a slave to her father's demands.

No man would have her if she had to work too hard to please him. Was Jasper that kind of man?

He looked to be in his mid to upper thirties. Close to her age at thirty-five.

"Have you ever been married?" she asked and then wanted to kick herself. She didn't need to know such a personal detail about him. Better if their relationship remained professional. Finding Bernie's killer had to take top priority.

"No." He got a faraway look, turning to gaze through the windows across the pool at the sunlight hitting the mountainside.

Heavy question.

"Serious girlfriend?" She couldn't stop herself. He tempted her like warm caramel-drizzled brownies.

"I've had a couple of those." He faced her again.

"Did they give up trying to keep you excited?" She didn't mean to sound crass but she was afraid she did. When he didn't respond, she was certain he'd taken it as an insult.

"I'm sorry. Sometimes my mouth gets ahead of me. Blame it on my father's blood coursing through my veins." She smiled to ease the sting.

His mouth slid up into an answering grin. "It's okay. I've just never thought of it that way before."

Did he think she had a point? That wouldn't be good news for him…or any woman who had the misfortune of falling in love with him. At least she knew early on. Nice to have a warning…

She stretched her right arm out along the top of the Jacuzzi and straightened her back, muscles pulling. She'd been shot just below her breast and every muscle in the vicinity protested. Shoulder. Chest. The fatigue had reached her head.

"I think I've had enough." She moved to stand and slipped on the bottom of the tub. Going down, she landed back on the seat, the jolting movement causing sharp pain. The wound felt as though it tore apart.

Strong, gentle arms scooped her up.

"There you go again, getting ahead of yourself."

She stared up at him, her hero. He made a good one. Without knowing him very well, she sensed an inner power about him, a toughness that didn't come from the street. His dominating presence came from a barometer of right and wrong and he stood only for right.

She looped her arm over his shoulder as he carried her out of the tub, her fingers resting on the back of his neck. Her breast mashed against his hard bare chest, smooth olive skin sloping over the manly ridges. The pleasurable sight eased the intense ache that radiated from her healing wound. She returned her gaze to his face and saw he'd been busy admiring her the same way.

The moment changed in an instant. Going hot all at once.

He stood with her outside of the tub, on the stone floor, unhurried to put her down.

Having caught several glimpses of him in her limited movement around the house, each time had caused a flutter. She thought he might be trying to keep their relations professional and give her time to recover. But there was an electrifying undercurrent linking them. Whenever they were close or their gazes connected, the current crackled to life.

Now in his arms, her body pressed to his, the heat

of desire mushroomed to life. He held her gaze in an inescapable stare. She wouldn't have looked away even if he had. He absorbed her face as she did his.

With the sound of the water fountain, he lowered his head and kissed her. She inhaled sharply with an unexpected jolt of desire.

The suddenness of his kiss and her reaction gave her a scare. She was always so careful about who she welcomed into her life. She hadn't dated since coming to Jackson Hole, nor did she have any plans to. Not that she'd plan that. She just wasn't ready for the complication.

He lifted his head and she fell into another long stare. Then he slowly, gently put her down. She left her hands on his chest, still mesmerized by him.

"I didn't mean to—"

"It's okay." She quickly dropped her hands. Lord, what a gorgeous body. "I better go."

Turning, she walked away. Solve Bernie's murder. No romance. Romance terrified her with all its unknowns. She loved her house in the Tetons because no one bothered her and she didn't run into anyone unless she chose to. She'd like to keep it that way.

Later that night, Jasper sat up in the family room with the television on low. He didn't know why he bothered. This house was big enough that Sadie wouldn't hear the sound. He could have gone to the theater room or the living room, but the family room suited what he was used to most. The staff had gone home. Sadie had her home to herself at the end of each day.

He couldn't get her blunt question out of his head.

He'd never thought of women in the context of excitement. Aside from sex, of course. Sex was exciting, but did he need women to excite him at other times? Granted, no one would fault him for not wanting a dull relationship, but to constantly need to be stimulated? Keeping a relationship new and sizzling became a challenge after several years with the same person, but if the foundation was strong, then those calmer times came naturally. Was he different? Maybe subliminally he sensed if a relationship with a woman would eventually go flat. Maybe he ended relationships when the woman no longer interested him…because she didn't excite him. It seemed shallow, but he had to admit much of his life had been shaped based on the level of thrills he received. Fighting for good had always taken precedence. Maybe his ambition bled into other areas of his life. Now he wondered why.

He'd always thought he'd do the marriage thing later in life. He'd never made a conscious decision, just forged ahead with his desire to be a hero. That had stuck with him since he was a kid. As a man he enjoyed women, and yet no one in particular stood out. Well, one did, but his relationship with her had been different…or had it? He'd definitely been excited with Kaelyn. Things had ended on a rocky note, the rockiest of all his relationships. Perhaps that was why she stood out.

He'd rather not travel too deep into that piece of his past. Someone had tried to kill Sadie and a man's murder had to be solved. He represented DAI now. He had a job to do.

Turning off the television, he left the family room

and headed for Sadie's fairy-tale stone castle-worthy stairs. A shadow in the foyer stopped him.

Dwight had just entered. He turned on a lamp on a table between two wing backed chairs. "I hoped to find you still awake."

The way the man regarded him put him on alert. He stepped into the foyer.

"Finley says you're getting rather cozy with the miss," Dwight said.

Had someone seen them in the Jacuzzi? He didn't respond. There was a reason Dwight had sought him out and if it had anything to do with Sadie, it was none of his business.

"I spent some time going over your background." Dwight stepped forward until he faced Jasper. "Quite impressive."

Still Jasper waited. The man had yet to reveal his purpose.

"Except one part."

Jasper looked away. So he'd bring that up, that dark piece he could never manage to shed. It followed him, haunted him. Then he looked directly back at Dwight. The man didn't trust him and was highly protective of Sadie. While he appreciated that, he also needed someone *he* could trust.

"My past has nothing to do with why I joined DAI," Jasper said.

"That's debatable," Dwight said. "You resigned from the Detroit PD. Why?"

That sounded like a leading question Dwight already had the answer to.

Jasper didn't talk about why. Dwight must have read some news article covering what happened.

"It was best for everyone involved."

"You shot a man while you were off duty. The details were kept real quiet, but it was your uncle. Who shoots their uncle, and why? Seems your boss liked you enough to spare your reputation."

"I left Detroit with my reputation intact."

"How is anyone supposed to know that? News said it was a family dispute. Your uncle attacked and you shot him."

"I just gave him a warning. I didn't kill him."

"A warning for what?"

That he wouldn't discuss. "He didn't press charges. My uncle realized his mistake and backed off. That's all that matters. He came to his senses and I didn't have to kill him." And he would have. His uncle had known it and thankfully he'd chosen to salvage what might be left of his relationship with his favorite nephew.

Jasper would never understand why his uncle had favored him. It could have been because he'd been the only boy in the family who'd pushed limits. Nothing scared him as a kid. Maybe that's all it took to please his uncle. But Jasper hadn't pleased his uncle. He'd never tried and up until he'd left Detroit, hadn't cared. He'd never respected his uncle, first of all. He was the polar opposite from his father. Jasper's dad had taught him how to be a real man, not one who needed money and women to feel like one. Jasper needed to impress no one. He only needed to stand up to evil in all its forms.

"Why did you shoot him?"

"My uncle had been drinking and lost control, just like the news said."

Dwight contemplated him a moment. Then he took an intimidating step forward, as though not satisfied with Jasper's vague explanation.

Jasper wasn't intimidated. He'd stood up to bigger, badder men. And he would give no more information on what happened that day. Or the days leading up to that.

"I'm only going to say this once," Dwight said. "If you hurt Sadie—in any way—I'll take the appropriate form of punishment into my own hands."

He didn't waste his breath by saying Dwight had nothing to worry about, at least not because of what happened between him and his uncle. He couldn't promise anything about his personal relationship with Sadie. He lived by truth—what truth he could reveal—and he wouldn't be telling the truth if he said he was sure he'd never hurt Sadie.

She wasn't one to engage in a casual affair and he wouldn't give her the impression that he'd offer anything more. But their attraction had alien power over him. He suspected she felt the same. He wouldn't intentionally hurt her, but if neither of them could resist passion, he might…when he walked away. Because that day would come. He may not understand why he needed the excitement of the new and unknown, but he did. Living so tucked away from civilization would drive him insane.

"It seems we both have secrets worth protecting," Jasper said.

"So you admit you have secrets."

"Not a secret, just something I'm not willing to discuss with just anyone. What about Sadie? What kind of secret are you keeping for her? What is she hiding?"

Dwight didn't respond, which only confirmed Jasper's suspicions. Sadie was hiding something all right. Was she a victim or a perpetrator?

"Maybe Sadie isn't the one in danger of getting hurt," Jasper said. "Maybe I should be the one taking things into his own hands."

Chapter 3

The following evening, Sadie found Jasper out on the turret-top patio. He stood with the setting sun spraying color across the darkening sky and the silhouette of jagged Teton peaks succumbing to blackness. But he didn't seem to be up here for the view. His head moved slowly, scanning the property below where lights illuminated carefully cultivated landscaping. Sadie hadn't wanted to build her castle in the middle of trees. She wanted to be able to come out onto a patio like this and see the landscape. Her security team hadn't complained. Like Jasper, they preferred to see the property.

"You're missing the sunset," she said as she came up beside him, leaning her forearms on the rise of a stone sawtooth.

"I'm not missing a thing."

She wasn't fooled. He hadn't come up here for leisure. He may have seen the setting sun but he hadn't *seen* it. "Do you ever savor the moment? Take in a sunset—and I mean really take it in? Smell the grass and flowers? Or is it all rifle scopes and gunpowder for you?"

"You do have a way with words, Sadie Moreno. Are you a secretly aspiring to be a writer?"

He liked how he joined in on the teasing. "No, but I do have an artistic streak in me. Must have gotten that from my mother."

"She was creative?"

"She painted. I saw her paintings from when she was a girl. She was pretty good." Clasping her hands over the stone wall, getting the feeling he'd asked to probe rather than out of genuine curiosity. He'd asked as though her mother was still alive and she'd already told him she died after she was born. She looked out toward the horizon. She'd steer clear of any more talk of her mom.

"What kind of creative streak did you get from her?" Jasper asked.

"Interior decorating." She looked over the stone wall toward what she could see of the lower levels of the house. "Maybe even exterior. I had a lot of input into the design of this house."

"It's a nice house." She caught him regard her warmly for a few second before he said, "I savor more than the sight through a scope or the smell of gunpowder. But thanks for that visual."

She turned to lean her back against the stone wall, elbows on the top sawtooth, taking in his wide shoulders. "What things do you savor, then?"

He looked down at her mouth and then lower. Then his eyes lifted and she felt the burn of the man inside. He didn't have to say the first thing that came to his mind.

Women. And he could savor her.

Sadie straightened and once again faced the view. Time to change the subject…real quick. "So…what made you bury yourself in work?"

She saw a subtle flash of unguarded surprise. She bet people rarely surprised him.

"Why do you think I do?" he asked.

She shrugged. Where had she gotten the idea he buried himself? "Just something about you. And the things you said. Meeting your match with Dark Alley Investigations. That must keep you busy."

"It does, but why does there have to be a reason to love what I do?"

"Do you love it?" All the death and sadness? Of course, that wouldn't be the part he loved. He loved being a hero. The good guy.

He took some time to mull over his response. She could see the calculation in his deliciously blue eyes.

"It satisfies my craving for excitement."

His gently mocking tone reminded her of when she'd asked if women gave up trying to keep him excited. She put her attention on the setting sun, the sky deeper tones of red and orange, lighting streaks of cirrus clouds.

"I shouldn't have said that. I said I was sorry and I meant it."

"Don't be. The truth is never something you should be sorry for."

Amazement brought her gaze back to him, the low

light shadowing the Nordic planes of his face. She wasn't sure if she'd call him humble, noble or chauvinistic. "You need women to excite you?"

He grinned. "What man doesn't?"

While he definitely charmed, she remained serious. He must have thought on this awhile after they last talked. Maybe he hadn't thought of himself that way before. Had he known what made him that way? Certain men avoid long-lasting relationships, but only as they matured. Some required more time than others, and maybe some men never graduated to the family level. Was Jasper that kind of man? He might only be about striving in his professional life.

Still, mysterious attraction, whether welcome or not, compelled her to be sure. "Is it really the excitement that keeps you from settling down? Or did a woman break your heart?"

His flirty grin wiped flat. The spark left his eyes and he turned to the darkening view. Perimeter lights began to dominate now.

"Don't want to get hurt again, huh?" She joined him in watching the last of the sun's rays give the show over to the stars. "Me neither."

When he didn't respond, she found she couldn't let go. "She must have been some lady."

Slowly he turned his head. The profound emotion struck her and penetrated deep. She felt it. Without even speaking he told her how much the woman had meant to him.

"I'm sorry," she apologized again, facing the grounds, the horizon a dark blue with the rugged black outline of the mountains.

"She was very special."

Startled that he'd responded, Sadie's curiosity only intensified. She didn't interrupt him, only let him take his time.

"Kind. Never jealous. She believed in herself, and that made her more than physically beautiful to me."

Sadie pictured the confident woman he described and felt the bond he had with her. Although he didn't say much, what he had said revealed the depth of his regard for the woman. How many men could say that about their women? Her father certainly had never spoken that way about her mother. Had Jasper had true love with his woman? It seemed that way.

"What happened?"

The warmth of memory faded as the end of something he'd considered good, if not life-lasting, came to an end. "The usual."

Someone's heart gets broken.

"Could she not handle your profession? The hours you work?"

"She could have handled it." Jasper offered no more. She'd already asked what happened between them and he clearly didn't want to say. *The usual.* But she had been strong and he'd admired her no small amount. Yes, she must have been quite a woman to capture this fascinating man's heart.

Sadie didn't welcome the flowering spark of envy. She rarely felt this way. When she was under her father's reign, she'd been too busy feeling sorry for all of his subjects. And afterward, too busy crusading for the homeless. No man had threatened her femininity that way, whether intentionally or not. In this case, Jasper hadn't intended to make her feel like that. She'd done that all on her own, and by no conscious will of her own. What an odd sensation.

She stood with him under the stars, seeing one of her security guards making his patrol on the inside of the fence, disappearing into some trees. It provided an adequate distraction.

"What about you?" Jasper broke the silence. "Has a man ever broken your heart?"

Broken her heart? Had she ever really loved anyone? "No one's ever broken my heart but I've been betrayed."

"An ex-husband?"

"Fiancé. He was an impulsive decision. We met and moved in with each other within six months."

"How long ago was that?"

"Five years. I had a really nice townhouse I left to be with him." She sighed. "You don't get to know anyone until you live with them, right?"

"My experience was different than that."

Meaning he'd known his woman well. "Then you were married?"

"No."

He'd had a lengthy relationship with the woman and something had split them up before marriage had a chance. Had the woman not felt the same as him?

"Did you meet yours in San Francisco?" Jasper asked.

Yours. Sadie would not think of her ex-fiancé in such kind light. He'd treated her like a piece of property. If anything, she'd been *his* whether she liked it or not. With her mind on that, she didn't have to sweat too much when she said, "Yes."

"What made you move somewhere so remote?"

She shouldn't have opened the conversation to this. "I've always loved the mountains." A partial truth.

"But you belong to social clubs and drive a flashy car."

Hearing his skepticism in the well-planted question—ever the detective—Sadie tried to counter. "You think it's odd I like mountains? Can't I be social and live re-clusively? I happen to enjoy my alone time as much as I do my friends. The car is an investment and I don't drive it very much."

"San Francisco fits a social, material-loving kind of woman more than all this does." His eyes went from her face down over her front and back up. "Flannel doesn't really match your tastes."

"You know my tastes?" Now he was being cocky.

He grinned and didn't answer.

Playfully cocky? She resisted how the discovery appealed to her baser instincts.

He'd interpreted her tastes with little or no pro-vided information. The Ferrari gave her away. Maybe she should park it in the garage and start driving the Jeep instead.

"I do love San Francisco." She didn't have to hide the truth in that statement.

"What did your ex-fiancé do?" he asked, more dig-ging.

He asked as a detective rather than an interested suitor. She had a quiet debate with herself over whether to answer. She toyed with the temptation her infatua-tion presented. But temptation might prevent her from making smart choices.

"He manufactured parts for spacecraft." At least that wasn't a lie. Talking about Darien depressed her.

Mostly because she felt so stupid and insignificant for being so easily duped. A girl was supposed to feel important with her man. Special. Like Jasper's lady must have felt.

"How did you meet?"

"He tripped me as I came out of a restaurant." She'd scraped her palm on the concrete and he'd retrieved an alcohol wipe and bandage from inside the store. "He didn't catch me like I starred in my very own fairy tale, either. I should have seen that as divine intervention, a sign to stay away from him."

"How did he betray you?"

He sure was quick with his questions, like he had them all planned ahead of time and had only to wait for her next answer.

She decided to echo his words. "The usual."

Feeling him linger on her profile, she sensed he hadn't missed her response and maybe suspected her betrayal may not have been all that usual. Maybe his broken heart hadn't, either.

The faint sound of breaking glass from a distance preceded Sadie's notice that one of the perimeter lights went out.

"What was that?"

"Someone shot out the light." As Jasper started to turn, the next light went dark along with more shattering glass.

Taking Sadie's hand, he rushed with her back into the house, where they ran into one of the security guards.

"Take her to her room!" Jasper said.

"Roger." The man took Sadie's other hand and Jasper let her go, seeing her look back at him as though she considered going with him. He was glad when she faced the other way and went with the guard. He'd fight to keep the attackers from getting into the house.

Jasper ran to the gatehouse where he'd seen an equipment room. On his way, he spotted Dwight running from another direction, intersecting his path and running beside him.

"You heard it, too?" Dwight asked.

"Saw it. Sadie and I were up on the turret patio." They reached the gatehouse, where the guard inside was on the radio talking to the guards in the mechanical room where all the surveillance cameras fed into.

"Dwight's here now." He dropped the radio and saw Jasper and Dwight enter and go into the equipment room.

Dwight tossed Jasper a body armor vest.

"Mechanical counted at least five on the video," the gatehouse guard said. "The silent alarm tripped with the first shot at the perimeter light."

Five? Jasper ignored what that implied and secured his vest. "Who's inside?" He'd left Sadie locked in her room.

"Jacobs and McKenzie." Dwight finished securing his vest. "They're with Sadie now. Two more are in the mechanical room."

"Where did they last see the intruders before they took out the cameras?" Jasper asked the gatehouse guard.

"Shooting out the northwest corner light. All the lights are out on the northwest side."

"They'll go after the cameras next." Jasper handed

Dwight a radio and connected his before going to the gun rack. "They're going to try to get inside."

Two other guards joined them. Jasper put on a helmet and Dwight handed him a night vision device. He strapped that to his head.

After checking his automatic rifle and pistols already in his waist and thigh harnesses, Jasper went to the video monitors and searched with the gatehouse guard for movement outside the gate. There was none.

"Have they breached the wall?" Jasper asked.

"Mechanical said no, not yet. But they disabled the sensors so we won't know where they'll try."

From his surveillance on the turret patio, the trees would hide them from sight, so they'd likely make the attempt somewhere along the fence in that location. He pointed to a section of fence where the trees were the thickest. "They'll try right there."

"How do you know?" Dwight asked.

"It's what I would do." He turned to Dwight and the other two guards. "You two go around the northwest side. Dwight, you come with me."

Dwight turned to the gatehouse guard. "Stay here and wait for police. You're the gate defense until then."

The guard's head bent with one determined nod.

Jasper ran from the gatehouse and Dwight ran beside him.

"If I wasn't going to suggest the same, I would have given the orders," Dwight said.

"This is no time for a contest of egos." Ignoring the other man's pinching mouth, Jasper ran toward the northwest fence and cluster of trees with an attractive walking or biking path meandering beneath the canopy. He stayed close to the stone wall and out of sight in dark shadows. Near the first shot-out light, he stopped.

Dwight stopped beside him, using two fingers to point from his eyes toward the house.

Jasper spotted the other two guards near the corner, giving an arm up sign that Dwight returned. Silent language no one had shared with Jasper, something that tweaked his ire but would have to wait until later to reprimand. Sadie's safety could be compromised with each piece of information they kept from him. They had to operate as a team.

The two guards disappeared behind some shrubs.

Jasper resumed his trek along the fence. Near the edge of trees, he stopped and listened. No sound from the other side alerted him, but that gave him no ease. The enemy could have already cleared the fence.

Dwight elbowed him and pointed. Jasper followed the aim and spotted an area of barbed wire that had been cut. The enemy had cleared the fence.

"Team twenty-two," Dwight said low into the comms. "The coyote is in the yard. Move out."

"Roger twenty-one."

Team twenty-one and twenty-two? They must have decided early on to use that code in the event of an attack.

Dwight used his hand to indicate to Jasper that twenty-two would flank the trees opposite from where they stood and they'd take this end.

Jasper nodded once and used his night vision to scan the trees. Nothing moved.

He ran to the first trunk and took cover, Dwight taking cover behind another. Night vision revealed no threat. Jasper moved along with Dwight deeper into the trees.

An explosion thundered and the pressure sent Jasper flying. He landed on his back on the ground, narrowly missing a fallen log. He scrambled on a backward crawl to take cover behind a tree. Searching for Dwight, he saw him the same instant he spotted darkly clad men armed with high-powered rifles rushing through a gaping hole in the rock wall. Some grass and a tree started on fire.

The cut barbed wire had been a diversion.

Dwight was slow to regain coherency.

Seeing a man storm toward Dwight with his weapon ready to fire, Jasper used his rifle scope and found the man through the high-tech optics. The man took two more steps with his rifle aimed, enough time for Jasper to find him in the crosshairs and fire. The man went airborne and fell to the ground, lifeless.

Jasper counted two, three, four more men scattering when they realized Dwight was covered. Jasper continued firing while Dwight regained his wits and scrambled to a tree trunk. Then Dwight began firing along with Jasper.

The other guards reached them, going to the opposite side of the gap in the wall. All four of them fired on the intruders. Bark flew off trees. Rapid gunfire exploded against the mountainsides.

The first of the four remaining attackers fled through the opening in the fence, leaping over the grass fire. The rest returned fire, forcing Jasper to duck for cover.

"Move!" Dwight shouted.

Jasper welcomed his vigilance. The enemy was getting away. He saw three figures jumping the fire and vanishing behind the fence.

He joined Dwight in running after them, seeing the other two guards close behind. Jasper jumped over the fire and took cover at the first tree he came to. Dwight and the other guards fanned out and they all searched with night vision. But there was no sign of the enemy.

Seeing movement in the trees, Jasper broke into a run. He heard an engine start. As he broke from the stand of trees, he stopped on the side of the dirt road leading to Sadie's house and saw the last of the remaining men get into a big SUV. The driver began racing away before the doors were all shut.

He ran out of bullets but Dwight and the other two fired at the disappearing vehicle. It had no rear plate.

When the SUV taillights disappeared, Jasper lowered his weapon.

Dwight leaned his upright against his shoulder and said to the two other guards, "Check the perimeter again and get someone out here to repair the fence. All of you stand guard tonight. We've got to make sure that opening stays secure."

"Roger that," one of them said and they both ran back into the woods.

"There were five of them," Jasper said.

"Yeah."

Jasper turned to have a look at the man's face. Stubborn silence met him, at least on that matter. Even now, after what had just transpired, he'd say nothing. Offer nothing in the way of an explanation, even if speculated. While that frustrated Jasper to irritation, he'd wait to get his answers. Right now all he wanted to do was get back to Sadie.

He started walking up the road toward the gatehouse.

Dwight walked beside him. "I owe you a thank-you. You saved my life. That man was going to shoot me."

He sure was. "No need to thank me." He wouldn't have done nothing. But Dwight might mean Jasper had kept a close, keen eye and had experience with this kind of violence.

"Why were there five of them?" Jasper asked.

"I don't know."

"It's strange, don't you think?" He hadn't expected an answer. Not yet.

"Yes. For a homeless man's murder, Sadie is attracting a lot of attention. More than she should."

Dwight sounded as though he'd said that on purpose, perhaps to throw Jasper off or keep him from asking any more prying questions. Jasper didn't operate that way. He'd ask the prying questions. "This has nothing to do with Bernie King's murder. Someone who murdered a homeless man wouldn't assemble a team of professional assassins to go after a woman for meddling in the crime investigation."

"Who do you think attacked?" Dwight asked, feigning innocence.

"I don't know, but I suspect you have a better idea than I do."

Dwight looked ahead. "That will have to come from Sadie." As if she'd be any freer with her information. Jasper was beginning to wonder why anyone had thought asking him here would help when no one gave him what he needed to do his job. Dwight had flippantly said maybe Bernie's murder was related, but Jasper hadn't ruled out that it wasn't.

* * *

Jasper found Sadie in the library on the second level, standing near a settee, arms folded and face sober, a lot different than her flirty looks when they'd talked on the turret patio. He had to subdue a rush of hungry attraction that fueled his gladness over seeing her just as he'd left her. Untouched. Beautiful. And safe. The guard walking along the window turned, the other at the door raised his gun as Jasper appeared with Dwight in tow.

"They got away," Dwight said.

Sadie's somberness intensified into worry.

Jasper put aside baser instinct that would have him going to her and taking her into his arms. "I'd like word with you in private." He needed to see what she had to say about the number of professionals who'd attacked.

She looked at Dwight and then him. "Anything you have to say Dwight can and should hear."

Dwight nodded to the two guards and they left the room without question. Jasper watched them incredulously. Everyone seemed rehearsed or trained on what could and couldn't be said and to do whatever Dwight ordered.

Sadie, it appeared, counted heavily on her security man. What about Steven? Jasper thought he was the top dog, but where was he in a crisis? In San Francisco?

"There were five men who attacked," Jasper said by way of introduction to what he was really after.

"Five?" Sadie's head jerked toward Dwight, who nodded once, grimly. "Oh, my God."

She didn't exclaim. But her shock defused a lot of his darker suspicion.

"Why are you really living in Wyoming?" Jasper demanded.

She stared at him, dumbstruck, for several seconds until she regained composure. "I...I told you." She moved to a chair and sat, leaving her hand on the armrest and staring across the room, still overcome by residual shock.

When he stepped toward her, Dwight moved to stand behind the chair, a protective measure.

"You like reclusiveness," Jasper said, glowering down at her. "Try again, Sadie."

Her eyes rose up, taking in his legs and torso before meeting his. "I feel safe here."

He had to work around a very male attraction to her caused by the touch of her gaze before he could find his voice. "You aren't telling me the truth. And I don't believe you feel safe here anymore. Why do you have an entire security staff?"

She clasped her hands in her lap.

"There's a room in the gatehouse stocked with weapons," he said.

"How many rich people do you know who don't have security?" Dwight asked, defensive.

Jasper saw how he put his hands on the back of the chair on each side of Sadie. "I'm not saying it's unusual to have security. But this feels like crime boss security."

Sadie eyed him wryly. "I'm not a criminal if that's what you're worried about."

"What are you, then? Your company headquarters

are in San Francisco. You live in a remote area with extreme security. What are you afraid of?"

"I'm not afraid."

"You're keeping something from me and after tonight, I think I should know what that is."

She stared at him awhile. Was she thinking of possible lies or would she finally tell him the truth?

"I'm exactly what you see."

"Why do you think five men attacked?" He couldn't keep his frustration out of his tone.

"I don't know."

He didn't believe her. "You must have an idea."

"She said she doesn't know," Dwight said.

Sadie averted her face. Unable to meet his eyes or something else?

At last she looked up at him again. "What if Bernie saw something?"

He had entertained that possibility but wouldn't tell her yet. The location of Bernie's body made him suspicious. Evidence proved the body had been transported there. The murder had taken place somewhere else. "Professionals attacked you tonight."

"Maybe professionals killed Bernie," Sadie said.

He saw her hope that she was right. She was reaching. Coming up with excuses. But nothing would deter him from his certainty that she was withholding something from him.

He knelt before her and put his hand over her now tightly clasped hands. "I can see you're scared, Sadie. You say you aren't but you are. Who are you afraid of?"

She blinked a few times and glanced back and up at Dwight.

He put a comforting hand on her shoulder and then glowered at Jasper. "Ease off on her. She's been through enough for one day."

Jasper ignored him. "If there's something you aren't telling me, don't keep it from me."

She only met his eyes again.

"You can trust me," he said.

After long seconds where she blinked some more and bit her lower lip, he thought she'd relent and start talking. But then she brushed his hand off hers and stood, forcing him to move back and Dwight to remove his hand from her shoulder.

She turned to face Jasper, a guarded mask now, hands at her sides, chin lifted, eyes fierce with determination. "I hired you to solve Bernie King's murder. Beyond that, nothing else about me is any of your business. Let Steven and Dwight take care of the attack if you don't think it's related to Bernie's murder."

He half admired and half cursed her. She stuck to her objective and didn't trust easily. She didn't know him very well and had hired him only to help with the murder investigation. She didn't argue that the attack could be unrelated. She didn't deny there might be more she wasn't saying. And he couldn't come down too hard on her since she did have a capable security team protecting her.

"Police are here," Dwight said, still with the earpiece in place. The gatehouse guard must have just told him. He started for the door.

Dread made her eyes and mouth droop a little more. The notion of talking to the police must not enthuse her. And all Jasper had accomplished was to provide her with a rehearsal. Now she'd know what to say to the police.

Chapter 4

After one of his outer perimeter patrols, Jasper entered the kitchen and went to the refrigerator for a cold bottle of water. The back door slid open. With bottle in hand, he turned to see Sadie come in. She stopped as though startled, not planning on running into anyone, least of all him. Her face wore a slightly startled look.

"It's a little chilly tonight," he said, twisting off the bottle cap and taking a long swig.

She relaxed, albeit a subtle change in her expression. "Yes."

Lowering the bottle of water, he saw she wore jeans and a red-and-black flannel shirt. He lingered on the shirt, unbuttoned in front to the top of a white T-shirt, low enough to reveal the first sign of cleavage. He didn't think even the modest exposure was intentional, just impossible to avoid at times.

To divert his attention elsewhere, he lowered his gaze and caught sight of her slippers. She'd worn slippers outside?

He didn't reveal he'd noticed. "No jacket?"

"The flannel is lined, and I was only out for a few minutes." She shrugged. "Breath of fresh air."

"Alone?"

She walked toward the kitchen entrance. "I was just outside the door."

He'd just come in that way and hadn't seen her. Why was she lying?

He put his hand on her upper arm to stop her. "Is everything all right?"

"Yes." She nodded and swallowed, hints to inner tension.

"Why did you need fresh air?"

"It's been an eventful day."

She thought going outside alone would help? Her attackers had blown up a good portion of her fence and she felt safe doing so?

He searched her eyes until she lowered them. As he dropped his hand, he saw a phone in the front pocket of her shirt.

"You get cell service up here?" he asked.

"I've got an external antenna and signal amplifier for that and internet. Coverage extends to the garage."

"Who did you call?"

"They called me. Business."

She was a terrible liar. If he wanted answers he was going to have to get them himself.

"I think I'll go up to my room."

She obviously was trying to escape him. "It's still early. Have you eaten dinner?"

"Yes."

"Sure you don't want to keep me company?" While he used the invitation as a deliberate enticement, he couldn't deny the sincerity, as well. He'd like to sit with her, to have her near and for a period of time when he could look at her.

He began to do that now, watching her eyes warm and become less tense. But the fleeting delight passed quickly and she seemed to gather defenses.

"I'm tired. Thanks, though. Maybe tomorrow night. We could have dinner together."

"It's a date."

"Good night."

"Good night." He watched her pass, trying not to enjoy her butt but failing completely. She had a really nice rear end.

Jasper went to the glass door and peered outside. The lights were on in the detached garage. There was a courtyard in the back with a flower garden. The driveway ran along its edge.

Sadie closed her bedroom door and kicked off her slippers, still cooling from Jasper's invitation. Had he invited her to buy more time to question her or did he want to spend more time with her? Wiggling her toes, looking down at the slippers, she realized why he had questioned her. And why had he been in the kitchen? He'd gotten a bottle of water, but had he just come in from outside? If so, he wouldn't have seen her near the door because she hadn't been there. She'd been in the garage.

Going into her closet, she found a pair of shoes and put them on. Grabbing a sweatshirt, she slipped that on and left the closet. She didn't see anyone in the hall and made her way to the end, opposite the direction of the curving stone stairs. She opened a door there and quietly closed it behind her. Narrow stairs led to the main level and a work room off the kitchen.

She peered into the kitchen. No one was there. Crossing the floor, she went to the back door and went outside. The garage light was still on. She ran to the open door and saw the guard she'd spoken with earlier. He was alone.

"Is everything set?" she asked.

"Yes. No one but me knows." He opened the back door of a black sedan with dark tinted windows.

She got in and he closed the door.

The guard sat behind the wheel and started the engine. "Are you sure you want to do this?"

"Yes. Let's go. We'll be back before anyone misses me." And she felt safe going with one of her guards. He'd come on board shortly after Dwight, another down-on-his-luck man who'd lost his job as a security guard at a big corporation. He'd had a run-in with one of the executives, failed to handle a visitor according to the arrogant man's wishes and was fired. Sadie trusted him with her life.

"Jasper might. I saw him walking the grounds before you came to talk to me." The guard backed out of the garage and turned the vehicle toward the driveway.

"Yes, I saw him, too." She was a little concerned about that but she had to make this meeting.

A few minutes later, they reached Jackson Hole and the twenty-four-hour diner where she always met Steven. The guard parked down the street. Sadie got out with him and he walked her to the door, keeping a lookout for any threats.

Through the window, Sadie spotted Steven already sitting at a table and went inside.

He stood when he saw her. "Sadie." He hugged her. "I've been out of my mind with worry ever since Dwight called."

She sat and so did he. She ordered a coffee, seeing he already had one.

"I'm fine. You shouldn't have insisted on meeting."

"You were attacked."

"Not me. Your team and Jasper fought them off. They kept me safe. Jasper saved Dwight's life."

"Jasper did?"

"Yes. Dwight said one of the attackers would have shot him if Jasper hadn't seen him and shot the man instead."

"Quick on his feet."

He was more than that. Sadie wished he wasn't, but to her, he was so much more. "He's a former Detroit cop. SWAT, Dwight said. He's a capable cop and detective. Dwight has a new respect for him, I think." And so did she. Despite her resistance to the contrary, he had a knight in shining armor halo over him.

"He always did need to be shown a man is trustworthy."

Jasper was trustworthy? Sadie didn't think of him that way, maybe because she didn't feel like trusting him with her heart. She probably wouldn't trust any man after all she'd been through with Darien Jafari, the man she'd lived with and almost married, a dangerous man she'd spent the last five years trying to purge from her life and bring him the justice he so richly deserved. But she was tempted to believe Jasper was trustworthy. What if she did? What if she allowed her desires to take her where they led?

Her coffee arrived and she took a sip, wishing she could get rid of the foolish fantasies that plagued her.

After a long silence, Steven said, "You know what this means, Sadie." He fingered his coffee cup but didn't lift it for a drink.

"Yes. Darien has found me," she said.

"I'm afraid he did so because of me." He looked down at his cup with regret.

"What? How? Do you think he followed you last time?"

"I can't be sure. I've been careful spying on him, waiting for him to make a mistake, looking for any connection to what he's done. Now I wonder if he's been on to me. I was always careful when I planned my trips to see you, but if he became suspicious, he could have found out."

Why would Darien become suspicious? Steven was his closest bodyguard. "But you were careful." Despair sank through her heart. If Darien had discovered Steven's allegiance to her, she'd never be free of him. Steve was her best and only hope of sending her evil and violent ex to jail where he belonged.

"Yes. But he's been acting strange lately. Asking me questions about you, like where you may have fled to. He said he intended to keep looking for you and asked that I help him."

"Did you agree?"

"Of course. I lied and said I would, but he must not have believed me. Now I'm afraid our association has been discovered. I'm sorry, Sadie."

She glanced around and looked through the window, not seeing the guard near the doorway anymore. Had he gone for a walk to secure the area?

"I probably shouldn't have come here," Steven said. "But I had to warn you and I couldn't do that with Darien near."

She was glad he had but he'd taken a risk. "You could be in danger, Steven. Where are you staying?"

"I'm not staying. I will fly home tonight."

Sadie reached across the table and put her hand over his. "Maybe you should come stay with me. We could tell Jasper everything. He might be able to help us."

"You want to take that chance? Are you sure he can stand up to a criminal like Darien?"

Sadie thought awhile. Jasper was good but he was only one man. His agency might have the resources but she couldn't be sure and the last thing she wanted was to put anyone else in danger. That, and the thought of trusting another man made her nervous.

"Darien would have killed me by now if he knew I've kept in touch with you. He must have found out another way."

"How?" That instilled a frigid wave of fear inside her. Darien had seemed like a gentleman when she'd first met him, but he was anything but.

"He's been searching for you ever since you got away. He's a mad dog."

Steven would have left his employ long ago were it not for all the trouble Darien caused them both. She would die if anything happened to him. And now he had a girlfriend he seemed to truly love.

"No more people can die because of me, Steven." Her eyes stung with moisture. That scared her more than all else. "Maybe you should get out now while you still can."

"I'm in until I stop him. There's nowhere I can go to hide anyway. He found you. He'd find me, too."

"But if you led him here…"

"Don't worry about me. Right now we have to decide what to do with you." He took out an envelope from his inner jacket pocket. "This is quick and dirty but it will get you somewhere safe until I can set up a new identity." He handed her the envelope.

She reluctantly took it, her heart sinking. "I can't go through that again, Steven. I can't." Uproot her entire life and go on the run? She looked up from the envelope, wiping a tear. "I can't do it."

His face sagged with answering sorrow. "I know what you had to sacrifice, Sadie. But your life depends on your actions now."

"Your life depends on it, too."

"I have a contingency plan. If Darien is on to me, I'll know and I'll get out in time."

"What about your girlfriend? Does Darien know about her?"

"No."

"Good." He kept her a secret.

"What are you going to do, Sadie? Take the passport and get on a flight tonight. Disappear. I'll wrap things up at your house."

"But… Revive… Bernie. I can't walk away from that."

"If you stay, you'll be killed. All Darien has talked about is how much he wants to make you suffer before he kills you."

"He tells you that?"

"No. He doesn't talk to me like that. I hear him."

Steven listened to his conversations. He took risks. And he didn't take them only for her. Darien had taken something valuable from him, too. His brother had been a security guard for him until he'd been killed during one of Darien's illicit business deals. He had a motive to see Darien taken down. For that, Sadie would always be grateful. But after so many years, would they ever find justice?

After Jasper didn't hear any voices, he pulled the trunk release and climbed out of the trunk of Sadie's car. At least she'd had the wisdom to take a guard with her. Closing the trunk, he searched for her and the driver. He saw the driver standing outside of a diner, smoking a cigarette. Jasper turned his back as the man's head began to turn in his direction. When he looked again, the man had started walking the other direction.

Jasper went to the diner window and looked inside. Sadie sat with Steven Truscott. She had her hand on his and seemed upset.

Why had she met Steven in secret?

Glancing up the street, he noticed the guard stop and begin to turn back. Jasper headed toward the sedan. Reaching the trunk, he checked the guard. The man had reached a bench outside the door of the diner and sat, looking the other way as he blew smoke.

Checking the street first, Jasper waited for a car to pass and then climbed back into the trunk.

Moments later, he heard Sadie get back into the sedan.

"Do you need me to take you anywhere else?" the driver asked after closing his door.

"Just get me home."

"What did Steven say?"

"I don't want to talk about it. Please. I just want to go home."

"Sure thing."

Jasper waited until the car engine shut off and the sound of the driver and Sadie exiting the vehicle and garage faded before opening the trunk again. After getting out, he searched the darkened garage. Light filtered in from outside the glass-topped door beside the windowless overhead doors. All was quiet. It was late enough that most of Sadie's staff had gone home.

He peered through the glass to ensure he wouldn't encounter anyone and then left the garage. The cameras would capture him but he didn't think anyone would question why he'd gone in and later had come out of the garage, at least not until morning.

At the back door to the house, he used his key to enter and avoid setting off the security alarm. Like the garage, the house was dark and quiet. He walked through the kitchen and into the living room. Hearing thudding upstairs, he climbed to the second level and saw a light on in the library. In the doorway, he stopped, seeing Sadie at a bookshelf, books scattered on the floor.

She held something in her hand, a photo, and he noticed her sad profile. Had her meeting with Steven prompted such reminiscence?

She must have sensed him standing there, her head jerking up and to her left. With a startled gasp, she knelt to pick up the fallen books. Putting the photo inside one, she stood and slipped the books on the shelf.

Jasper walked into the library. "Can't sleep?"

She shook her head, still with her back to him.

"Who is in the photo?"

"My mother." She sounded crestfallen, and even embarrassed at being caught looking.

Why keep it hidden? Come to think of it, he hadn't seen any photographs in the house.

Slowly she turned, wiping under her eye. "I can't bear to look at it all the time so I keep it in a book."

She'd never known her mother. Why was she so sentimental about it? He supposed a person might lapse into melancholy over never knowing their mother. But why could she not bear to look at a photograph?

"What are you still doing up?" she asked.

Riding around with you in the trunk. What are you still doing up?

"I did another patrol," he said.

Sadie rubbed her arms and looked across the library. Jasper could see her unease. The attack and whatever she and Steven had discussed definitely upset her. He'd picked up on that on the ride back here. He almost forgave her for her deception. He'd already decided not to press her on why she'd sneaked out. She wouldn't tell him anyway. While that frustrated him, her mood switched on a protective reaction. He could not hold her secret against her when whatever she hid affected her this way.

"Are you sure you're all right?"

"It's just been a long day. I have a lot on my mind." She averted her gaze and gave her arms another rub, as though thoughts of a haunting piece of her past made her chilled.

He curbed his urge to go to her, hold her and tell her he wouldn't let anyone hurt her. But he had to have answers, and if she wouldn't give them to him, his next move had to be his own secret.

Still, he couldn't stop his natural response to her. His softening regard led to an unintentional sweep down her body. First her small, sloping nose above those full lips, then the hang of her wavy dark hair. Even filled with sadness or dread, her brown eyes flashed seductively. Her breasts pushed out the flannel shirt that hung over a pair of jeans, and her long legs made him want to see them bare. How he could find her so attractive when she lied bewildered him.

Her head turned and he watched her realize he'd been observing her. A deep, intimate awareness of his desire for her but so far had managed to prevent any interference with his job began to get the upper hand.

As he began to try to control the feeling, his gut talked to him again. Whatever trouble she was in—and he was starting to think she was in some big trouble—he didn't get any bad vibes from her as a woman. Right now, the vibes went along the lines of her needing help—serious help—escaping whatever danger had led her to this remote Wyoming hideaway and had finally caught up to her.

That mystery intrigued him. Made him want to protect her. To be her hero.

Her eyes locked with his all the while his thoughts roamed into this new territory, opening to the possibility of them together. Her. Him. Naked and then seeing where it went from there.

What if he sampled some of this excitement? What harm would it do? None if both of them had no expectations afterward. He was too curious not to at least try out a kiss. How would she react?

The heat building in him intensified when he saw her notice what his thoughts were doing. Her lips parted ever so slightly with the need for more air and her cheeks took on a faintly rosy color.

Slowly, reluctantly averting her gaze, she moved to the window, lowering her arms.

Jasper didn't think she went there for the view.

He followed, stopping behind and to the side of her.

He brushed a few soft tendrils of hair off her neck. "I hate to see you so down."

She turned with his touch and he fell into another enchanting spell.

He moved his hand to her cheek, wanting to feel the soft, alabaster skin. "I wish you would tell me everything."

Closing her eyes, she rubbed her cheek against his palm, as though being able to tell him would be a dream.

"I can protect you," he said.

She opened her eyes for another deep, intimate look.

"I want to protect you." He felt the truth of that all the way through him. He wanted to protect her as a man, as her man.

He slid his other hand to her lower back without thinking. When she raised her hands up to his shoulders, he pulled her against him. Lowering his head, he kissed her. The instant his mouth caressed hers, he knew they both would be lost to the night if one of them didn't stop.

Chapter 5

Sadie awoke to bright sunlight streaming in through her bedroom window. The angle and brightness told her it was well into the morning. She stretched her arms above her head and legs straight, arching her back. Blinking awake, she caught sight of bedcovers in disarray beside her.

Going up onto her elbows, she stared at the spot where someone had slept. A man.

Jasper.

"Oh, my stars!" Sadie threw the covers off her and sprang up off the mattress. Standing beside the rumpled blanket and sheets as though they'd come alive with all the images that replayed in vivid color and had enchanted her dreams.

Jasper and that first kiss. He'd swept her away into a sensual state of being. She hadn't thought to stop.

No, stopping hadn't entered her mind. She'd fallen right into bed with him, and he was a good lover. The way he kissed mesmerized her, moving over her mouth and making hers join him for a slow dance. The way he took her hand and asked with his eyes if he could take her to the bedroom.

Sadie showered and dressed, remembering that first contact of skin, naked torsos and legs, Jasper's caressing kisses and hands and his slow buildup to entry. And even then, he'd taken her slowly. It had all been a dream. No other way described it better. A dream.

No wonder she hadn't once thought to stop him.

Going downstairs, she didn't find him in the kitchen. She was almost glad, not wanting to face him just yet. Best if that stays a fantasy for as long as possible.

"Good morning, miss."

Finley approached from the kitchen. "Good morning."

"Will it be breakfast or lunch at this hour of morning?"

Gracious, it was almost eleven. "Where's Jasper?"

"Packing, he said."

"Packing?"

Just then, Jasper appeared in the kitchen. "Good. You're ready. We're leaving in one hour." He went to the counter where Finley always had some kind of sweet cake cut up in bite-size pieces on a pretty plate. Popping one and then a second piece of scone into his mouth, he looked at her as though nothing had happened between them last night. He was in detective mode, driven and determined to get going.

"Wh-where are we going?"

"To San Francisco. I can't solve anything from here."

Now that she was healed enough he felt safe in traveling with her. Had he delayed his investigation for her? Maybe not delayed, he'd worked as much as he could from here, but of course he had to be more hands-on.

She glanced at Finley, who immediately recognized her ire and gave a nod.

"I'll leave you to it." He left the kitchen.

Sadie folded her arms and faced Jasper, who'd now poured himself a cup of coffee and returned to the plate of scones.

As he chewed and sipped from the steaming cup, his eyes found her and stayed, his keen insight registering her mood.

"What?" he said after a swallow.

Was this how a typical man behaved after earth-shattering sex? Her ire flared even more when she felt a tickle of affection. He was happy, she'd give him that.

"I woke up alone." She instantly regretted saying that. Dropping one arm and waving her other hand, she left the kitchen.

"Yeah, but I wasn't far." He stepped toward her and pecked her mouth with his. She smelled and tasted apple scone.

She couldn't help smiling softly.

"Go pack," he said above her mouth.

The last time Jasper lost control with a woman, he'd gotten himself into big trouble. The whole experience had taught him he had enough going on in his life without adding complications women gave him. While Sadie's trouble might be a lot different than his last brush with love, trouble was trouble. Protecting her might be a necessity, but that didn't include having sex with her.

The day was bright and birds chirped with the onset of spring, happy and cheery and in stark contrast to the turmoil going on inside him. He walked along a quaint San Francisco residential street in a fog—he'd left Sadie at the hotel with a DAI guard he'd arranged for this very purpose.

He couldn't believe how easy it had been for an irresistible kiss to lead to carnal throes of passion. He was pretty sure Sadie had fallen under the same agonizing spell. While he took some comfort in that, he couldn't forgive himself. It had been that easy the first time, and had he made a mess of that.

Reaching the address a DAI team member had sent him, Jasper went to the door and rang the bell, smelling freshly cut grass and blooming flowers. Deloris Moreno answered. She lived in an upscale neighborhood but not so upscale that one would think she'd gotten a sizable divorce settlement. Perhaps in line with what Sadie had told him about her father. He might have hired a cutthroat attorney or forced her to sign a prenuptial agreement.

"Mr. Roesch?" the woman queried.

While Sadie slept, he'd phoned ahead to explain why he needed to see her—manufactured a bit. "Yes."

She came out onto the porch and indicated the outdoor furniture, an all-weather charcoal love seat and matching chair with a table between, a vase of fresh perky yellow tulips in the center.

He went to sit on the chair and she on the sofa.

"So, you're the private investigator looking into a murder case?" She gave him a staged once-over. "My, I wasn't expecting anyone so handsome." She waved her hand in the air, a downward swipe. "And I wouldn't have invited you to my home if I hadn't verified your employment and purpose."

Any smart person would do the same. "Thank you for seeing me."

"Who is this murdered person?"

He'd get to that in a minute. "How long were you married to Mr. Moreno?"

Her animation dimmed considerably. "Not long. Just five years. We divorced some ten, eleven years ago. Worst time of my life. I never wanted to remarry after him. He gave me all the taste of marriage I want."

"He wasn't a nice man?" Jasper recalled all Sadie had told him.

"Oh, he was nice, just not to me. Everyone had this rosy image of him. That used to infuriate me. He cared a lot what others thought of him, but at home he was a different man. He loved embarrassing me at parties or whenever we were with groups of people."

He was *nice*? He *cared* what people thought of him? That didn't match what Sadie had told him.

"One time he corrected a word I mispronounced and laughed and joked about how I never went to college," Deloris went on. "Nobody thought anything of it, but when we went home he went into a rage about how I should learn English so I wouldn't make him look bad in public. He told me he married a stupid woman and should have married someone smarter."

Now that was more in line with what Sadie's version of her father. "Did people at work like him?"

"Yes, of course. Like I said, his image was important to him. He had to have people like him. No one at any of the holiday parties complained about him and none of the other executives' wives gossiped as such. But I was married to him. Why would they tell me? I just know what a jerk he was home."

"What about other women? Women who worked for him?"

"He especially had to have them like him. He flirted with women in front of me. Promoted the pretty ones. It was disgusting."

That also didn't jibe with what Sadie had told him. "Was he married before you?"

"Once, but not for very long."

"And he had no children from that marriage? He told me he didn't have any children."

"He did have one child." Deloris hadn't been married to him long enough to be Sadie's mother. "Sadie Moreno."

She sat back as though puzzled. "She's his daughter? He didn't have any children. I never met anyone. He didn't have a daughter. I'd have known."

Didn't have a daughter.

"Are you sure? Maybe he had an estranged daughter." He had to have known about her or he wouldn't have named Sadie as his sole heir.

She adamantly shook her head. "George didn't want kids. In fact, when he died, he left the majority of his fortune to charity." She all but spat the last word.

Charity? Jasper stared at her a long while, pole-axed that Sadie had lied in such a huge way. Who the hell was she?

"Sadie said she inherited his fortune."

Deloris's puzzled look returned. "Who is Sadie Moreno? I've never heard of her. And no, he didn't leave his fortune to anyone."

Clearly she had never met Sadie. "How did you fare in the divorce?"

"I think you know the answer to that." She glanced back at the house. "He had his expensive attorneys. I'm sure he enjoyed crushing me one last time." She paused and Jasper could sense her thinking back on those times. "I was glad when I heard he died, but a little angry he didn't leave me any of his fortune. It wouldn't have caused him any trouble to take care of me better than he did. He never remarried after me and I never did, either, so I was able to claim his social security. That's all I got from his billions." She shook her head. "What a jerk."

She had the same sentiment toward George Moreno that Sadie did, but not his poor ethics at work.

"Who is this person you say was murdered?"

"Bernie King. He was a homeless man."

"Homeless?" Deloris frowned her confusion. "George got himself involved with a homeless man?"

"He was last seen at Sadie Moreno's Revive Center," he said, hoping she wouldn't ask too many more questions.

She fell silent for a few seconds, no doubt thinking over what he'd explained so far. "So you think this Sadie person's money has something to do with the murder?"

"I'm not speculating yet. I appreciate you talking to me. You've helped me better understand Sadie's relationship with her father."

"You mean, there is none," Deloris said. "George isn't her father. She lied to you about that."

After a moment wondering why she had lied, Jasper said, "Yes."

"It's impossible this girl is his daughter. If she is, then George never knew of her."

And could have never given her his fortune. "Thank you, Ms. Moreno." Jasper stood.

"That girl stole George's money," Deloris called after him. "She didn't inherit any."

Jasper highly doubted Sadie stole the money, but he did agree she probably hadn't inherited any, either. She'd already had money, and for whatever reason had made up a new identity. Somehow she'd hidden her money, probably in some offshore account, and moved to Wyoming to hide.

Anger simmered in his chest but he also worried for her. What kind of trouble was she in?

He left Deloris on her front porch. Had Sadie told him the truth about anything? He'd kept to himself how much their night together impacted him. He'd felt shaken the next morning. And then he'd decided the time had come to get the case moving, and moving fast. If he kept busy, he'd keep his mind off her. He'd planned to give her a few more days to recover but that night changed everything. He couldn't book them flights fast enough.

But before he delved full-steam into the case, he had to know the truth. If this next stop didn't produce the answers he needed, he'd go get them from Sadie, and this time she'd talk.

At the Revive Center, Jasper was taken aback by its size and grandeur. A striated earth-colored brick structure, overhanging rafters extended from an uneven roofline. The front entrance sat forward from the rest of the building and was made mostly of glass. He entered through the revolving door and stepped into an atrium full of trees and plants. A stone pathway led to an open area and a directory.

The facility had a medical clinic and a mental therapy staff. A physical fitness center that included rehabilitation. An entire floor was dedicated to reentry into the job market. He didn't see any listing for staff.

A door opened to his right. A homeless man walked toward the exit holding some papers and a few brochures. He didn't look at him as he passed and exited the building.

Jasper glanced toward the door and noticed a framed poster on the wall. *Enter here to start your new life.*

Moving around the directory, he saw several displays built into the walls. A homeless person could come here and learn about the facility before ever coming into contact with a person, a nonthreatening way of drawing them in. No one had to know they'd come to check the place out.

Jasper went to the door and pushed it open. Sounds and sights hit him. The large space functioned as a giant living space and cafeteria. Several televisions hung on the walls and food service personnel were busy getting ready for the dinner crowd.

"Can I help you?"

Turning toward the voice, Jasper spotted a dark-haired women behind a counter, racks of brochures behind her and a computer on the counter.

"I'm just checking the place out." He'd rather not let on who he was just yet. "I drive by here every once in a while and I heard what a success it's been. I was thinking about volunteering, maybe getting a job if an opening is available."

The woman smiled wide, her white teeth flashing. Light reflected of her sleek black hair and her brown eyes may as well be the same color as her hair. "We never turn down a volunteer. How familiar are you with the operations of the Revive Center?"

He gave her his best apologetic face. "Not very much. You take in homeless?"

She laughed briefly and moved from around the counter to come and stand beside him. "We start with this room. It's deliberately casual. Some home-less have been on the street for a long time and the idea of something new might be frightening. Others are just scared it won't work. Many are plain happy to have the chance."

He surveyed the room and all its occupants, some eating, some watching television, others seemed to be just waiting.

"If they decide to take the next step and come in here, we greet them and get them acquainted with the program. First we take care of immediate needs like food and medical and clothing, then we develop indi-vidualized plans based on the level of attention each person requires. Some need more help than others."

"Who's in charge of the operation?" Jasper asked.

"Carol Smith. She's the general manager."

"Who's the owner?"

"It's a nonprofit founded by Sadie Moreno, but she isn't here very much anymore. She leaves the day-to-day operations to Carol." She led him across the room to a set of double doors, using a badge to enter.

So far much of what Sadie had told him was true.

"This is the administration area, where all the clients are processed and assigned housing."

Jasper saw men and women busily working, passing one office where a homeless man sat before a woman typing into a computer. He wasn't as interested in that as he was digging for information.

"As you may have seen, the second floor is job placement assistance and the third is rehabilitation."

Jasper half listened to that part of her narrative.

At the end of the hall, she led him into the staff break room, not as large as the main cafeteria but large enough to hold four tables. The far wall was all windows and he could see another building, taller than this one but the same basic design. He'd seen part of it from the street.

She began to move toward the exit of the break room. "Let me take you to Carol. You'll have to talk to her about onboarding. Nothing goes forward without her okay."

"She sounds like the one I need to talk to, then," Jasper said. The woman had no idea he wasn't talking about volunteering, either.

"Right this way." The smiling woman who clearly was proud of her job walked ahead of him down another hall.

On the way, he pointed to her badge. "Who issues those for you?"

After glancing down and idly lifting and fingering the plastic-covered badge, she said, "The facilities manager."

"Is he or she in charge of security here?"

"I don't know." At an office door, she stopped. "This is Carol. She'll be able to answer all your questions and get you set up as a volunteer or see if any openings fit your qualifications. I'm sorry, I didn't get your name yet." She held a hand in the air with an upward lift of her eyes. "How rude of me."

"Jasper Roesch," he said to the woman with short gray hair and glasses inside the office who'd looked up at they appeared in the doorway, hand still on her computer mouse.

She smiled at him. "Come on in."

Turning to the other woman, he said, "Thanks," hoping she'd hear the dismissal.

She must have. "Anytime. Looking forward to seeing you around." As she backed up her eyes roamed over his body briefly. She faced forward and walked down the hall.

Jasper entered the office and sat on one of the chairs packed between the wall and Carol's desk and looked back at Carol.

"What kind of work are you looking for, Mr. Roesch?"

"Something in security. I've heard of the man who heads it up. Is he here today?"

Her reaction resembled his tour guide's. "We have a facilities manager. Is that who you mean?"

"Steven Truscott?"

She looked confused. "Steven Truscott? That name

doesn't ring a bell." She used her mouse to check a database.

Jasper didn't tell her it wasn't necessary. Sadie had lied. Again. Steven had lied. Even more significant was that Sadie hadn't breathed a word about Steven to anyone here. He was a secret.

"I'll give you some forms to fill out. Bring them back when you're finished and we'll get you all set up. Why don't you come back tomorrow?" She stood from her chair. "I can walk you back out."

Jasper left the office and waited in the hall for her to go with him.

"We miss Sadie around here," Carol said as they walked. "She used to come here more often but ever since Bernie's murder she's worked from home."

"Really? Why do you suppose that is?"

"Probably because she was so upset about it. And the police are getting nowhere with the investigation. I heard on the news they have no new leads."

"A cold case?"

"I suppose so." Carol opened the cafeteria door and kept talking as Jasper spotted Sadie just then entering on the far side, commanding in a runway model black hat and black pantsuit. Behind her, the security guard he'd posted outside their hotel room lifted his arms and shook his head wryly. Sadie must have insisted on coming here.

When she saw him she stopped short with a fuming look.

"Oh my, look—it's Sadie. I can't believe it," Carol said. "What a coincidence."

Carol walked with him to Sadie. She stood speechless. He could imagine her mind racing, wondering how much he'd learned and what she should and should not say right now. She was pretty when she was mad. He took in her dark hair clipped up with a few stray tendrils hanging and eyes that met his head-on. Damn, what this woman did to him!

"Sadie," Carol said. "We didn't expect to see you here."

"I didn't expect to have to come," she replied, no longer flummoxed, anger coming out just a bit. She did a good job of covering it for now.

"This is our newest volunteer, Jasper Roesch," Carol said.

"Volunteer?" Sadie questioned with a mocking tone. "That's what he told you?"

Carol faltered, and from the counter to his right, he watched the other woman glancing over as she greeted a homeless man.

"Y-yes," Carol stammered.

"He's a private investigator I hired to look into Bernie's case," Sadie said. "He came here to fish for information." She all but hurled the last at him, accusatory and incensed.

He raised his right hand as though on trial. "Guilty as charged."

The counter woman had abandoned her conversation with the homeless man and Carol stared at him in disbelief.

He lowered his hand and put on his best boyish charm. "My apologies, ladies. I wouldn't be a good detective if I didn't do a little anonymous sleuthing."

After a moment Carol's expression smoothed. "Oh, you are good, Mr. Roesch. You certainly had me going."

"Me, too," the woman at the counter said, clearly pleased to learn Jasper was more than a volunteer— rather a sexy private detective.

Jasper noticed Sadie turn to look at the smitten girl.

"Volunteer." Carol laughed as though at herself. "You didn't look like a volunteer to me."

"Not to me, either," the woman at the counter said, smiling in a flirty way.

"Can I get the rest of the brochures?" the homeless man asked impatiently.

Jasper watched Sadie's gaze return to his, her temper cooling. She now seemed to brace herself for what was to come. Questions. Would she finally answer them?

Chapter 6

After Jasper bade his drop-dead gorgeous, charming farewell-for-now to the ladies, he ushered Sadie out of the center's great room and into the lobby. Marching along the stone path to the exit, she pushed through the revolving door.

Out on the sidewalk she rounded on him. "*What* are you *doing* here?"

"Getting answers I wasn't getting in Wyoming."

"You could have brought me with you."

"Could I have?" he challenged, silencing any further argument.

He'd asked about Steven. She'd kept Steven a secret along with her past. He was part of her past, and now Jasper had uncovered some of it. "You're supposed to be solving Bernie's *murder*, not nosing your way into my *life*!"

He moved closer, so his face was above hers. "Well, the beauty of working for Dark Alley is I don't have to follow any rules. You better get used to that."

Ooo, he was incorrigible. "I didn't hire you to invade my privacy."

"Your life—the secret part of it—has everything to do with Bernie's murder," Jasper said. "I don't appreciate you lying. You're hindering my investigation."

Was she? He seemed so sure Bernie's murder was linked to her past. She hadn't been convinced. She wasn't sure she was now.

Maybe she denied the possibility, because if Bernie's murder was linked to her past, her life and the loves of anyone close to her were in danger.

Sadie couldn't get enough air all of a sudden, picturing Darien appearing before her, evil face conveying his desire for revenge—and to permanently silence her.

"Why didn't you tell me why you really wanted to come here?" she asked, not liking how much that bothered her. Even after Darien's betrayal, she still harbored the hope that trustworthy men existed.

"Why did you meet Steven without telling me?" he countered.

"Steven is none of your business. I only need you to find Bernie's killer."

"You may as well give that up, Sadie. I'll solve Bernie's murder. He's the innocent one in all of this. But I'll also find out whatever it is you're hiding."

"Why?" All her frustration over not being able to make him back off came out in the question. He didn't know what he would open, what he'd bring down upon himself—upon her.

"Why not just tell me?"

As he waited for her response, she struggled for a way to end this conversation. But the longer she took, the more aware she became of him standing so close, of the masculine planes of his face. Wide jaw, blond stubble and wise, strong blue eyes.

Vivid memory of him over her in bed seized her. Only the light of day differed. The shadows had helped keep reality at bay last night.

She noticed a change in him as she continued to stare up at him, captured just as she in this unexpected moment.

"Why did you leave the room without telling me?" she asked.

Why did she ask that? "It was time to get the investigation going in high gear."

"No, that's not why, Jasper. You needed to escape. You turned to the nearest thing that would capture your attention—anything other than me," She watched his face carefully. "Tell me I'm wrong."

For a moment he absorbed her face, making her wish she could climb inside his head and see what he was thinking.

"It was time to get going on the investigation."

Disappointment curdled inside. While that was true, the timing might have been different if they hadn't become intimate. "Would you have wanted to fly to California if we hadn't had sex?"

"Sadie, don't go there."

"Why not?"

He sighed and she saw his growing irritation.

"Would you have?" she demanded.

"I don't know."

"You wouldn't have. Why can't you admit it?"

"We don't know each other very well." He put his hand on his hip. "That night was…intense."

That made her feel marginally better. He'd felt that, too. She hadn't been alone. "That unsettles you?"

"Doesn't it unsettle you?"

She had to be honest. "Yes."

"Because you don't trust men."

"And you're petrified of commitment."

After a few seconds, he said, "I wouldn't use the word *petrified*."

He said that with such charm she couldn't be offended. Still, she had to be smart for her heart's sake.

"Do you regret it?" she asked after a while.

"That's a loaded question. I could ask you the same."

She wasn't sure if she regretted last night. When she didn't answer, he looked around as though checking to make sure they were still safe. Then he spotted the guard who had accompanied Sadie here. He cupped her elbow and gave a hand signal that he was taking her with him. The guard saluted back and headed for his own vehicle.

Jasper started walking toward the parking garage. She allowed him to guide her there.

Inside the garage he took her to the car he must have rented and opened the passenger door. "Get in."

Again, he scanned every inch of the garage before looking expectantly at her when she didn't do as he said.

They weren't quite finished with this discussion. The one about last night, yes, but not the other. "How did you know I met with Steven?"

"I was in the trunk. I saw you with him."

She moved her head back a fraction, stunned he'd been with her the whole time. "Really?"

"Please. Get in the car, Sadie." She heard his tight tone and realized he dealt with his own frustration over her keeping secrets from him.

"We aren't finished yet." She wasn't sure she wanted to get into any car with him.

"You're right about that," he said. "Steven isn't your security officer."

Of course, that was why he'd paid a visit to her company.

"I also had an interesting conversation with George Moreno's ex-wife."

A second bomb. How many would he detonate? Sadie didn't even flinch that time. She supposed she should have expected him to unearth that much. So much. She had hired him, after all. She'd hired the best, but she hadn't anticipated Bernie's murder being linked to her past. Would she have done anything different had she known or at least suspected?

She leaned her head back and closed her eyes, unprepared for all he dredged up from her dicey past.

"George didn't have a daughter," he continued with the third bomb.

She lowered her head. "He didn't know about me." She had to make him believe her. If he didn't, then he could find himself in more danger than even he could handle.

Jasper stepped closer, again looming over her. "Cut the bull, Sadie. George didn't want kids. He gave his money to charity and a portion of it to his ex-wife, the closest person he had to family. You aren't his daughter." After that forceful assertion he asked, "Who are you?"

The most dreaded question anyone could ask her. "Don't." She started to move out from between him and the car.

He took her arm, a little rougher than before. "You didn't get your money from George. Where did it come from?"

She didn't respond. She couldn't. Instead, she tugged her arm. "Let go."

He pulled her to him, so that his arm hooked her by the waist and she had no choice other than to put her hands on his chest.

"It didn't take much effort for me to find out," he said. "Whoever you're running from could have easily done the same."

Did he think that someone had? She didn't stop her alarmed inhalation.

"Who are you?" he repeated.

"You have no idea what you're asking." She felt clammy with rising anxiety. If she told him…then what?

"Tell me who you really are, Sadie. Why are you running? Who are you running from?"

As she stared at his urgent, coaxing face, she almost felt compelled to spill everything. Somehow after their night she felt closer to him. But she could not mistake a night of passion as a green light to blindly trust.

She pushed against him. "Let me go, Jasper."

At her solemn voice, he looked deep into her eyes and must have seen not only her resolve but also her helplessness. She could not tell him.

He released her and took a step back. "Who is Steven?"

Another question she couldn't completely answer. "He is my security officer. I didn't lie about that."

"Just not for the Revive Center?"

"No."

"Then how do you know him? Where is he from? Who is he?"

"Stop asking questions I can't answer." She walked toward the garage exit.

He walked beside her. His guard had already left but she could catch a ride from someone at her company.

"Why can't you answer them, Sadie?"

Could she reveal that much? She didn't think he'd back off otherwise. "Because doing so might get you killed."

For a moment she thought he might concede she had a valid reason for keeping secrets.

"You're running from someone dangerous."

That was an understatement. She didn't respond, not feeling she had to.

They left the garage and walked along the sidewalk, back in the same direction they'd come.

"I can protect you," Jasper said. "DAI has professionals who deal with people like that. You have to trust me, Sadie."

"I can't trust anyone. And I will not risk another person's life by involving them in my situation."

"Another person? Someone was killed other than Bernie? Who?

"I can have a team of former Delta soldiers here tomorrow," Jasper went on. "Nobody will get past them. It would take an army of thirty or forty."

"The person who'd like nothing more to see me dead and anyone next to me has the means to send a lot more than that."

"He sent only five to your house."

"He wasn't anticipating you and my security team. Next time he will."

"Nobody that powerful sends anyone in without already knowing what kind of security you have."

That made her falter. She slowed her steps and glanced at Jasper.

He took her arm, stopping her completely. "Trust me, Sadie. Please. I know how this works. I've seen DAI in action. Their security team is among the best in the world. We have the best security lead any company like ours can find. He's been in war-torn countries, fighting where there is no US support. These aren't former homeless people or corporate security guards. These are men who know weapons and war. They're fighters."

She heard his heavenly words and wished she could just throw up her arms and say, "Okay, send them in." But there was too much on the line. "I can't risk anyone else's life. I can't." On that she could not bend. "Steven is my inside man. If anyone can help me bring Darien down, it's him."

"Darien?"

She inwardly cursed her slip and averted her face.

"Trust me, Sadie."

She wanted to. She wished she could let down her guard and hand over her troubles to someone capable. But she could not. Not only her fear of Darien stopped her. She wouldn't trust anyone unless she felt sure she could.

"I can't," she whispered. She backed away. "You already know too much."

He searched her eyes, willing her to stop denying him. But at last his persistence waned. He seemed to accept she wouldn't tell him anything more.

"Let's go back to the hotel and talk," he said.

About Darien? She wasn't prepared for that, or ready.

Jasper took her hand and gently tugged her back in the direction of the parking garage. "Come on. We don't have to talk about Darien until you're ready."

While his words soothed, they delivered his full intent of making her tell him everything.

"What are you going to do?" she asked. And she wasn't asking about what he'd do once they reached the hotel.

"I'm going to protect you and find out who killed Bernie."

She believed him. Part of her shied away from how good that felt and part of her exulted in awe over such a powerful man...a good man...a man nothing like Darien Jafari.

Jasper didn't bother Sadie all the way up to the top-floor penthouse. He'd chosen this hotel because it required a room badge key to take the elevator to the top floors. But once there, he looked for easier things to talk about, to get things going.

"I asked Dwight to fly out. He's in the next room. Backup."

"Good." She nodded idly, distracted.

She moved awkwardly around the living space.

"Tomorrow I'd like to question the homeless people who saw Bernie the day of his murder and also the day before."

"The police already talked to the other homeless people," she said. "Why go and talk to them again?"

"I'm not the police."

She didn't comment further. He sensed her contemplating the night ahead, with last night still so fresh between them.

Making another pass in the living area, she caught his look and stopped. As with other times, she didn't turn away and neither did he. A sizzle crackled the air.

She faced the window, another repeated action. "Can we do something? I don't think I can just hang out in this room the entire night."

He heard the unspoken *with you* in her statement.

"I'd rather not risk being seen any more often than we have to."

Facing him, she hugged her middle with one arm and bent the other to put her index finger along her cheek, thoughtful but inventing a way to avoid boredom—or time alone with him.

At last she lowered both arms. "Since we can't do anything fun, let's have fun right here."

"Order room service?" He didn't add that fun might lead to another tumble on the sheets.

"No. Make candy. Chocolate." Her face lit up. "I haven't made chocolate in so long."

"Candy?"

She went to the phone and spoke to the concierge, who must have agreed to arrange for someone to go get all the ingredients.

"Why do you want to make candy?" he asked.

"It will take my mind off…everything."

He knew exactly what she meant. But in the meantime they had a while to wait for the ingredients to arrive. "About that…"

She held up her hand. "Let's not talk about it. Let's just agree not to let it happen again."

"I don't think either of us planned it in the first place. And I think we need to talk about it."

"Are you all right with chalking it up as something casual? A one-time thing?" she asked.

"Are you?" He didn't believe she would be.

"Yes. I am."

"What if it happens again?"

She had nothing to say in response to that. If they hadn't planned the first time what would stop them from partaking in a second? He wouldn't be against it but he had to know what her expectations were.

"Then we don't have very strong willpower."

"I normally do," he said. "Except not with you." He let her fill in the blanks that his concern was he wouldn't be able to stop if there was a next time. And he suspected she felt the same.

"What are your expectations?" she asked.

"I have none. When my investigation is finished, so are you and I."

She visibly flinched. "Are you always this charming with women you sleep with?"

"I didn't mean for it to sound so harsh."

"Well, don't worry. I'm not ready for another serious relationship, and I don't know if I ever will be."

They at least shared that in common. But he felt he needed to clarify. "I'm not saying I'm all out against a serious relationship. But I'm with you on feeling that I'm not ready."

"Good."

The way she said that made him wonder if he'd insulted her or hurt her somehow. That hadn't been his intention. And he was pretty sure that even if he had offended or hurt her it wouldn't change her sentiment. She didn't want serious and neither did he.

A hotel staffer came to the door with a bag of ingredients. Sadie took it to the kitchen and began taking out things she'd need. Placing a baking pan on the counter, she lined it with tinfoil.

"Are you going to help?"

She wanted him to? "I'm not much of a baker." He joined her behind the island counter.

"Get the graham crackers," she said.

"I can take orders from a pretty woman, though." He grinned as she glanced over at him uncertainly.

The she got busy greasing the foil.

He removed some crackers.

"Line the entire pan with a layer of them."

He worked at doing as she asked, hoping she'd relax enough to trust him with the truth. "What got you started baking?" What did she like about it?

"My... I grew up doing this. My father's kitchen staff let me bake with them. What kid doesn't like licking the spoon?" She retrieved a saucepan. "This is for the caramel and half-and-half."

He took that out of the bag and she put some of both in the saucepan, heating the mixture and stirring. He believed when she spoke of her father she told the truth, but what about her mother? She had told him her mother was dead. The way she'd looked at that photo, the way she kept it hidden, and now the way she'd stopped herself. *My*...would she have said *mother*? Was her mother really alive and she avoided talking about her or had she told the truth and simply had difficulty talking about her?

"Is this your recipe?" he asked.

"Yes and no. This recipe has been around but the baker in the Philadelphia house added a few touches. She was my favorite to bake with."

He didn't think she realized her slip. "I thought you grew up in San Francisco."

Her stirring slowed a fraction. "We had more than one house."

He bet that was true. Still, she seemed to cover for herself. And they both knew she wasn't Sadie Moreno. He doubted she was from San Francisco as she'd said.

"You must have made it a lot. You don't need the recipe."

"I've made it a few times." After the mixture was melted together, she poured it over the graham crackers.

"What are you making?"

"*We* are making caramel stacks."

He noticed her begin to relax and smothered a smile.

She retrieved another pan and began melting chocolate, moving like an expert chef.

"Why do you like baking?" No one could fake this. Someone other than Sadie Moreno had learned to make candy.

"I don't know. I just did."

Vague response. Lie. He buried his initial disappointment.

Pouring the melted chocolate over the caramel layer, she spread an even layer on top of the caramel.

He handed her the nuts from the bag and she sprinkled them over the chocolate.

With a peaceful, content smile, she bent over and smelled the still warm chocolate and caramel, a true lover of sweets.

"Now we let them sit awhile." Sadie cleaned her mess while Jasper watched her. Her dark hair flowed over her shoulders and her striking brown eyes needed no liner. Making candy was something she really enjoyed. A hobby? She seemed so experienced.

After a few minutes she went to the pan of candy and lifted the foil with candies and placed them on the counter. Next she found a knife and began cutting the chocolate caramel into squares.

When she finished, she picked one up and offered it to him on the palm of her hand, all with careful love, eyes admiring the piece and then rising to his.

He took the candy and met her eyes as he took the whole thing into his mouth. Simple but good.

"If I had a better equipped kitchen, I'd make you something really spectacular."

"You've had a better equipped kitchen before?"

That almost tripped her up. The love for candy creation left her face. "At home."

He wondered. Did her kitchen in Wyoming match whatever kitchen she'd had prior to becoming the mysterious Sadie Moreno? Like the one she'd grown up in?

She lifted a square and put it into her mouth. After chewing with her eyes closed, she said, "It's been so long since I've made chocolate."

"What's the last thing you made?"

"Caramel-filled chocolate. Gooey and good."

"When was that?" He thought he'd test her out with a few probing questions.

"A long time ago."

"More than five years?"

She lifted a second piece of candy and popped it into her mouth with less love than the first time. "Are you fishing for information, Detective Roesch?"

"Yes." He grinned, pleased with her sharp mind.

She smiled back. "They say the devil is charming."

"You should think of me as more of a guardian angel."

She handed him another chocolate caramel stack, wariness in her eyes.

"I'm on your side." He took the candy and popped it into his mouth.

Without responding, she took two more chocolates and wandered out of the kitchen.

"Isn't this better with champagne?" he asked, going to the wine cooler and choosing a bottle.

While Sadie eyed him with her candy in hand from the living area, he took out a plate and piled up several more squares. Then he carried the bottle of champagne and plate with flute stems between his fingers and joined her before the sofa. She took the plate from him and placed it on the coffee table. While he righted the flutes and put them next to the plate, she sat down. He uncorked the bottle of bubbly.

"Are you going to try to get me drunk so I'll talk?" she asked.

"That could be exciting." He poured champagne into one glass and then the other.

She laughed briefly and then opened the file he'd put on the table earlier.

"You highlighted a few things in here," she said, flipping the copied pages until she came to the one where he'd highlighted the note that Bernie had a lot of cash in his wallet.

"Bernie was going to buy a new car the next day," she said.

He nodded. "Whoever killed him wasn't after money."

"Why do you think his murder is related to those men who attacked?" she asked.

She'd carefully avoided mentioning her past and Jasper let that go. "The location of the body. It was moved there on purpose."

She sat back as he stepped around the table and took a seat beside her.

She flipped to another page. "Why did you highlight this witness? He said he didn't see anything."

"He saw Bernie leave the Center and go to the parking lot."

"But he didn't see Bernie go into the apartment building."

"The witness noticed a woman walking toward Bernie. He described her in great detail, right down to her Fossil purse and two-inch heel boots."

"So?"

"With that level of detail, the questioning officer may have missed writing something else down."

"Ah, very good." She crossed her legs and sipped her champagne.

Those long, slender beauties drew his eye, the black material of the pants tightening along the slope of her thigh and rear. She'd removed the jacket after they'd arrived.

Very good indeed.

Sitting this close to her, smelling her, heating up with the sight of her, Jasper had to take a couple of seconds to remind himself she might not be forthcoming about her past, what had brought her to Wyoming. Who was she? He knew only what she'd revealed, and he had serious doubts about how much she withheld. Hell, maybe everything she had told him was a lie. He had to be careful not to put his heart too much at risk.

Chapter 7

Chad Long lounged back in his newly purchased supercenter chair with a content smile that lit his bright green eyes. He always smiled with his lips pressed together and laughed for no apparent reason, not an outburst kind of laugh, just a little laugh after he spoke sometimes. Chad had a mental instability he now treated with medication and could function normally in society.

Sitting beside Jasper on a black microfiber sofa, Sadie noticed the other touches Chad had added since she'd last been here. While the apartment lacked decorative adornments, he did a fine job of putting together a home with discount center furniture. Like Bernie, he was about to move from the Revive Center's living quarters into his own place. While he'd come along after Bernie, he was another special case to her.

"I got a job at HomeGoods Center," he said, flashing some of his teeth briefly. "I start Monday."

"That's fantastic," Sadie said, noticing through glimpses that he must have been to the dentist. "Your teeth look great. You should show them when you smile."

He did show them this time. "I'm so used to hiding them I forget I can now." He chuckled a little. "Doc has me on a gradual plan to get the rest of them fixed up."

"That's truly wonderful," Sadie said, feeling Jasper watch her.

"Where have you been?" he asked. "We've missed seeing you at the Center."

She caught Jasper's anticipatory look and could see he waited to hear what she'd say. She'd always worked remotely but hadn't maintained her regular visits since Bernie's murder. "Something kept me away. It is good to see everyone again, and I'm so happy to see how well you're doing." She did get great joy when people succeeded. When she'd first opened the center, she didn't anticipate caring so much. Her main goal had been to do something good and not for money, something that would epitomize the antithesis of corporate greed. Helping the homeless reclaim their lives did that in abundance.

He looked at Jasper as though catching his scrutiny. "I never thought I'd find a way off the streets. I didn't think I could. Usual shelters have capacities and don't let you stay indefinitely. They also don't treat disabilities. That's why Sadie's center is such a miracle."

She heard that a lot. While she wouldn't attach a word like *miracle* to what she did, she understood what her facility did. Jasper said nothing in response but

Sadie could tell that he saw her with new eyes. That much she hadn't withheld from him, her passion to do something good, to be what her father wasn't and never could be. Chad made him see that.

As he continued to meet her gaze, the moment shifted, warming and gravitating back to that instinctual level where their hearts navigated the path forward.

"It's a big part of who I am now," she said to him, but for Chad, too. "It was always in me, I just didn't have the chance to explore until I moved to Wyoming."

Jasper's eyes moved away as he digested her words. Then he seemed to gather himself and zero in on why they'd come here.

"Chad, I'm Jasper Roesch. I'm a private investigator Sadie hired to help solve the case. We came here today to talk to you about the last time you saw Bernie King."

"All right. I'm not sure how much I can help but ask away. One of our own was killed."

Jasper relaxed against the back of the sofa with one arm stretched along the back and one ankle propped on his knee. "I'd like you to revisit what you saw that day. Don't leave out any detail even if it doesn't seem related to Bernie, like the woman you saw with the Fossil purse."

"The only reason I knew she had that kind of purse is I saw a girl in the mall once who was looking at them. They stood out because they were so colorful. I remembered thinking how I wanted my life to be that colorful again."

Jasper nodded. "It's that kind of detail I need. Walk

me through everything from the time you left the Revive Center."

Chad crossed his legs and put his thumb beneath his chin with his forefinger up along his cheek. "Well, I'd just finished a Back to Work Module and was going to come back here for dinner. I remember it was a beautiful day. No clouds and warm, a slight breeze. It tickled my hair right here." He laughed a little.

Sadie checked on Jasper to see if he noticed the funny quirk. He simply waited, listening and not judging. She loved that about him, how he stayed straight and true.

"There weren't many people out. It was late for dinner. My module was an evening course. Bernie must have had one, too. I saw him leave the building ahead of me and followed him to the parking lot. Not on purpose. He walked through the middle of the lot and I walked on the sidewalk like I always do."

"What about other people or cars?" Jasper asked.

"Yeah. There were other people and cars. People walking on the sidewalk and cars driving by, some parked on the street."

"Did any of them stand out like the woman with the purse?"

He thought a moment. "There was a slicked-up white Mercedes parked in front of the building. It stood out because nobody living there had anything that nice. I thought maybe it was Sadie or someone she knew paying a visit."

"Is there anything you can tell us about the Mercedes?" Jasper asked.

Chad thought a moment. "It was a Maybach S600.

Long body. V12 engine. Sweet machine. Told the cops but they didn't think anything of it."

Probably because they'd assumed the same as Chad.

"Did you see anyone inside the car?" Jasper asked.

"No. Windows were tinted."

"What about the license plate?"

Chad tipped his head up as he thought. "I don't think they were local. Most of the plates here are red and blue. There was no red on these. Might have had blue writing. I can't be sure." He thought some more. "I think there was only one sticker on it, too. In the upper right corner."

"How far away were you?" Jasper asked, sounding eager.

"Maybe a hundred feet?"

Close enough to see the level of detail he had, but he hadn't retained the numbers. He hadn't had a reason to remember them.

"Where did you last see Bernie?" Jasper asked. "What was he doing?"

"It was a nice day, so I decided to go for a longer walk. I passed the lot and kept going on the sidewalk. I didn't look at Bernie again. He must have been somewhere in the parking lot, heading for the entrance to the apartment building."

"Was anyone else in the parking lot?"

Chad shook his head. "There was a couple across the street. They were close and into each other." He laughed a little. "And they passed the parking lot about the same time I did."

Bernie must have reached the sedan by that point. Had someone forced him inside?

"No one else in the parking lot?" Jasper asked.

Chad again shook his head. "No one."

No one from the apartments facing the parking lot had seen anything, either. No one had looked out the windows at that time, and the building hadn't been very full at that time.

"Thank you." Jasper stood. "You've been very helpful."

Sadie stood with him.

"It was good to see you again." Chad leaned in and hugged Sadie.

"Keep doing well," she said.

Jasper led the way to the door. After saying farewell, they took the stairs to the entrance. Outside, Sadie walked with Jasper past the tree-and-shrub-lined sidewalk and then around a janitorial supply delivery truck. Clearing that, she spotted another formerly homeless man approaching from the small parking lot. Sadie recognized him from an initiation session she'd provided several months earlier.

A tall, lanky man with wiry gray-blond hair and light blue eyes, Eddy Anderson smiled big white teeth when he saw her.

"Hello, Eddy. How are you doing?"

"Hey, Miss Moreno. Going good. Just finished my rehab and now I qualify for a place here." He nodded up at the apartment building.

"Good for you."

"Hey, I heard about Bernie. Been meaning to tell you how sorry I am. It was clear to all of us how much he meant to you."

"Thanks, Eddy."

Eddy turned to Jasper. "Never met anyone with as

much warmth in her heart as Sadie. I hope you're taking good care of her."

"Jasper is the investigator helping the police look into Bernie's murder," Sadie said by way of introduction.

"Pleased to meet you." He bowed his head to Sadie. "Best of luck finding Bernie's killer."

"Thank you."

"Well...good to see you." Eddy held his hand up as a farewell.

"Bye, Eddy." Sadie watched him walk away.

"How does everyone know you so well if you work remotely?"

Ever the detective, Jasper would ask that question. "I make a point to meet every client and when I traveled here, I met with them to see their progress for myself. There are too many to spend one-on-one time with all, but I find the meetings benefit the newer clients." She walked a few steps with him beside her before she added, the Revive Center. "I was a lot more interactive before Bernie's murder." Bernie's murder made her realize how vulnerable she was, and how much of a risk she took being so visible. As with Jasper, the location of his body really set her off. It was as though the killer had tried to send her some kind of message. But what message was it?

Before they reached the sidewalk, Jasper took her hand and tugged her into a small courtyard beside the building. Trees partially concealed them from the road and a bench offered a moment of relaxation among a curving bed of early spring flowers.

"Sit with me." Jasper gently pulled her along with him and sat.

She sat beside him. "What are you doing?" Did he plan on romancing her—now?

He used two fingers to move her head so she faced his. "Don't look. There's a car parked on the street with two men inside. I saw it park there on our way into the apartment building."

He had? She hadn't noticed him observing their surroundings that closely. "Did they follow us from the hotel?"

"No. They were waiting down the street and saw us park. Do you recognize them?"

He'd seen them parked there and hadn't said anything. Sadie looked at the car. The tree branches made it difficult to see. The driver was bald and probably stocky in shape, but that was all she could tell. She couldn't see the passenger other than in silhouette. "Did they see us leave the apartment building?"

"I don't think so. There are trees outside the entrance and a delivery van was parked in front. That kept us hidden until we ran into Eddy, and then a big SUV parked in the lot might have blocked their view."

She watched him glance toward the street. "You're sure?"

"They don't seem to notice us. If they saw us they'd be looking at us now and they aren't."

"If they can see us." Even if they couldn't, they might have seen them walking through the parking lot. Maybe they'd noticed Jasper's alert vigil and now feigned nonchalance.

"Do you recognize them?" he asked again.

She glanced back toward the car, squinting in an effort to see better. Then she finally shook her head, giving up. "I can't be sure but I don't think it's anyone

I recognize." Darien wouldn't come in person anyway. He probably had countless henchmen working for him.

As the driver's head began to turn toward them, Jasper stunned her by twisting a little more and bringing his face very close to hers. He did this to both block the men's view of them and put on a show, but Sadie experienced a surge of sexual awareness nonetheless.

His blue eyes lowered to her mouth and then came back to her eyes with the glimmer of fire. Sadie caught her breath. She wanted to run her hands into his blond hair and pull his head to her, make him kiss her. She soon discovered she didn't have to. He put his hand on the side of her head and brought his mouth to hers, satisfying her intense craving.

She ran her hand up his arm, feeling the hard muscle of his biceps beneath his jacket, and then moving inside to his chest. She opened her mouth as he began to devour her, igniting the craving into something far more lethal.

He seemed to gain control first, resting his forehead against hers and ending the fiery kiss.

"Where did that come from?" she asked. Holy crows. She couldn't get enough air and heat burned low in her abdomen. Instantaneous passion.

"I wish I knew." He glanced back at the car and then returned for another kiss, although he didn't let this one sail them away. "Is there a back entrance to the Center?"

"Yes." They'd parked in front of the building and walked to the apartment complex. She realized then that he'd taken her to this bench on purpose so he could get her close enough to try an identify them—or see if she'd tell him. Should she be offended?

He stood and took her hand, leading her toward the side of the building. A sidewalk there provided cover, also landscaped with several trees and shrubs. At a door near the middle, Sadie stopped and used the badge she had hanging from her neck by a Revive Center lanyard. Inside she led him down an empty hallway and then turned to follow another until they reached the lobby, greeting two workers who passed them along the way.

At the front door, Jasper stopped her. She let him go first and followed him out onto the sidewalk, then he hurried her to their car, Jasper's rental.

Sadie craned her neck as he sped them away. The other car didn't follow. They'd successfully eluded them. But who were they? Sadie shuddered, already knowing.

Back at the hotel, Jasper arranged to meet with Dwight about the tail. He didn't like how easily he and Sadie had been spotted. They'd decided to meet in Dwight's room. Jasper knocked and Sadie's head security guard opened the door. He had insisted on coming out so Jasper had sent his own guard home.

Jasper put his hand on Sadie's back as they entered. It was an automatic thing, until she looked back, eyes smoky with desire. He stepped inside the hotel suite, this one a little smaller than his and Sadie's but still with all the luxuries.

"Make yourselves at home," Dwight said, going into the kitchen area. "Anything to drink?"

"No thanks," Sadie said.

Jasper shook his head and turned back to the living area. *The Good Dinosaur* played on the television. Dwight was a Disney fan. Go figure. Jasper stepped farther into the open room, watching Arlo yell in his high-pitched voice with two T. rexes, Nash and Ramsey.

"It lightens the spirit," Dwight said from the kitchen.

"Dwight always picks the animated films on movie nights," Sadie said with a smile a sister would have for her brother.

"I can see how that would get the mind off darker thoughts," Jasper said. "Or pasts."

"Dwight was Special Forces," Sadie said.

"Exactly." Jasper didn't add that certain Special Forces types didn't cope with civilian life so well once they left the Warfighter Theater. He didn't have to. Without seeing Dwight's reaction he knew the man medicated himself on animated films. It was an outlet. A healthy one, if he didn't bottle up too much.

"I didn't watch them until I met Sadie," Dwight said. "She saved me."

She'd saved a lot of people. That made it exceedingly difficult for Jasper to hold her lies against her. He looked over and saw her innocent wariness, gagging him.

"That car in front of the Center," Jasper said. "Let's talk about that."

Dwight brought drinks to the living room, holding three sodas with both hands. He placed them on the coffee table.

"I know you said no thanks, but…" He ran his hand

through the air, down low toward the cans. "It's root beer."

Jasper couldn't stop a half grin and saw Sadie smiling, too. He picked up a can of soda and cracked it open.

Sadie reached for a can and sat back, watching the movie for a bit.

"I followed you," Dwight said. "Sticking to the shadows like we agreed."

"I saw you." He'd made sure to watch his surroundings, to protect Sadie.

"You're the only one who did. Those two blokes in the parked car didn't see me. They saw you and Sadie, though, walking in the parking lot. They didn't see you park, just walking."

Jasper had realized that.

"They didn't see you leave. I stayed and watched them after you left. Eventually they got out of the car and went to the apartment building. They talked to a couple of tenants in the parking lot and then went inside, piggybacking after someone badged through the door. They were inside for about thirty minutes and then came back out. Stayed in their car until another one arrived. They work in shifts watching the Revive Center."

They were waiting for Sadie. They probably hadn't attacked because she was with Jasper. Or maybe they would have tried to tail them back to the hotel, find out where she was staying and get her that way. They'd tried before, at her remote home in Wyoming.

As always, why the homeless man was killed troubled him. If the two were connected, why kill a homeless man and then attack Sadie? Sadie cared about

Bernie. The killer may have known that. Depending on how long the Revive Center had been under surveillance, the killer could have.

"I followed the first car," Dwight said, jarring Jasper out of his thoughts. "They're staying at a hotel not far from the Center."

"Maybe we should go pay them a visit," Jasper said.

"My thoughts exactly."

Chapter 8

Jasper wouldn't let her stay at the hotel by herself, so Sadie tagged along with him and Dwight. She was a little anxious over how they planned to get information out of the men who'd staked out the Revive Center. She wasn't crazy about confronting people who were capable of killing.

The hotel had a lounge and they checked that first. The men's car was parked in the lot so they were in the building somewhere. Jasper and Dwight had guessed right. Although Sadie hadn't seen the men close up, she recognized the driver's bald head and stocky build. The man sitting next to him at the bar laughed at something the smaller man said. He was thinner and taller and had short dark hair.

Dwight approached one side of the duo and Jasper the other. Sadie stood back to Jasper's right. The two men looked from one man to the other and then both froze when they saw Sadie.

"I'd introduce ourselves but you already know who we are," Jasper said.

"We've never seen you before," the bald man said.

"Let's cut the bull. You were parked in front of the Revive Center. Why?" Jasper pulled open his jacket a fraction, just enough to show he was armed.

"You must have us confused with someone else," the thinner man said.

"I followed you from the Center to this hotel," Dwight said. "We know you were watching for Sadie."

"Sadie?" the bald man repeated, sliding a glance toward her.

She lifted her chin, refusing to crumble with his subtle challenge. Sadie wasn't the name he'd been given.

"Our business is our business." The bald man stood, having to look up at Jasper. "You'd best be minding your own."

"Or what?" Jasper asked. "Who do you work for?"

"Or you may find yourself in a lot more trouble than you think."

The thin man stood and took his partner by the arm. "Let's get out of here."

"Who sent you here?" Jasper asked.

"Have a good night," the thinner man said.

As they started to walk away, Dwight stepped forward as if he'd go after them, but Jasper stopped him.

"You have it backward, by the way," Jasper called after the men. They paused and turned to look back. "You both may find yourself in a lot more trouble than you think. Tell your boss he better back off."

The bald man scoffed and the thinner man grinned cynically.

"The big guy has a sense of humor," the bald man said.

Around them people began to take notice of them, conversation fading as the music continued to play.

"I think you know who you're talking to," Dwight said.

"Jasper Roesch from some highfalutin PI agency." The bald man nodded. "Yeah. We know all about you."

Sadie saw that Jasper was neither surprised nor alarmed. He must have expected them to know about him. They had, after all, staked out Sadie's company and probably at least knew of the attack at her home.

"Then you're not as smart as I suspected," Jasper said. "Tell your boss he's been warned." He stepped forward until he loomed over the bald man. "And none of you will get another chance."

"That's awfully big talk for one man," the thinner man said, still wearing that creepy grin.

"You assume there's just one?" Jasper's grin was much more shrewd and fearless.

"You have no idea who you're dealing with," the bald man said.

"Then enlighten me."

With a scoff, the bald man turned, the thinner man following.

Sadie wondered if either man realized Jasper had only tried to dupe them into revealing who'd sent them. She could tell him, but then she'd have to tell him the rest and not only did she not trust him with what he'd do with that information, she feared the consequences.

"Well, that was a waste of time," Dwight said, coming to stand beside Jasper.

"Not entirely. A message will be delivered."

"You may have poked the sleeping tiger."

Jasper turned to look at him. "Which tiger would that be?"

Bernie's killer or the one that sent attackers crashing through her fence?

Dwight looked away, meeting Sadie's eyes. He wouldn't say a word unless she gave her consent. And she wouldn't, at least, not yet. Not until she had no other choice.

"I hope park benches don't become a regular thing for you," Sadie said, sitting on the Warren Park bench facing the lake.

Today she'd abandoned her flannel for an eye-catching white sweater dress, gray over-the-knee boots and a stylish matching gray hat with a brim that angled over her sexy dark eyes. She'd left her hair down and the thick, wavy mane covered her shoulders and tops of her breasts. That narrow path of thigh between the hem of the dress and the top of her boots had drawn his attention more than once. She wore tights for warmth but her legs might as well be bare.

"Being in the same environment as the killer sometimes helps me piece together clues," he said, choosing not to let his mind wander back to their kiss on the last bench they'd shared. "What was the killer thinking, bringing Bernie here? Why this park?"

"Is anything coming to you?"

"Not yet. But it must have meant something to the killer. He had a reason for choosing this place."

Sadie turned away, her gaze going over the park and lake. Could she tell him anything that might help? Would she? Jasper had brought her here not only for himself. He hoped some of her guarded shell would crack enough to give him some kind of clue.

After several seconds, she faced him again. "You really do think Bernie's murder is related to those men tailing me, don't you?"

She must not have believed it when she'd made the suggestion herself after the attack. "Because of where Bernie's body was placed, yes."

"Why?"

"It was too deliberate. It's as though Bernie was chosen because he meant something to you."

She drew in a breath. "No. That can't be." Denial made her react that way. She may have wondered if Bernie's murder was related to the attack but she'd never considered someone would be killed because she cared for them.

He was on to something. She knew of a reason or someone who would have a reason to go after her through her precious homeless people. "Why not?"

"My comings and goings at the Revive Center were not made public." She was reaching again, making up excuses.

"You came to the Center in secret?" he challenged her.

She averted her face, once again taking in the grounds.

"Damn it, Sadie. Give me something." He couldn't leash his frustration any longer. "Who would hurt someone you care about?"

When she turned to him again, he could see her

fearful hesitation along with her own frustration. Just when he thought she'd open a door, she abruptly stood and began walking away.

He easily caught up.

"You brought me here on purpose," she said. "The perfect setting to get under my skin. The killer brought Bernie's body here for a reason and you wanted me to see it up close and personal."

She blamed him for trying? How could she be upset with him? She was the one lying, not him.

"You need to come clean with me about your past," he said. "I did bring you on purpose but I also came here to get a feel for the killer's intent." He hadn't lied about that. Coming here had reinforced his hunch that Bernie's murder was related to her attack.

She walked without responding.

"Why won't you trust me?" he asked.

Stopping, she faced him with troubled eyes. He wanted to make her feel safe so she wouldn't ever have to look that way again. She frustrated him to no end with her secret-keeping but her stunning Spanish beauty and glimpses of vulnerability deflated that.

He took her hand and tugged her to him, slipping his arm around her and then running the backs of his fingers along the soft skin of her face.

"Who would hurt someone you care about?" he asked again.

Closing her eyes, she moved into his caress as though the touch drugged her. If this continued he'd be on to other things in a hurry. He put his fingers beneath her chin and waited for her to open her eyes.

"Trust me with that much, Sadie."

She closed her eyes again, tighter, but then opened

them again, looking straight into his eyes for many more seconds.

"The last man I trusted turned out to be someone I didn't know," she said at last.

Okay, now they were getting somewhere. He lowered his hand from her face, holding her loosely. "What did he turn out to be?"

She gazed down at her hands flattened on his chest between his open jacket. "When I met him he said he owned a company that manufactured high-tech components that go into spacecraft. Military electronics. He took me to nice restaurants and was always a perfect gentleman. He spoke like an educated man and made lots of money." She looked up and into his eyes again. "But I found out he had no college education and his closest friends were either addicted to drugs or dealing them. He had a criminal record, mostly related to drugs. My father hated him so I didn't think to do a background check on him. I felt this perverse kind of thrill that I would fall for a man so unlike my father. It was the dumbest decision I've ever made."

"You married him?"

"No. I told you the truth about that. But I moved in with him. That was enough to put me in danger. I barely got out of there with my life."

Elated he'd gotten that much out of her, Jasper ran his hand up her back in an encouraging rub. "Why did you have to leave that way? Was he abusive?"

"And a liar. And very dangerous. He went ballistic when I confronted him on the drugs and afterward refused to let me go see a doctor. I was a prisoner in my own house."

Everything was starting to make more sense. "How badly did he hurt you?"

"He smacked me a few times, mostly slapping my face. He never punched me and actually was proud of that. He threatened to, though. He liked to use that against me, his threats to start punching or kicking me. I got away before he could. And I have to stay away."

Jasper couldn't wait to track this guy down and teach him a thing or two about how to treat a woman. But he had to tamp down his rage and stay in line with what she finally revealed.

He had so many questions he had to take his time choosing the one he needed to ask first. "How did you get away?"

"Steven helped me escape," she said.

"Why Steven?" Was he her friend or someone else?

"He works for…him."

Jasper didn't miss how she'd carefully avoided saying the abusive man's name. "He still works for him?"

"Yes."

She admitted to her lie that Steven had been head of security at the Revive Center.

"Who was killed trying to help you?" he asked.

Her eyes lowered and he felt her slipping away, retreating back into her protective shell.

"You told me once that you didn't want to risk anyone else's life," he pressed. "Who was killed, Sadie?"

She lifted her gaze. "A police officer."

He couldn't believe she'd told him. "You went to the police over the abuse?"

She hesitated and he saw her work for a reply, which told him all he needed to know. She wouldn't tell him the truth about that.

"Yes."

No, she'd gone for another reason, something that involved her ex. "What's his name?"

She shook her head.

"What about your ex? I need his last name, Sadie."

And that's when he saw her go behind her shell again. He'd get no more out of her. He let her go when she gave a gentle push.

She started walking again. He fell into step beside her, satisfied he'd gotten much more than he'd anticipated, but he wasn't quite finished with their talk.

"A hero never hurts his woman," he said. "A hero never hurts anyone. A hero protects those close to him. They don't have to be close to his heart. They can be close in proximity. A hero protects the innocent and tears down the guilty. Especially for those closest."

"You think I don't know that?"

"I'm just saying. There's a difference between a hero and a guy like the one you were with." Jasper hadn't said it but he'd tear down her ex if he ever found him. And she should know by now that she could trust him.

She walked in silence a few steps, the sidewalk winding through a grassy area fringed with flowers that would burst into color this summer.

"You of all people should understand how hard it is to trust after someone you loved betrays you." Just before they reached the parking area, she stopped walking. "When I asked you what happened between you and that woman you loved, you said 'the usual.' I don't know what happened, but I do know that it wasn't *usual*. We share that in common, Jasper. I picked up on it then and I feel it more than ever now. Your situation may have been much different. I ran from an abuser who lied to me about who he really was, and you…? What happened in your situation?"

Was that what drew him so inexorably to her? This inner sense that their hearts were linked because of past experiences? Injured souls didn't trust again easily but maybe that abated with someone who'd been through something equally damaging.

"There was one thing I left out on my list of things heroes do," he finally said. "Heroes respect their family. But that's one area I don't own bragging rights."

"The woman you loved was part of your family? Was she married to your brother?"

"My uncle. Didn't Dwight tell you?"

"Dwight knew?"

"He knew part of the story. Not all of it." People passed them in both directions along the path. Jasper put his hand on her back and guided her to another bench. When he sat, he leaned with his forearms on his legs and looked out across the park and the parking area. "My uncle is a lot like your father." That was as good of a place as any to start this tale. Jasper sat up and looked at Sadie, whose beautiful dark eyes searched into him with heartfelt interest. "He made his fortune selling cars, opening several dealerships around the country. He liked me when I was a kid, I think because I was always such a daredevil. He took risks in business and respected others like him. But he was selfish, like your father, and treated those he considered beneath him with condescension. He embarrassed me at times, whether at family events or whenever he attended school functions. He wore his wealth like a badge, in a gluttonous way." Jasper let a few of those memories pass through him. And then those led to other memories, filling him with a familiar ache, a familiar sorrow. And plenty of regret.

"He married a woman much younger than him," he said. "He was my father's older brother. He wasn't older by much but you do the math. Kaelyn was just a few years older than me."

"She was the woman you loved," Sadie said without judgment.

"I didn't plan on anything happening, but the more I talked with her, the more I fell in love with her. At least I thought it was love. Sometimes I wonder if the wrongness of it gave me a thrill I couldn't resist, and maybe I justified my actions based on my lack of respect for my uncle. One thing led to another and pretty soon we were sleeping together."

"Did she love you?" Sadie asked.

No one had ever asked him that and it came with a piercing stab of regret. "Yes." He'd always felt she loved him more than he loved her, something else that made him believe he hadn't truly loved her, which only intensified his remorse.

"I found out he was hitting her and wanted to kill him," Jasper said. "She wouldn't leave him because she was afraid. I told her I'd help her, but she was too concerned over his reaction, me being his nephew and all. He found out about us and came after me with a gun. I got the gun away from him and he kept coming after me, so I shot him in the leg. The chief didn't release any information on it, but my uncle spread plenty of lies about what really happened, saying I came after him over a family dispute." Jasper grunted a cynical laugh. "He said it was over money, not his wife. I resigned in the wake of all the publicity. I broke things off with Kaelyn when I went to work for DAI. Kadin doesn't view those kinds of actions as wrong. He sees through a lot. He gave me a chance and I've worked hard to earn his respect."

"You didn't mean to hurt your uncle."

"Didn't I?" he countered.

"Respect is important to you," Sadie said.

Why did she pick that part out? "Both ways. Yeah, I suppose it is, among other things." Loyalty. Faithfulness. Honor. Integrity.

"You loved that woman," she said. "You didn't use her to get under your uncle's skin. You didn't use her to punish him. You loved her."

"Maybe," he had to concede. "It was hard to tell through all my guilt."

"Why did you feel guilty?"

"Sleeping with my uncle's wife? Any decent fool would feel that way. I should have backed off when things started to get intimate. After that first kiss, I should have stayed away. But I didn't. I didn't respect my uncle and even though he was a jerk, I still should have respected his marriage. Not for his sake, but for hers. I could have helped her get away from him. I could have." This was the part he could never talk about, the part that ripped him in half and destroyed him.

"You're talking as though..." Sadie stopped as realization popped her eyes wider. "You aren't saying she...that your uncle...did he kill her?"

"No, but he may as well have. She hanged herself after he beat her one last time, this time for trying to leave. She had her suitcase packed and in the car. He dragged her back inside, according to neighbors. The next day she made it to the hospital and pressed charges. I went back to Toledo and gave him a dose of his own medicine. Told him if he ever went near her again I'd kill him. He stayed away from her and it looked like she'd finally be free of him. But the charges she filed didn't result in jail time. When I came back after finding out she was in the hospital, Kaelyn begged me to take her with me. She begged me to start a new life with her in Wyoming where I had moved. I denied her. There was already too much drama. Everyone in my family was on me for having the affair in the first place. That only made the abuse worse. I told Kaelyn I'd get her somewhere safe and make sure my uncle never hurt her again. She agreed to meet me the next day. I had everything planned. But she never showed up. My dad called and told me she'd hanged herself. My uncle blames me."

"That wasn't your fault! He was abusive and she felt she had no way out."

"She did, though. I was her way out." But he'd abandoned her by refusing to take her with him, citing that the two of them staying together would cause too much tension in the family. He had to do the right thing. He knew his uncle didn't deserve her, but long-term if Jasper had stayed with her it would have torn the family apart. Jasper ending their relationship had nothing to do with how he felt about his uncle. It had everything to do with honor. Honor for himself and for Kaelyn.

"She didn't hang herself because you let her go, Jasper. You can't think that."

He met her imploring eyes and knew she meant it with all her heart. She was a woman who'd survived an abusive man. She must know how desperate a woman would feel in that situation, how helpless and stuck, unable to see a way out.

"That was at least part of it. She loved me. I know she did. And I abandoned her at her lowest. She needed me and I wasn't there for her."

"But you were. You would have gotten her somewhere safe. She must have known that. Her husband had her beaten down so much that she couldn't reason her way out of her despair."

"It doesn't matter anymore," he said. "What matters is she's dead."

"You didn't kill her."

"No. But she's dead." He could tell her he missed the woman but he wasn't sure he'd be completely honest. What they'd had was wrong. Any regrets or sadness he felt stemmed from that more than his love for her. The wrongness. He still couldn't believe he'd allowed something like that to happen. Him. A man who valued heroism.

Sadie put her hand along his face and moved toward him. Before he could stop her, she pressed a soft kiss to his lips, nothing sexual, just supportive. She couldn't know how much more powerful that was. He almost took it to the next level. Except she cooled everything when she drew back and said, "Let's go get chocolate."

Chapter 9

Sadie couldn't stop thinking about everything she and Jasper had talked about yesterday. She finally gave in to them and reclined on the sofa, facing the darkened window and listening to the rain patter.

She never talked about Darien with anyone. Not only did that bring up too many bad memories, it was dangerous talking about him. Talking about him could lead down a slippery path. But what stayed with her long after they had left the park was all he'd revealed about the woman he'd once loved. He'd wanted to save her and couldn't. That touched a soft spot inside her and made her think of Steven.

She'd never told anyone, but he had feelings for her and that's what made him help her. She'd told him she wasn't interested, though. At the time she hadn't thought she would be interested in any man for a very long time, and she hadn't been, not until Jasper came along. He'd awakened something in her, something she couldn't shake, and now she felt drawn to him more than ever.

He felt responsible for Kaelyn killing herself. Sadie had thought about that all night. That poor woman had lived in an abusive marriage and then had met a man like Jasper, a chivalrous man, a strong man with a righteous mind. She must have been in awe, maybe full of disbelief that a man like him would love her. And then when he'd turned her down she must have been crushed. She must have envisioned a life doomed to never being free of her horrible husband. Sadie had felt that way with Darien.

Sadie could well understand why Jasper felt guilty. But Kaelyn taking her own life was not his fault. He'd cared about her and would have helped her. He just couldn't give her his heart. What would it take to capture his heart? The adventurer, the thrill seeker. The lawman. The Good Samaritan.

When her core tickled with imagination, Sadie forced herself to stop.

Hearing a phone ring, she twisted on the sofa to see Jasper still sitting at the kitchen island where he'd been working on his laptop. He answered and after a few seconds he turned sharply to Sadie.

"When?" he asked the caller, and then listened for a longer period of time. "We're on our way."

She stood as he did, alarmed and full of apprehension. "What is it?"

"Eddy Anderson has been kidnapped. A ransom note was left in his apartment."

Sadie sucked in a breath. "He was taken from his apartment?"

"It appears that way."

Wouldn't that mean he knew whoever had taken him? Or had he been accosted outside and forced at gunpoint from then on.

"The ransom letter demands one million and the abductor will call the Revive Center one hour from now with instructions on where to make the drop."

"Ransom?" That made no sense. First murder, then the attack and now this?

"The letter contained a threat not to involve police."

"Or the kidnapper will kill Eddy?"

Jasper nodded soberly.

Sadie put her hand to her mouth. She could not endure another loss like that.

Jasper walked with Sadie to the front entrance of the Revive Center, carrying his laptop case and hurrying to get them out of the steady rain. He didn't like seeing Sadie so stressed. His desire to make her happy redoubled, to keep the sadness out of her eyes. Their intimate talk must be to blame. He had no other explanation for this inner rise of protectiveness he felt for her. Talking about Kaelyn had never been easy for him, but with Sadie the words hadn't been as difficult as he'd expected. Maybe that was due to the similarities they shared. Life had a way of making sense in retrospect. Some things seemed to happen for a reason. Had fate put him outside DAI when Sadie drove up in her Ferrari? He wasn't sure he was ready for that kind of fate.

"Those men saw us talking to Eddy," Sadie said.

Jasper passed through the revolving door with her. "I don't think they did. Remember their view of us was blocked. They didn't see us on the bench."

He took her hand as they headed for the inner offices. Going through the door to the reception room, they ran into Dwight, who'd been the one to call him about the kidnapping. After they'd confronted the two men who'd staked out the Revive Center, he'd gone back there to watch the men who'd taken over the night shift. The room was empty of all but them.

"This doesn't make sense," Sadie said. "Why kill Bernie, attack my home, spy on me here and then kidnap another homeless person?"

"I'd like an answer to that question myself," Jasper said, taking his laptop case behind the counter. "It's almost as if someone is toying with you."

"So far there's been no contact," Dwight said, following Jasper. "The message said the call would come here."

While Jasper took out his laptop, Sadie meandered through tables, passing vending machines and the two refrigerators in the kitchen area.

"Boot this up for me, will you?" Jasper asked.

"Yeah, sure." He sat on the stool and went to work.

Sadie went into an alcove where a few more tables offered a little more privacy, disappearing from view. Jasper left the front counter and headed toward the alcove. Reaching that, he saw she had stopped by the far windows, darkened since the sun had set hours ago. Hugging her arms, a shudder seemed to pass through her. Her shoulders rose and fell with a slight tremble.

He went to her, glancing at Dwight, who'd sat down on the chair behind the counter, passing time with a

magazine as he waited for the phone on the counter
to ring. Standing behind Sadie, Jasper put his hand
on her upper arm. She must have heard him because
she didn't flinch at his touch. He looked through the
window. The reception area was dim, with after-hour
lighting. Through the glittering reflection of rain droplets clinging to the glass, he could see lights from the
adjacent building and part of the apartment building
to the right. Some trees in the landscaping along the
Revive Center blocked some of the view.

"What if Eddy is killed?" she asked.

"He won't be."

She tipped her head up. "How can you be so sure?"

"I'm not sure how, I'm just sure that whoever kidnapped him wants money and that's not in line with
Bernie's murder."

"You don't think they're related?"

"We're going to find out."

"I can't bear another of my clients being killed,"
she said.

"If I have my way that will never happen."

She faced the window again, looking at him
through the dimly reflected light on the glass, freck-
led by droplets of rain. He met her gaze and a shot of
warmth sizzled through him. Her face was so beautiful. He lifted his free hand and fingered strands of
her hair between his fingers. That led to the desire to
brush the rest of the strands away from her slender,
soft neck. First he kissed the skin there.

Hearing her increased breaths, he kissed her jaw-
line. Then he tipped her chin up with his fingers and
kissed her mouth. She turned and looped her arms
around his neck, her fingers going into his hair. Her

breasts pressed just below his chest. He held her to him, kissing her the way he longed to as soon as he'd seen her face in the reflection. When she began to make sounds that told him she was more than ready to take this somewhere with a door, he withdrew from the kiss. Breathing with her to calm their passion, he couldn't resist touching her hair one more time. He put his hands on each side of her head and rested his forehead against hers.

"Jasper?" She sounded breathless and aroused.

"Yes?" he answered in a raspy voice that was equally aroused.

"What are we going to do about this?"

"I don't know. Maybe just let it run its course?"

She moved her head back and searched his eyes, a question in them. What if the course never ended?

The phone rang in the silent reception room, abruptly ending that conversation.

Sadie rushed to the front counter as Dwight picked up the phone.

Jasper wrote down the number displayed in the caller ID filed of the phone.

After Dwight listened awhile he said, "We need proof of life."

With that, Sadie moved a few slow steps closer, eyes wide with apprehension.

Jasper resisted his urge to go to her and went to work on his computer.

"Eddy? E—" Dwight must have been cut off. After a moment he said, "Yes." And then hung up.

"What is it?" Sadie asked.

"We have twenty-four hours," Dwight said.

Sadie didn't balk at the amount. "Is Eddy all right?"

"He sounded scared but in one piece." He looked at Jasper. "It was a woman."

Their enemy could have arranged for anyone to make that call. Or his instinct was dead-on and this had nothing to do with Bernie's murder.

He finished working with the triangulation software. It picked up on four towers with the strongest signals and outlined the area on a map. When he realized which neighborhood the call had come from, he went utterly still. No. It couldn't be.

"What's gotten into you?" Sadie asked as Jasper drove them to a private airport she never even knew about until then, the windshield wipers a monotonous rhythm.

"We're going to get Eddy back."

He'd been evasive when she and Dwight asked why he'd seemed so shocked looking at the results from the cell tower triangulation report. Then he'd told Dwight to stay at the Center in case another call came in and taken Sadie with him.

The private airport had a small terminal building.

"Why are we here again?" asked Sadie. "You've been such a fountain of information since we left the Revive Center."

Outdoor lighting illuminated the parking lot and double door entrance, enough for her to see his frown at her sarcasm. The rain had abated some, but still sprinkled down steadily.

"As soon as Dwight called with the ransom demand, I got a hold of Kadin. He's sending some… necessities."

Sadie didn't question him, just went inside the terminal and walked with him toward the only counter there. An Asian man stood there, looking up from a tablet he must use to pass the time at this hour of night.

"You Jasper Roesch?" the Asian man asked.

"Yes."

"Your plane is arriving now. They're approaching the runway. Gate Three." He pointed. "That door."

"Thanks."

Sadie walked with him through the waiting area to the other side of the terminal. "Wow, people know who you are here."

When he reached one of five pairs of doors, he held one open for her. "DAI has contracts with certain private airports."

By certain she was sure he meant the airport allowed them to bring in things others wouldn't. And when had he arranged all of this? He must have called right after he'd talked to Dwight, maybe when she'd gone to change before going to the Center.

Standing outside beneath an overhang to stay out of the rain, they waited a few minutes. Then Sadie spotted a plane taxiing toward them. A sleek white jet came to a stop at Gate Three. Moments later, a door opened and stairs were lowered. A big man appeared. With dark hair in a buzz cut, he carried a duffel bag and stepped down the stairs. His long, ground-eating strides brought him to them under the overhang.

"Sadie, this is Jamie Knox, DAI's head of security."

Jamie's clever blue eyes found her with a nod. Sadie sensed a good but powerful man in him, one who upheld justice with the same righteousness as Jasper.

"This is Sadie Moreno."

"Nice to meet you in person, Sadie, I've heard all about you."

Sadie glanced at Jasper. How much had he told him? She had to assume everything.

"Did you get the call?" Jamie asked.

"We did. I have tracking capability on the phone. Looks like the abductor took Eddy to her house. This is no professional."

"Her?" Sadie eyed Jasper accusingly.

At last he relented. "Deloris Moreno lives in the vicinity of the triangulation," he said.

Talk about things one never expects to hear. The ex-wife of the man she'd assumed her false identity as his daughter?

"Why didn't you tell me that already?"

"Why didn't you tell me you weren't really George Moreno's daughter?" he shot back.

"There'll be time for lover's quarrels later," Jamie said, looking back at the inclement weather. "I'd like to get this finished and get back to my own lover."

"Uh... We're not—"

"Reese tried to say the same thing for a while," Jamie stopped her with a knowing grin. "Funny, how after you fall in love you can recognize it on other people right away."

Sadie was the opposite. She could recognize people in love because she'd never been in love.

Two more men stepped out of the plane, one of them finishing with his combat vest, fastening an ammunition pouch.

"We located the kidnapper. We won't be dealing with a career criminal." Jasper got down to business, clearly not comfortable with that kind of talk.

"Who is it? You know the person?" Jamie asked.

Jasper glanced over at Sadie with a little frustration. "Sadie's supposed ex-stepmother."

"Supposed?"

"I'll explain later. Let's get a move on."

The other two men joined them and Sadie was relieved she wouldn't have to get into any details of her past just yet. But she knew the time had come when she would have to.

"This is Mark and Doug. Both former SEALs. They've done several hostile rescues. Mostly Middle East. This will be a walk through a daisy field for them."

Sadie saw how the compliment didn't faze either man. She felt a little disconcerted to be in the company of such dangerous men. She also felt empowered. Eddy would be rescued tonight.

Jasper forced Sadie to wait in the rental while he and Jasper's team surrounded Deloris's house. Jamie had come amply armed with automatic weapons, night vision and communication. He even had a radar that showed two people inside the house, one who moved around in a nervous way and another who sat on a chair, presumably tied there.

Deloris thought she had until tomorrow night, when she'd meet them for the drop. Jasper almost pitied her for also thinking she could get away with this. She'd been smart enough to use a disposable phone but not enough to know her location could be traced.

Jamie's plan was simple. Two men would go in from the back and he and Jasper would go in the front. This would be over quickly. Jasper looked forward to the questioning—before the police would arrive. The plan was to call 911 when they were finished with Deloris. Then he'd take Sadie back to the hotel room, where she'd tell him everything she'd left out so far. At least, that was how he hoped it would go.

Jasper made hand signals to Jamie for him to get the door ready. Jamie planted an explosive near the lock mechanism and then they waited for the second team to give their ready word through the radio.

"Team Beta in position," came the voice over the radio.

"Alpha going in hot," Jamie said, gesturing to Jasper to take cover.

Jasper turned his back and did take cover along the wall, Jamie doing the same on the other side of the door. The explosive was just enough to shatter the door from the frame—and enough to cause Deloris the shock of her life. Jasper didn't know that yet. He only imagined it, but he was pretty sure she'd be shocked.

Jasper entered with gun drawn, covering Jamie as he followed. Eddy sat in the living room, tied with his hands behind the chair and feet to the legs. He breathed fast through his nose and his eyes had bugged out from the unexpected explosion. He also had duct tape covering his mouth. As he must register they weren't here to harm him but rather help him, Eddy nodded toward the kitchen.

Jasper moved in sync with Jamie there. Deloris stood frozen, wearing a Kiss the Cook apron and holding a frying pan in one oven-mitted hand. She'd been in the middle of serving dinner. The idea sort of threw Jasper. She was an older woman who didn't fit the profile of a kidnapper and ransom demander anyway, and here she was falling right back into her everyday life. Had she planned to feed Eddy one of her home-cooked meals, too?

Team Beta came smashing in through the back sliding glass door, startling Deloris further so that she dropped the pan, a creamy chicken dish splattering all over the floor, steaming.

"Hands up," Jasper told her.

She complied while Team Beta rushed into the living room where Deloris had left Eddy to prepare dinner and began untying him and ripping the duct tape off his mouth.

"Get me away from that crazy woman!" Eddy said.

"Are you all right?" one of the other operatives asked.

"Yeah, I'm all right. If I'd have known Grandma here was my abductor, I'd have fought her when she put a gun to my head."

Jamie went to Deloris and pulled her hands behind her as she began to sob. "How did you find me?"

Going to stand in front of her, Jasper met her defeated eyes. "It was easy. What were you thinking trying something like this?"

She sobbed as her tearfulness intensified, bowing her head. "After you came here and told me that woman stole all of George's money, I just got so angry. I was angry after George died and found out he left me nothing. I've never gotten over it. I treated him well. Why didn't he take care of me?"

"Deloris, Sadie didn't steal George's money. She only assumed a false identity with a believable enough story to explain her own wealth." All she'd needed to do was hide from the man who frightened her.

Sadie appeared through the front door, going to Eddy, who stood by the two ops men.

"Eddy! Are you okay?"

"I'm fine, Miss Moreno."

"You're not a Moreno!" Deloris shouted, shaking her finger in anger. "How dare you steal what's not yours!"

"Come on, Eddy. I'll take you home."

"Hold on, Sadie," Jasper stopped her. "The police will be here soon."

"What?" She looked horrified.

She was afraid of being caught with her fake name.

"We can probably resolve this without the cops," Jamie said.

Jasper agreed. He just wanted to rile Sadie up enough to loosen up her tongue for later.

"I swear I won't try it again," Deloris said.

"You're right, you won't," Jamie said, walking toward her with menacing strides. "Because we'll be watching you. The rest of your life, I'll know if you get anywhere near anyone close to Sadie."

"And I won't let you near her," Jasper added.

Jamie thumbed toward Jasper. "He's the guy you need to watch. Don't cross him again. Take my word for it. When a man like him loves a woman, he'll do anything to protect her." He leaned forward a bit. "That includes killing for her."

Deloris gasped and drew her head back. Then she jerked her gaze from Jamie to Jasper.

"You never know when or where we'll appear, Ms. Moreno," Jamie went on. "One day you might think we aren't watching and imagine giving another ransom another try. Or maybe you'll go after Sadie herself."

Jamie moved his forefinger back and forth. "Don't make that mistake."

"We'll be watching," Jasper said.

Deloris's eyes shifted from each man as they spoke. "I won't. I swear. No police. I won't survive a day in prison."

Neither would Sadie. Jasper looked over at her, not even trying to subdue his scowl.

Just then his cell phone rang.

"We've got this," Jamie said. "Take Eddy and your lady home."

"Thanks, man."

"We're a team."

And a fine one at that. Jasper was proud to be part of that. He answered his cell on his way to Sadie.

"Mr. Roesch?"

"Yes?"

"Dwight Mitchel asked me to call you. He's been shot and is on his way to the hospital."

"Who is this?"

"Carol. From the Revive Center. There's been an incident. Someone left a dead animal in the lobby with these Loredo candies dumped on it. Dwight caught the man and he was shot."

Jasper cursed. "Where is the man now?"

"He got away. Police are here now."

Candies. The person who'd left the dead animal had left candies.

Loredo candies.

The sun was coming up behind a blanket of clouds when Jasper finally sat in front of his laptop doing an internet search on Loredo candies. He and Sadie had gone to the hospital and waited until the doctor finished surgery on Dwight. After finding out Dwight would survive his gunshot wound to his abdomen, they'd returned to the hotel.

Sadie had gone straight to bed, exhausted and at the end of her endurance. He'd resisted comforting her, fearing that would escalate to something else. And he had another agenda. He hadn't told her about the candies, only that a dead animal had been left at the Center.

Now he finished reading a news article, one of several he'd found on the Loredo family and the confectionery corporation founded by Matias Loredo. *Loredo Confectionery Corporation*. Matias and Ana Sophia Loredo had a daughter, Catalina Loredo. Jasper stared at a photo of her. Dark hair slicked back, no makeup and wearing an inflexibly prim gray pantsuit, she possessed a stunning presence. Tall, slender, head held high. Controlled. Confident. Ruthless businesswoman. Unapproachable in every way. She looking nothing like the long-haired tussled beauty he'd seen get out of a Ferrari in a sexy black dress, but he had no doubt she was the same woman. Anyone who looked close enough would recognize her.

While he'd expected her past would be something like this, he still couldn't believe all he'd learned. Sadie did have a mother and a father who were both very much alive. She was an only child and had run a branch of Loredo Confectionery Corporation in Toronto, Ontario, Canada. The company's headquarters were in Philadelphia. Her love of candy now made sense. Apparently, she'd inherited more than a love of money from her father. She also loved chocolate.

She'd been engaged to be married to Darien Jafari, a successful high-tech component manufacturer from Toronto. She'd lived with the man up until her disappearance five years ago.

Jasper also read an article about a murder she'd witnessed and reported to the police. The article also reported the detective assigned to the case was shot. Police hadn't given out much detail, only saying the killer hadn't been found and with Catalina's disappearance, they had no other witnesses. Police touched on the possibility that the detective's murder was related to the one Catalina witnessed and that Catalina had gone on the run, fearing for her life.

Catalina's fiancé appeared devastated over her disappearance. He'd cooperated with police and expressed his anxiety to the press. So had her mother. Jasper spent long moments studying photos of her. The resemblance to Sadie was evident. Her mother had met Matias at a Philadelphia art show early in his career. He'd emigrated from Mexico with his parents. The photos of him revealed a confident man who seldom smiled. Quotes of things he said revealed his selfish, ruling nature. Sadie's mother portrayed someone of the opposite nature. She seemed so lost, and not because of her daughter's unexplained absence. She didn't seem happy in any other photo prior to Sadie's vanishing.

Sadie had told him the truth about certain things, most intriguing, about her father. She couldn't hide that emotion. Lucky for her, George Moreno had died a wealthy man she could portray him personally any way she wished. She'd reported the murder and the killer had gone after the detective and probably her.

Fear had driven her into hiding. She couldn't testify until the killer was captured. He couldn't hold that against her, but he also couldn't help feeling resentment. Maybe resentment was too strong of a word. Injured. Was his pride hurt that she hadn't trusted him enough to confide in him? He had a personal reaction. His feelings for her, his deep attraction, caused this friction. He didn't like how that clouded his professional ability to solve Bernie's and now these other two murders.

Chapter 10

"Have you been to sleep yet?"

Jasper looked up, startled that Sadie had jarred him from thought. He still sat in front of his laptop, ruminating over all he'd learned about the woman who'd so enchanted and captivated him. He was attracted to a beautiful woman…who lied.

"No."

Her eyes, still sleepy and waking up, shifted to his laptop and the darkened screen, then to the coffee cup and two empty bottles of water. He'd clearly been busy with his night owl time.

Without comment, she went into the kitchen area, retrieving a cup and pouring some coffee still left in the pot he'd brewed. After that she faced him, holding the steaming cup in both hands and leaning against the counter, watching him. She seemed wary.

He didn't even know where to begin. Mostly he felt cornered with all his feelings about her. He would not abandon her but he wished he could shut her out of his heart.

After a couple of sips, Sadie stepped toward the table, her long white nightgown transparent enough for him to see her legs and a glimpse of the apex of her thighs. Of course the man in him took special notice of that.

She sat across from him and the man in him appreciated her breasts without a bra for a moment or two.

"My real name was Catalina Loredo," she said.

Her unexpected declaration surprised him, refreshingly. She lightened his tired mood in an instant. She was going to tell him? He didn't have to pry it out of her?

"My father is Matias Loredo. My mother isn't dead. I'm sorry I lied to you about that. George Moreno's wife died so I had to stick to that story."

Jasper didn't say anything when she paused. If she wanted his forgiveness he wasn't ready to give it.

"My mother's name is Ana Sophia," she continued, not seeming bothered that he hadn't responded. "Other than Steven, she's the only one who knows why I had to disappear."

"Your household staff?" he asked succinctly.

"They know why I had to disappear, but they don't know my real name." She met his eyes as he waited for her to continue, weirdly vindicated in making her do all the work. "I know you probably read all about me, but there are things you wouldn't have been able to read."

"And now you're going to tell me?"

Somberly her eyes lowered before lifting again. "I don't want to. But you already know, so it doesn't matter now. You're in this with me. Your life is in danger no matter what I say or don't say."

"My life is my own and danger doesn't scare me. You should know that, Sadie. You should have known that from the start. You can't protect me, but I can protect both of us." He didn't mean to sound pompous but his frustration made him spell out the truth for her.

Holding her coffee cup with both hands again, she slowly lifted it and took a sip, as though gathering her thoughts along with savoring the warm, strong flavor.

"And for the record," Jasper had to add, "I'd like you to tell me because you trust me. Because you want to tell me." Not because she felt she had to, that she was forced.

Her eyes met his with new contemplation. He felt her honestly assess why she would finally tell him.

"I trust you with the case, Jasper," she said in a soft voice. "And I don't want anyone else to die."

"I'm not going to die," he said with conviction.

Her eyes closed in a slow, believing blink. Then she drew in a deep breath, let it go and began. "When all of this started, I reached a point in my life where I desperately needed change. I could no longer stand the sight of my father. I hated the sound of his voice. I loathed everything about him. He gave me the Toronto office and at first I thought it was a great career advancement and might be the change I was looking for. It was, at first. I had just met Darien and living in Canada was exciting. But running a confectionery wasn't what I aspired to do with my life. That was my father's dream. I always felt I was missing something, that I was meant to do something else, something that meant more to me. I had to make a change in my life. Darien and I were getting closer. He was different from my father. Considerate. Polite to others no matter who they were. He was successful, but not obsessed. He asked me to move in with him and told me I didn't have to work. He preferred that I didn't. That was all the encouragement I needed." She stopped talking as she must have drifted off with whatever memory that triggered. She shook her head slightly. "Looking back, I can see why I made the mistake of jumping into a serious relationship with him so quickly. He was a lifeline, a way out. An excuse." She looked up at Jasper, spearing him with her striking dark eyes.

"I flew back to Philadelphia and after visiting my mother, I went to the Loredo headquarters and told my father I quit." She breathed a wry laugh. "He flew into a rage. 'What do you expect me to do with the Toronto office?' He yelled at me. 'I can't replace you overnight!' I told him I didn't care and left. I went back to Toronto and Darien. Turns out he was furious with me, too. I couldn't believe I had fallen for someone like my father. I didn't tell him I was flying to Philadelphia until the morning I decided to do so. That was the first time he hit me. I was shocked. He was nothing like the man I had met. My father wasn't physically abusive so at least I can claim a difference there. I realized Darien had been playing a role all along. He knew how I felt about my father and was careful not to behave the same way, when in fact he was my father and worse." She averted her face, still cupping the warm cup on the table. "When I told him I wasn't accustomed to sharing my life with anyone, he only grew angrier. He told me if I ever did that again he'd lock me in a room. I packed a suitcase that night. But when I tried to leave, his guards stopped me. He did lock me in a room then. He told me the only way I'd ever leave him is if I was dead."

Jasper imagined how good it would feel to wrap his hands around that coward's neck. Weak men were the worst of any society.

"I kept a low profile after that, and at the same time began to spy on him. We reached a point where he began to trust me again. I could come and go as I pleased. He continued to threaten me. He said I could go wherever I wanted as long as I told him, but if I tried to leave him, he'd find me and kill me."

"Was he ever married before?"

She shook her head. "Not that I know of. I discovered he was running a drug operation and most who worked for him feared him intensely. One day I followed him to a bar in downtown Toronto. It wasn't like any place he'd ever gone to with me. It was run-down. Small. Old. And attracted a low-income patronage. I went inside and there was no one there, but I heard voices coming from the back. I stood out in the hall next to the door to an office and listened to Darien talking to a man who sounded like he was in pain. I peeked inside and saw Darien and another man had their backs to the door. They faced someone else tied to a chair. He was bloody, beaten. He saw me watching but didn't let on he did. Darien accused him of stealing from him. When the man tied to the chair denied this, the other man with Darien picked up a clear wrapped package of drugs and asked him where he got it. The tied man repeatedly said the drugs weren't his. But

Darien ordered the man with him to kill him. He did. He put the drugs down and drew a gun and just…shot him." She paused as though remembering in vivid detail what she'd seen, which must have been shocking and intensely disturbing. "The man looked at me right before that. He was looking at me when he was shot." She bowed her head with a shudder.

Jasper reached over and put his hand over hers. "Is that when you disappeared?"

Sadie lifted her head. "No. I ran from the building and went straight to the police. I told a detective how dangerous Darien was, how he abused me. I was afraid. He wanted to send me somewhere safe. But I was too scared. I believed Darien would kill me if I left. So I went home and pretended I knew nothing. The detective began to investigate the murder. He questioned Darien who of course denied everything. He kept asking the detective who witnessed the shooting. The detective wouldn't tell him. I found out a few days later that the man who was shot was one of Darien's suppliers."

"You stayed in the same house with him?" Jasper asked.

"Not for much longer. Darien was beginning to get more and more suspicious of me. I flew to Philadelphia to wait for the detective to capture the shooter. He never did. I think the shooter found him instead. Darien sent someone after me. Three men. One of them was Steven. He kept the other two from roughing me up, but they all brought me back to Darien. I think that's why Darien trusted Steven. He helped bring me back home. But Steven didn't know Darien was beating me. He found out, though, after he brought me home. He forced me to admit what I saw. I thought he was going to kill me. The next few weeks were pure hell. That's when Steven helped me plan my escape. He saw what Darien really was, and it wasn't a successful high-tech component manufacturer. If it wasn't for Steven, I might still be there…or dead by now. He arranged for my new identity and for my money to be transferred to an untraceable international account. First he put it in an account under my name and then transferred it to one in my new name. He knew someone who helped bury the transactions."

Jasper had a new respect for Steven and might even forgive him for lying. The lies had been necessary to protect Sadie.

"I stopped in Philadelphia to say goodbye to my mother and then went to Wyoming. I started the Revive Center and everything was fine until…Bernie."

"What about the murder in Toronto?" Jasper asked.

Her face drooped with regret. "That's why I kept in contact with Steven. He tried to help me get something else on Darien. Police didn't have enough to make an arrest and still don't."

"Another cold case."

Slowly, Sadie nodded, eyes moistening but not tearing completely. She turned her head.

She must have lived in constant fear of Darien finding her. Standing, he walked across the room to the window. Now more than ever he yearned to choke the life out of Darien Jafari. Men like him didn't deserve the air they breathed. Weakness made them monsters. A bully disguising an insecure man.

Solving Bernie's murder became infinitely more important to him. Now it was personal. Darien had harmed Sadie and still threatened her life. Jasper had to crush him. But something about Bernie's murder bothered him in light of the murder Sadie had witnessed. Her ex-fiancé was obsessed enough to haunt her by killing someone close to her, but why place the body in Warren Park? Jasper needed to know that if he ever hoped to solve the case.

Sadie watched Jasper standing at the window. The rain had stopped but clouds still hovered. He returned to the table, seeming oblivious to her while she felt waves of relief for finally letting go of her secret. She also felt closer to Jasper, as though she'd connected more with him. That came with some reservations, mainly because the last time she'd felt this euphoria she'd moved in with a madman.

Sitting down, he opened his laptop. Curious of what he was doing, she stood and moved beside him. He opened a map of Warren Park.

"The body was found here." Sadie pointed to a bridge that crossed a narrow part of the lake.

He studied the photo for endless moments.

"What are you looking for?"

"Something," he said. "Anything. There has to be something here we're missing."

She scrutinized the map with him. He switched to a satellite view and zoomed in, going over the entire area where the body was discovered.

Something in the water caught her eye. "What are those?"

He zoomed in more over the objects. "Poles."

"Trees," she said.

"What are we missing?" Jasper asked in frustration.

The answer slammed her. "Toronto."

Jasper looked up at her.

"Toronto got its name from the Mohawk meaning of trees in the water. Trees grew where a narrow body of water connected Lake Simcoe to Lake Couchiching. Look. This lake narrows where the bridge is located, and there are posts in the water near where Bernie's body was found." The more Sadie thought of it the angrier she grew. "That bastard was taunting me, sending me a clue." *Hello, darling, I'm coming for you.* "I should have seen that from the start."

"Don't be too upset. We're not exactly dealing with a sane person." Jasper stood and went back to the window. "He had a good time toying with you and then tried to kill you. When that failed, he arranged for the attack."

She walked across the living area to him. "He shouldn't have made the clue so hard to figure out. If I'd have died I'd have never known who wanted me dead… Well…I know Darien wants me dead, but I didn't anticipate he'd go after my friends."

"He didn't want to get caught. Maybe he liked the idea of you not figuring it out until he had you. Then he could have his fun letting you know."

She nodded. "Yeah, that's Darien's way. He needed to always feel in control." She wandered away from the window, hugging her arms.

"The witness who last saw Bernie," Jasper said, "The one who saw the expensive car and the license plate. Ontario has one sticker in the upper right and the writing is blue. Darien must have been the one to abduct Bernie."

She glanced back at him. "Or his assassin. Remember he had another man kill his supplier." And that man was still running free.

Jasper turned from the window. "Let's talk about him for a moment." He walked toward her. "We know why Bernie was killed. Why was that man?"

Turning to face him, Sadie shrugged as he stopped before her. "He stole drugs."

"Did he? Tell me about him."

Why did he want to know? As a detective he'd have lots of questions to ask but she failed to see the importance. Besides, thinking about him always upset her. "His name was Henry Barnes." She felt ill even saying his name. That poor man. "He had a wife and two kids." She would never forget the look in his eyes as he was being shot.

"What did he do for a living? You said he was Darien's supplier."

"He was a buyer for an aerospace company."

"He went to meet Darien about a business deal?"

Where was Jasper going with this? "Must have."

"But you said he was killed over drugs."

"Maybe that was his other reason for meeting Darien." Who knew what people did in their spare time? Even the most reputable of characters have been found to have bad sides.

"That doesn't make sense."

Sadie didn't follow him. "Why not?"

"He had a good job. College educated most likely. A family. Why steal drugs from a man who bought his company's components. Aerospace components. Rocket engine parts, I read."

"You never know with people," Sadie said, voicing her earlier thoughts.

"A guy like that wouldn't travel all the way to Canada to steal drugs. How would he get them back across the border?"

Good point. "Maybe he sold them while he was still there. Darien acted like he was threatened, like Henry had infringed on his territory."

"He was threatened all right, but not over drug turf."

She'd never considered that Darien would have another reason for killing that man. Had he told his bulldog to plant the drugs? Make it look like that's why the man was killed?

"Did you ever notice anything else about what Darien was doing?" Jasper asked.

"Illegally?" She shook her head. "But he was good at deceiving me."

As she began to think of how deeply Darien had scarred her, Jasper took her hand and gave it a gentle squeeze. The touch communicated he understood all she said beyond what she actually did say. Darien had done more than deceive her from the moment she'd met him. He'd hurt her. Physically.

Warmth suffused her and she felt a soft smile spring up onto her face, put there by the melting of her heart.

Jasper leaned in, a mischievous glint taking over the light in his blue eyes. "So…what should I call you?"

Her smile expanded. He made light of her own deception, and with his affectionate way, he told her he knew she'd done it innocently. "Sadie." She'd thought about this a lot over the last five years. "Even if I forgive my father and keep the Loredo name, I will always be Sadie. Catalina did whatever her father wanted. Sadie isn't that woman. I stopped being Catalina a long time ago."

"All right then. Sadie it is." He lifted her hand and kissed the top just above her knuckles, tickling her insides.

"What are we going to do now?" she asked.

"I'm going to Toronto. You should go see your mother."

"My mother?"

"I can't have you with me in Toronto. I'll send agents with you to Philadelphia. You can wait for me there."

Many mixed emotions passed through her. Seeing her mother resonated like a beacon of hope. Seeing her father had her recoiling. That Jasper would arrange for her to see her mother moved her. Despite her lies, he cared for her.

She missed her mother. Seeing her again was worth the unpleasantness of running into her father.

"I'll wait for you there," she said.

He smiled at the way she said it. "It will take time to plan. We can lay low here for a few weeks and then go. I need to study Darien before I meet with him. I'll put some surveillance on him and then decide how and where to meet with him."

What would they do in the meantime?

Chapter 11

Sadie stayed in bed longer than usual. She didn't feel very well. Maybe a little extra sleep would calm her churning stomach.

Over the past few weeks, Jasper had been busy studying Darien. He watched video surveillance and looked through photos and read reports from whoever his company had sent to observe Darien. He probably knew more about her ex-fiancé than she ever did… well…except for his illegal activities. Darien was an expert at covering his tracks. She'd learned that in the five years she'd been in hiding, working with Steven trying to expose his involvement in the murder of one of his suppliers and the detective.

Her stomach churned some more, not getting better. She rolled onto her back and put her hand on her belly, moaning to the wave of nausea. What had she eaten the night before? The smell of sweet cinnamon rolls filled her next breath. Immediately after, the nausea overwhelmed her. She flung off the covers and propelled herself off the bed, racing to the bathroom. She barely made it to the toilet before losing what little was in her stomach.

After rinsing her mouth out, she brushed her teeth and then hopped in the shower. Standing under the spray, the cause of her sickness plagued her. She didn't feel like she had food poisoning. Dinner had been freshly prepared and brought to their room. Hotels like this didn't serve bad food. She'd stayed here many times and had never gotten sick. Another possibility kept pushing forward but she kept it at bay. She'd wait and see if the nausea continued.

She dressed and left the bedroom. Out in the living area, Jasper paced with a phone to his ear. In dark slacks and a light blue button-down dress shirt with a shoulder gun holster he always wore, he captured her as usual. Sometimes he wore jeans but mostly he dressed professionally like this. Her favorite shirt color was blue because it brought out the blue of his eyes. His blond hair was combed but a slight wave to it made him appear a bit messy. He walked slowly toward the double glass doors open to the dining room. The dining room table was full of papers, two laptops and radio communications equipment.

He'd kept busy with the investigation and had also worked others. Sadie had taken a few trips to the Revive Center but worked mostly from the hotel room. Both of them had dived into work, she suspected, as a way to avoid getting too intimate. She'd enjoyed having him nearby, though. He provided a pleasant view whenever she had a pause in her busy days.

Dwight had been released from the hospital weeks ago and Sadie had arranged to have him transported back to Wyoming, where Finley would take good care of him. He'd been ornery and protested right up until he'd been put onto a private plane. He wanted to help, but he would be of no help while he healed from a gunshot wound. He hadn't been able to argue against that. And he'd seen how Jasper had stepped up security. Sadie had never felt safer. Jasper was more than capable of protecting her. Just take a look at the dining room. Darien, or any of his thugs, didn't know where she was and Jasper had placed a few undercover security guards on them and the Revive Center and was in constant communication with them all.

"He goes to the coffee shop every morning on his way in to work," Jasper said into the phone. He must be talking to someone at DAI about the surveillance he'd been conducting on Darien. "Home by six or seven. Sometimes he has meetings at the bar. Did you get anything on the bar owner?" He paced toward her, saw her and lifted a hand in greeting, those eyes she so loved staring at smiling even though his mouth didn't. "He's probably being forced to let him use it." After his gaze traveled down her body and back up, he paced back the other direction. "No, I think I've got enough to make arrangements."

He always gave her a tickle whenever he looked at her that way.

After ending the call, Jasper faced her. "There are cinnamon rolls on the counter. Might want to heat them up a few seconds."

When the idea of eating cinnamon rolls sickened her, Sadie put her hand to her stomach. "I'm not hungry."

"Don't like cinnamon rolls?"

"Not this morning." She reached for the pot of coffee and then got a whiff of the strong smell. What was wrong with her?

She'd have orange juice.

Retrieving the container and a glass, she poured some, pleased when the smell or the idea of it didn't repulse her. Taking a drink, she finally allowed herself to acknowledge how odd it was to be sick over the smell of cinnamon rolls and coffee. Then the thought slipped in that she hadn't had her period in a long time. She usually had a light one but not this time. Her implant was good for up to three years.

Oh, no. Sadie put down the glass.

Had it been three years since she'd had the matchstick-sized etonogestrel implant put in her arm?

She did the math and felt herself go cold in the face. Three years, six months and a week or two. Plenty of time to become fertile again. She was so accustomed to not worrying about her birth control that she'd forgotten to go in and get another implant. There had been no urgency, since she had no plans to rush into another relationship. And Jasper had come along so unexpectedly.

The smell of coffee and cinnamon exacerbated her rising panic, assaulting her nose and senses. Combined with the shock of realizing she could be pregnant, her stomach protested mightily.

She ran to the bathroom, barely making it again.

* * *

Seeing Sadie run off into her bedroom, Jasper ended his next call before finishing the number. What the...?

He went to her open door. He'd been sleeping in a connecting room, proud that he'd managed to restrain himself with Sadie. It hadn't been easy. She tempted him no matter what she wore, be it pajamas that covered her from neck to ankle or skinny jeans. And the flash of her sexy brown eyes whenever he caught her looking at him had more than once nearly overpowered him. When he caught her looking at him with that unmistakable desire, he had the toughest time doing battle with his male urges.

"Sadie?"

Hearing her finish vomiting and then turn on water, he went into the bathroom to see her bent over the sink.

"Are you okay?" he asked.

She rinsed her mouth out and used mouthwash. Then she leaned on the counter and stared at him through the mirror.

Had something she ate gotten to her? The longer she stared without talking, the darker the mood became between them. He felt his uncertainty gradually transcend into knowing. Realization sank in like a dense fog in the dead of night. Denial fended off panicked questions.

"Did you eat something that didn't agree with you?"

She didn't answer, seeming to be in denial herself.

What if...

She couldn't be.

No. Not now.

And then denial no longer worked. If Sadie was pregnant, what would he do? What would they both do? None of the limited options appealed to him.

She straightened and turned, still using the counter as though needing the support.

"How long have you been feeling like this?" he asked.

"I've been queasy for about a week now. This is the first time I've thrown up and I realized I'm late by about two or three weeks." She didn't track her periods.

She was late. Jasper held on to sanity. "Are you taking any birth control?"

"I have an implant but it's…it's probably…no good anymore."

The air whooshed out of him. He couldn't even begin to fathom how this would change his life. A tractor loader may as well have dumped a pile of rocks on his head.

He stared at her and she stared at him.

"I'm normally not forgetful about that sort of thing," she finally said, seeming to need to talk about something. "I never planned on having kids…at least, I didn't when I worked for my father. I guess I haven't put any further thought to it since then. Things are so different for me now. My life is more open for kids… having a family…I suppose…but I…I don't know if I want kids." She looked at him funny, eyes squinting in her confusion. "Do I?"

While she babbled on in a near hysterical fashion, his mind did the same in silence. He didn't feel trapped in his body very often but he sure did now. One of them had to get a grip, though.

"Okay." He held up his palms. "Let's remain calm."

Calm. How could he remain calm?

"Do you really think you're pregnant?" he asked.

She raised her palms. "You ate the same thing as me last night."

"But you might not be, right?"

She lowered one hand and scratched the side of her neck. "Anything is possible."

They shared another stare and he just knew her thoughts paralleled his. Her implant had expired. Her period was late. And she'd just gotten sick. They could not deny the signs.

He watched her crack under the realization. Her eyes widened. Her breathing quickened. "Oh, my stars. What if I am?" She began to hyperventilate. "Jasper."

She was as freaked out as him. Unfortunately, hysteria would not get them anywhere. Jasper took her clammy hands and pulled her to him. Holding her, he looked into her frantic eyes. "Sadie. Breathe slower."

She shut her eyes and took a great big breath and let it out. Repeating that a few times, she regained control of her nerves and then opened her eyes.

"Let's not panic until we have facts." Moving back, he let her go. "Let's go get a pregnancy test."

"Right. Good thinking. It might be something I ate." She followed him out of the bedroom. "The cook might have done something different to my dinner."

When that didn't ring true in his gut, Jasper wished

he didn't have such acute instincts. He wanted to ignore this one.

By the time they returned they'd both have had time to assimilate what Sadie being pregnant meant. They'd have time to get some perspective.

All the way to the store, Jasper kept trying to imagine himself becoming a father. The only things that came to him were pictures of him holding a baby straight out in front of him; looking down at a baby crying in a crib and not knowing what to do, the ear-splitting sound reverberating in his head; driving a minivan with a car seat in the back; and Sadie breast-feeding. The last defused all the others. In his mind's eye, she looked angelic, face radiating love only a mother had for her baby. A baby he had given her. That image stayed with him as he parked in the market lot.

"You don't have to go in with me," she said.

"What?" What was she talking about? "No. I'll go in with you." This would be his baby as much as hers. He wasn't the type of man to walk away, no matter how appealing that seemed right now. Long-term, he knew he'd regret not stepping forward, straight up against this life-altering situation.

He walked with her toward the entrance. A grocery store never seemed so ominous before. He didn't want to go in there. He didn't want to buy what they had to buy. Because later, that moment of reckoning would come.

Sadie groped for his hand and entwined her fingers with his as though he was her lifeline. He held her hand as they entered.

A woman at one of the checkout counters saw them and smiled.

Could she tell why they were here? Jasper didn't mind if she did, he only wondered if their nervousness was obvious. He felt like he was back in a junior high health class being taught about what happens when boys have sex with girls.

Each step closer to the correct aisle felt like a suffocating walk to his doom. Still holding her hand, he walked with her toward the pregnancy tests. They stopped together, checking out the options. And then he looked at her. She looked back as though as hesitant as him.

A shopper pushed a cart down the aisle. Jasper paid the woman no attention until she slowed and he saw her adoring smile.

"Is this your first?" the five-foot-tall, chubby-cheeked woman asked.

One glance at Sadie confirmed the question only flared her anxiety. Maybe the trip to the market wouldn't give them enough time to gather perspective.

"Yes," Jasper said.

"Oh," the woman's face glowed like the moon with affection. "You look like such a perfect couple. And you came with her to get the test."

"Wouldn't miss it for anything." He began to have fun with this. What else could he do? He'd deal with the consequences later. He didn't have to think of them now. Besides, playing as though he and Sadie were married and had planned to have a baby was so far from the truth it had to be funny.

"How long have you been trying?" the woman asked.

Obviously she had a very poor "appropriate question" barometer. He felt like responding with something like, *we've been going strong every day for a year.*

"Not long," he said instead.

"Babies can be a little daunting to new parents, but once they arrive they have a way of casting a spell of awe over everyone. They are such a miracle."

"We can't wait." He hoped his sarcasm didn't come out.

"Congratulations." The woman smiled and went on her way.

He noticed Sadie's gaze following the woman until she disappeared around a corner. Her anxiety had calmed and now she seemed contemplative. Then her catlike dark eyes shifted up and the softening ended. She turned back to the tests.

Jasper took the initiative and grabbed one. "Let's go."

Sadie took the test into the bathroom after drinking a tall glass of water. She was about to shut the door when Jasper put his hand on it.

"What are you doing?" she asked.

"I want to be part of this."

"I'm going to pee on a stick."

"And that stick is either going to have a plus sign or a minus sign and I want to be there when it does."

"Why?"

Why? Why was she asking him why? "I could be a father today. It's kind of a big deal."

"I'll let you in after."

"Sadie, I've seen you naked. Just let me stand here." When she still seemed to recoil out of shyness, he moved to the other side of the wall beside the door. "How's this?"

She laughed briefly. "Much better."

His supportiveness must be working to alleviate some of her stress.

A few seconds later she finished and when he heard the toilet flush, he moved into the bathroom. She'd put the test on the counter and he bent over to see. It was already starting to change color. She leaned next to him and he smelled her sweet scent and felt her warmth. Her long hair tickled the side of his face. He glanced at her. She glanced at him. A moment of that mysterious, potent attraction passed between them.

Together they watched a plus sign emerge.

Sadie swore three in a row.

Jasper straightened and looked through the mirror at the woman who would be the mother of his first child. "I don't believe it."

She looked back at him. "I don't, either."

He left the bathroom. Out in the living area, he walked to the window and then walked all the way into the dining room, circling the table. Then he leaned over the table, trying to come to terms with this explosive reality.

"You don't have to worry about making any drastic changes to your life."

Jasper looked up and saw Sadie standing in the open double doorway. "I just need a few minutes."

Her stoic expression didn't change. She sure had come to accept this a lot faster than him. In just the short walk from the bedroom to the dining room she seemed to have come to some decisions.

"We both know you won't have time to settle down

and raise a child. You won't want that. You need excitement and your job gives you that."

He put aside her mention of his need for excitement. "You're going to exclude me?" He'd just insisted on being present for the test. Didn't she understand he'd want to be a part of every stage of her pregnancy?

"Your job is too demanding…and dangerous."

He also heard her thinking she didn't trust him or any man. She'd gone the last five years living alone and independent, with no one to direct her path forward anymore. He agreed this was a bit sudden, but he wasn't going to ignore his responsibility.

"Why do I get the feeling this is more about your father than Darien?" he asked.

She moved farther into the dining room. "What do you mean? This has nothing to do with my father."

"You were all too happy to leave your life in Toronto. You left a lead position at a foreign subsidiary at your father's direction. Always at your father's direction. You ran, and now you're hiding and you prefer to keep it that way."

"Yes. I did love getting away from my father. But I don't want to hide forever." She spread apart a few pages that were lying on the table, something idle to do as she likely suspected what he meant. "I don't see what that has to do with us."

"You won't trust anyone not to take over your life again. Your experience with Darien only made that threat worse. I didn't understand why a woman like you would choose to live somewhere so remote. But it all makes sense now. No one can control you there."

She moved her hands from the papers to face him.

"You're right I won't let anyone control me the way my father did, but I also won't control anyone else."

"You wouldn't control me if I decided to be our baby's father."

"Yes, what kind of hero would you be, after all, if you didn't?"

Her aloofness disconcerted him. Few people could do that to him. His attraction to her must be to blame. She'd created a soft spot.

"What's wrong with doing what's right?" he asked.

"Nothing if you don't need excitement all the time." She stepped over to him and put her hand on his chest as though that would soften the blow. "I won't let you tie yourself down with me and a baby when we barely know each other. We aren't in a relationship. Neither one of us is ready for that."

"Are you ready for a baby?"

She dropped her hand with a scoff. "No."

"Well, neither am I, but that won't stop a baby from coming. Our baby. This is just as much my problem as it is yours."

"And when this case is solved, what then? Will you live here?"

He had a house in Rock Springs and an office at DAI. He didn't know how he'd reconcile that but he'd find a way.

"Are you going to be happy sacrificing everything for this baby?" she asked.

"Are you going to let me take on some responsibility?" he countered. "What if I don't give you the choice?"

"I can't stop you, you're right. But I don't think you

trust yourself with something this big," she said. "You still blame yourself for Kaelyn's death. You aren't over that. Jumping into a family won't help you. You'll only feel trapped and wish you could move on to more exciting things. Do you even realize how you use excitement as a crutch because of Kaelyn's suicide?"

Now she was starting to make him angry. She was being insulting. "I never said I'd give up my job to be a family man. My job is enough and excitement isn't a crutch."

"It isn't? Why do you need it then?"

He couldn't answer that. She'd already gotten him wondering if he'd fallen for Kaelyn because of the wrongness, which in turn gave the affair an exciting thrill. He didn't like thinking of himself like that, but his affair with Kaelyn had been exciting.

"My job is enough."

"Am I enough, Jasper? Is any woman enough for you?"

Although he could see where she was going with this, he didn't think he was the only one with baggage. "Is any man enough for you, Sadie? You're the one running away from us together for the baby."

"Because I'm not ready for that."

"Neither am I."

"Then…" She let out an agitated breath.

"We don't have to get married. But I can still be a part of our baby's birth and life," Jasper said. "Don't even try to exclude me from that."

He wouldn't stand here and argue with her anymore. He stormed out of the dining room and left the hotel room, feeling safe in doing so, given he had plenty of security roaming around.

Sadie almost regretting saying the things she had, except they had to be said. She didn't trust Jasper to be reliable enough to commit to a baby. And did she want him to? He was right, she had run from her father and she felt like running away from Jasper. Did that mean she'd become so independent that she couldn't open her heart to another man? Giving her love again did scare her. She wasn't afraid to admit that to herself.

"I don't want a man in my life," she said to the empty hotel room. Hearing the words aloud, however, didn't convince her they were true. Did she not want Jasper in her life? Maybe it was too soon to tell. Maybe she did want him in her life—for now. That didn't mean she'd grow to want him permanently. A baby was permanent.

She went to the window and caught herself looking down the many floors, searching for a tall blond-haired man. She almost felt abandoned. Would he come back? She wished he hadn't left at all. Maybe she should have chosen her words more carefully. She was too high up to see enough detail on the street below. She missed him already and he'd just left.

Could she take him into her life for the baby? The idea of living with him ignited her anxiety. So where did that leave them? Starting off with dysfunction right out of the gate?

Why was this happening? Had she done something wrong and now was being punished?

How could she think of a baby as punishment? She and Jasper had created a life. A living soul grew inside

of her. What the woman from the grocery store said
played back again, as it had a few times before now.

They are such a miracle.

Maybe, but this didn't feel like a miracle. She was
pregnant and the baby's father had just walked out on
her. She'd driven him out.

Just as depression began to sink into her, the hotel
door opened. She turned to see Jasper coming toward
her, his face set with determination.

Her breath stopped along with the exhilaration of
seeing him. As he reached her, he slid his arm around
her waist. Pulling her against him, his stormy gaze
held hers in a fierce connection.

"I'm not going anywhere. You can talk all you want
about how you don't think I'll be happy settling down
and it won't matter. I could never abandon you or my
child. You're just going to have to learn to accept that."

This must be what he felt like when something
thrilled him. "Okay."

That eased all the tension out of his face. He lowered his head and kissed her.

She looped her arms over his shoulders and relished
how he melted her insides and sent a delicious tickle
shivering through her. She met his hard kiss until it
turned needier. Then he drew back, looking with fiery
eyes into hers.

A baby really complicated everything, but for now
she'd take this moment and run with it. There might
come a day when he acknowledged he would never
be happy living in isolation. Sadie could no longer
live any other way. She had left the exciting world
of nonstop corporate action and the demands of her
overbearing father. She would never return to that

way of life. She might enjoy driving fast cars and expensive accessories, but she loved the quiet beauty of the mountains and her home that had become her sanctuary.

Her nonprofit company was nothing like the renowned, nationally famous private investigation agency where Jasper came from. He needed to be out in the world, and that had nothing to do with his sense of failure where Kaelyn was concerned. She couldn't send him away now, but she didn't think she'd have to. She only had to protect her heart in preparation for that day.

Chapter 12

That kiss and another as he left Sadie with two body-guards on the circular drive of her parents' mansion kept going through his mind. While he stood by the decision to stick by her and the baby, he felt evermore drawn to her. And the discovery that he was going to be a dad in nine months did strange things to him. One minute the notion touched and intrigued him and the next terrified him. It helped that Sadie dealt with similar feelings. He'd rather not try to predict what the future held.

Darien entered the Black Bean coffee shop, a quaint little cottage-style business on the corner of two busy downtown Toronto streets. Yellow with white trim, four small café tables with white umbrellas charmed the front patio. Jasper passed the patio, void of people on this chilly spring day. The car Darien had left remained parked on the street, two men inside. He didn't recognize either one.

Stepping into the coffee shop, Jasper spotted Darien at the counter ordering coffee. Fairly tall at just over six feet or so, he wore an expensive suit and had dark hair except for slight signs of graying. Jasper waited for him to get his steaming cup and find a table. Then he approached. Darien looked up from his tablet. His dark eyes stayed on Jasper but nothing changed in his expression. The fact that he kept staring indicated he recognized him.

"May I?" Jasper pulled out a chair and sat across from the man.

"Do I know you?" Darien asked.

"Let's cut the bull, shall we?" Jasper opened his jacket enough to let Darien see his shoulder gun holster.

"I have a few of those nearby, as well."

"I saw them in the Buick," Jasper said. "I've been watching you for a few weeks now."

The way Darien's head angled ever so slightly and his eyes grew more guarded told Jasper he'd caught him by surprise. Darien hadn't known anyone had spied on him. The men Jamie had sent were good, better, probably, than anyone working for this clown.

"That's something I've noticed men like you always overlook," Jasper said. "Insecurity makes you stupid."

"Where did Catalina find you?" Darien asked. "Or should I call her Sadie now?"

"She knew where to look."

A couple took a seat at the table next to them.

"What's your name?" Darien asked. "My people have been trying to find out with no luck."

"You can call me Jasper."

"All right, mysterious *Jasper*. First of all, I am not insecure. I am a very successful businessman."

"Anything else you're up to other than drug dealing?" When Darien simply stared at him, Jasper said, "Yes, I know everything about you."

"Perhaps not everything." He picked up the phone on the table and entered a text message, probably letting his goons know he might need them.

"I know you murdered Bernie and left a clue that would lead Sadie to you. I know you murdered a man over planted drugs. And I know you like to slap women around. Only weak-minded men do that. I'm pretty sure the only reason you can call yourself very successful is however you cheated your way there, in which case, I wouldn't call you successful at all."

Darien put down his phone. "You're righteously bold, aren't you? Someday you may find you regret coming here attempting to threaten me."

Leaning back, Jasper saw the couple engaged in a low-volume, intimate conversation. "I'm not threatening you or trying to. I wouldn't waste my time. I'm here to ask you about the supplier Sadie saw you kill. And how about that policeman? You shut them all down and drove Sadie away. Why?"

"That supplier as you call him tried to steal from me, but I didn't kill him. You're crazy if you think I killed anyone. Bernie? Who is that?"

Jasper wouldn't try to make him admit to murder. "What did your supplier know about you?" He had a view of the street from his seat and noticed the two men get out of the car.

"I believe we're finished with this conversation."

"Almost, yes. Just one more thing. You'll never get close enough to Sadie to hurt her ever again. If you doubt me, I've got a message for you." He looked out the window and saw two of Jamie's finest intercept the two men who'd gotten out of the car, covertly sticking guns to their sides and giving an order to back off.

"Who the hell are you?"

Jasper stood and looked down at Darien. "You can't win this one. I can see how this is going to turn out and it isn't the way you picture it. While I'd like nothing more than to choke the life out of you, I'm going to take you down the honest way. And believe me, you will go down. Nobody hurts a woman I care about and gets away with it."

"I never hurt Sadie. What are you? Her new boyfriend? What kind of stories has she been telling you?"

Jasper didn't respond. He turned and walked away, having said all he'd intended to say. All he wanted was for Darien to see the face of the man who'd hold him responsible for all the evil he'd inflicted on innocent people.

"She was a fool for leaving the way she did," Darien said to his retreating back. "She had everything she could ever possibly want. But she had to turn her back on her father and me. That's the trouble with her. Nothing is ever good enough."

Jasper looked back when he reached the door. The couple had stopped their exchange to stare at Darien, as had a few other patrons in the coffee shop.

"All that tells me is you don't know Sadie at all." Jasper pushed open the door and left.

Outside he nodded once toward Jamie's watchdogs. They nodded back. They'd hold Darien's men a few minutes longer and then let them go, long after Jasper left the vicinity.

He walked down the street and turned at the corner. Almost at his rental, a man appeared from an alley. Jasper stopped in the act of reaching for his gun when he recognized Steven.

Steven stepped toward him and extended a piece of paper, looking up the street in the direction Jasper had just come. "Meet me here. Now." With that, Steven returned to the alley, walking down the middle toward a parked car.

Jasper read the address and got into his car. He drove the short distance to a mom-and-pop café. In an older brick building tucked between a row of other connected businesses along the cracked sidewalk, Dave and Charlene's didn't offer much in the way of aesthetics.

He entered the café. A long row of red-topped stools lined a counter with a view of shining stainless steel in the kitchen. The sound of frying food and the smell of bacon greeted him along with the smiling face of a waitress passing him with handfuls of dishes. Seeing he'd arrived before Steven, he found a table out of sight of the front window.

Less than two minutes later, Steven opened the front door and walked toward him, looking out the window until a wall blocked the view. He carried a laptop case and put that on the floor before extending his hand.

"Jasper."

Jasper shook his hand. "Steven. I wasn't expecting to run into you on this trip."

"I wasn't expecting you, either. I've been tailing

Darien whenever I can. He took a trip to California during the same time that the dead animal turned up at the Revive Center."

"Is that why you wanted to meet?"

Steven settled in on his chair and told the waitress he'd like coffee and nothing else. Jasper declined to order anything.

"How is Sadie?" Steven asked.

Pregnant, but other than that…

"She's well. Right now she's visiting her mother."

Steven went still. "Alone?"

"With two bodyguards."

He relaxed. "Oh, good. I know she misses her mother."

Jasper waited for him to get to the purpose of this meeting. They probably shouldn't meet for very long. Steven shouldn't draw too much attention to himself with any lengthy, unexplained absences.

"I've been trying to figure out a way to get some things to you and Sadie." He leaned over and retrieved something from the laptop case. "Regular mail didn't seem very secure and couriers leave a trail." He sat up with an envelope.

Jasper took it but didn't open it. "What am I going to find in here?"

"A receipt from a Loredo candy store and some creepy pictures of a secret room in Darien's castle of a home. He's clearly got a severe obsession with Sadie."

"He's a serial killer wall type?" That Jasper hadn't expected. Criminal business deals and drugs, yes, but freak-show stalker? Nope.

"Without a doubt. There's something else." Steven

glanced around the café and toward the door. "He also took a trip to Iran I found highly suspect."

That didn't necessarily mean anything.

"I don't have any proof, but I heard him on the phone before he left, talking about some equipment he was bringing with him. He called them cryogenic accelerometers. I looked them up on the internet. Those types of components are used in ballistic missile propellants and liquid-fuel rocket engines to measure acceleration at low temperatures. Sounds illegal to me."

Rocket engine components sent to Iran? The sanctions probably didn't include technology like that. "Darien's motive for killing one of his suppliers just got a lot more interesting."

"I'd say," Steven said. "That's the first time I started to feel scared working for him and spying. He's into some serious illegal activities. Drug dealers can be clever but rocket engine sales to sanctioned countries takes things to a different level. Now I understand why he's always so careful, and why I couldn't help Sadie these last five years. Darien trusts no one and does his technology sales himself. I knew he had dangerous friends but I never saw this coming."

"Why don't you get out of here?" Jasper said. "Get away from Darien. Now. If you keep spying you're going to get caught."

"I will." He smiled at Jasper. "Now that I know Sadie will be safe and you have what you need to get Darien."

"You're awfully loyal to her." Everyone close to her was.

"There was a time when I would have been romantically involved with her, but the timing never worked out. She had to get away from Darien and emotionally wasn't in a place to start up with someone new."

He didn't say she still wasn't.

"And I'm glad nothing ever did happen between us. I might not have met the love of my life. Sadie isn't the kind of woman you leave." He sent Jasper a man-to-man look.

He couldn't comment on that. Leaving Sadie wasn't an option now. And as he imagined doing so without the baby, he had mixed feelings. He couldn't say he'd leave after the case was solved. It wasn't an issue of excitement, either. Maybe Sadie had been right when she said that was a crutch and he avoided the relationship itself. He supposed he'd never denied that. Neither one of them was ready for that, were they? And yet, here they were, with a baby on the way.

"It doesn't happen when you're looking for it," Steven said.

Which only worsened Jasper's rising sense of dread.

Sadie spent most of the day catching her mother up on what she'd done since leaving Loredo and her life with Darien behind. Her mother had wanted to go out for a special lunch but Sadie had promised Jasper she wouldn't leave the house. Instead her mother had asked her serving staff to prepare lunch here. For two hours Sadie had enjoyed the most delicious salmon salad and a long conversation.

They now sat on a rooftop patio overlooking the city, drinking iced tea. She'd called ahead to let her know she was coming so it wouldn't be such a shock. Her normally quiet and reserved mother had screeched in delight. They'd hugged and cried and blurted how much they missed each other and then settled down for some good quality girl time.

"Tell me more about this man who's helping you rid yourself of that monster," her mother said.

On this a warm May day, Ana Sophia wore diamond-accented sunglasses and a wide-brimmed hat with her semi-revealing silk dress. It seemed she'd taken on the same thirst for showy clothes and accessories as Sadie had when the occasion warranted. Even apart they still had similarities. Sadie had dressed up today as well, wearing something sexy and stylish that would surely displease her father.

Her mother's long, slender legs were exposed from the knee down. Her beige silk shorts and matching top were tailor-made, but there was something different about her. Sadie didn't know if her contented smile was because she was happy to see her daughter or if other things put it there.

"What do you want to know?"

"Well, for starters, what put that look in his eyes when he said goodbye?"

She'd noticed something romantic between them? Sadie recalled how Jasper had looked at her. He didn't seem happy to be leaving her behind. And there had been that heat to his eyes that she often saw.

"We…there's… I think we're attracted to each other."

"You think?" Ana Sophia laughed softly. "You don't have to think, sweetheart. He looks at you like you've already gone to bed together."

"Stop being such an intuitive mother," Sadie said. "Since when do you speak like that anyway?"

"Ever since I had your father served with divorce papers."

Sadie sat up from the recliner and gaped at her mother.

"Yes," her mother confirmed. "A few months ago I finally had enough. Took me long enough, huh?"

"But…you said you signed a prenuptial agreement." Her father wouldn't give her a dime.

"My lawyer pointed out a condition in the section that outlined the money I would and wouldn't receive if I divorced him. It said unless there were children involved, I leave with what I entered with. I'll clean him out of half of everything and I won't feel an ounce of shame."

Her father deserved what he had coming. "I guess he'll just have to work harder to make up for it. Divorce should suit him just fine." Sadie laughed and her mother laughed with her.

"Karma."

Yes, karma. But deep down Sadie still harbored hope that her father would change his ways and work at becoming a better person.

Her mother reached over and curled her fingers over Sadie's hand. "I know, darling."

Sadie marveled over her mother's keen insight. She knew her daughter's thoughts without any words. Ana Sophia likely hoped the same. She'd loved Matias at one point in her life. Sadie had loved her father, too, but the darkness in him had become too much to bear. It had poisoned her for too long. Her mother, too.

"Your father named you. Sadie is a name I would have come up with."

She still held her mother's hand. "Love you, Mom."

"Oh, and I you, my dear. When do I get to come see you? You can't make me go another five years and I'm dying to see your house."

"As soon as it's safe." She would not have her mother walking into an attack. "Knowing Jasper, it won't be that long." He'd have Bernie's case closed soon now that they knew Darien was behind it all. Then only the baby would keep him around. Sadie wished there was no baby, that she could see if what they had was real or not.

Catching her thoughts going down a path she preferred to avoid, she cut them off. She wouldn't think about a life with Jasper and how that made her feel all panicky inside. She withheld her trust for a good reason. She didn't know Jasper that well. Trusting him too soon would be foolish. He was nothing like Darien, though.

And the baby...

Sadie rolled her head to look at her mother. Her mother did the same.

"What is it?" her mother asked.

Sadie had to tell her. She wouldn't have another chance until it was safe to start freely talking to her.

"I'm pregnant," she said.

Ana Sophia's mouth formed a deep O. Then she sat up, her hand slipped from Sadie's. "For real?"

Sadie swung her legs over the edge of the chair. "Yes."

When her mother's delighted face smoothed into concern, Sadie realized she must not appear happy.

"It happened too soon?" her mother asked.

Sadie nodded.

"Well, he seems like a nice man."

"Yes, seems."

"Surely you don't think he'll end up like Darien."

"That's just it. I don't know and not knowing scares me."

"Don't be afraid, Sadie. There's something—"

"Excuse me, madam."

At the interruption, Sadie turned to see one of her mother's servants dressed in formal attire. Her mother hadn't lost her taste for that.

"Matias is in the foyer, asking to see…" He glanced at Sadie, flummoxed.

"Sadie," Sadie said.

"Y-yes."

"I don't want to see him."

"Maybe you should," her mother said. "Don't deny like I did for so many years. Confront him. Tell him how you feel. If he doesn't acknowledge that, then you can rest easy knowing you did all you could."

"Is that what you did?"

"Yes. I wasted too many years trying to *fix* him. I thought my love for him would change him make him more concerned about me and you than…money."

If Ana Sophia had truly confronted Matias, then it hadn't changed his selfish way. He'd chosen his corporation, his money, over his wife.

"How did he know I was here?" Sadie asked.

Her mother looked away.

"You *told* him?"

"Before you get upset, try to put yourself in my shoes. As a mother. I don't want you to live the rest of your life with…negative thoughts that might hinder you, keep you from finding happiness."

"Mother!"

"I know you don't want to talk to him, but you need to. Don't wait as long as I did, sweetheart." She nodded to the servant.

Sadie glanced back at the two men Jasper had left with her. They moved to block the servant's path.

"Just talk to him," her mother said. "Show him all you've become without him."

Would she still be running from her father if she didn't talk to him? She didn't have to say anything she didn't wish to say. She didn't have to allow him to control her anymore. Funny, how even after five years he could still induce fear and that inexplicable need to constantly please him. Yes, or endure the wrath of his temper and distain.

She stood from the recliner and faced the two bodyguards. "It's all right."

They moved aside and the servant vanished inside.

Sadie walked to the stone railing that resembled that of a turret in a castle. She and her mother shared that taste in architecture.

Ana Sophia remained on her chair, sipping tea and taking in the view.

Sadie's heart palpitated in anticipation of facing her father, the great Matias Loredo. Dressed in a dark gray suit that must have cost thousands with a smooth blue tie, his dark beady eyes didn't seem as penetrating as she remembered and his short black hair had a few gray strands now. She heard him step out onto the patio but didn't turn. She waited for him to appear beside her. He didn't say anything at first and she wondered if for once in his life he took time to choose his words carefully.

"Catalina," he said at last.

Then Sadie faced him, feeling her confidence burgeon. She had nothing to fear from this man. "My name is Sadie now."

"Yes, I heard you changed your name." A flicker of displeasure crossed his expression, the slight hardening of his eyes and tightening of his mouth. "Your mother wouldn't tell me what it was. She didn't want me to find you."

She didn't offer any more.

"It's what led to our divorce."

"Just that? My escaping you did all that?"

His brow lowered at her tone. She'd never spoken to him this way.

"I thought it was Darien you escaped. The murders…"

"That was part of it." Did he really not realize how his tyranny had ruined her?

"I gave you everything."

"That's what Darien said when I tried to leave him the first time."

"You ran the Toronto office. You could have taken over for me when I retire."

He bewildered her. "That was your dream, not mine. I'm living my dream now, and you'll never take that away from me. I'll never be your puppet again."

"Pup…" He seemed genuinely shocked. "I never treated you that way. I didn't micromanage. You made the Toronto office a success all on your own."

"You never told me that before now. The only time you communicated to me was when I wasn't doing things your way, or when you had something disparaging to say about your workers. I got so tired of watching you look down on them. You made me sick."

"Most people don't put their full effort forward unless they're pushed."

"There are other ways to push than make them feel puny. It's called encouragement. Incentive. Positive reinforcement. Things you're incapable of showing because you don't care about anyone other than yourself."

"Now that's enough." His temper finally flared. "I gave you every advantage. You should be thankful."

She expected her blunt, insensitive talk to work that way. She couldn't believe she was standing here saying all she'd thought of him. It felt freeing.

"The only thing I'm thankful for when it comes to you is that you never found me."

"Good God, what prompted all this hatefulness in you?"

"*Your* hatefulness."

"I have no hatred toward you. You're my daughter."

"No, your hatefulness toward everyone else, anyone you saw as beneath you."

She watched him take several seconds to think that over, reflect on where she drew her accusations.

"I'm your daughter. The title is what got me where I was in your kingdom. Not love you had for me."

"That's pure nonsense. I love you."

She scoffed.

"I'm a leader. An entrepreneur. People like me don't cater to weaker sentimentality."

"You don't have to be a tyrant to make people do what you want." She sighed. She was wasting her breath. He'd never change. "The only reason I agreed to see you is to tell you why I left. I have. I don't care how you see it or if you disagree. I've told you and now I'm finished talking to you."

"You ungrateful dissident. I should have you cut out of my will for this!"

"Go ahead. I make enough money on my own. I don't need you." She walked toward the two guards who still waited by the door.

Her father caught up. He took her arm and stopped her, a little roughly. "What are you doing? Are you living off the interest on the money I gave you?"

"I used it to start up a homeless shelter and program," she said.

"Homeless...what made you decide to do that? You can't possibly be making very much money, if any."

"I receive donations. I don't make what I made at Loredo, but it's enough. I don't need money to feel successful and fulfilled. I'm not like you that way. I actually care about other people. So I guess that's what made me do it. Seeing you not care made me care."

A look of outrage consumed his face, his skin turning a shade of red. "I came here today to talk to you and find out how to get you back to work at Loredo. Your mother told me about the man who's helping you resolve the murders. I wanted to offer my help."

She didn't need his help. Didn't he see that?

"I'll never go back to Loredo and do what you dictate," she said. "I have a new life. *My own* life. I'm *happy*. Nothing you say or offer will make me give that up."

"So that's it. You're just going to walk away and never see your father again."

She considered him a moment, not sure that is what she intended. She hadn't thought that far into the future. She'd only wanted to be free of Darien once and for all. Escaping her father had been a bonus.

"I might consider it if you can genuinely be happy for me and my own choices. I can't tell you what to do with your company but I'd ask that you at least think about how you treat other people."

"You can't talk to me this way!" he roared. "I'm your *father*!" He gave her arm a jerk. "You *will* come back. I'll see to it that you come to your senses. You're a Loredo. You belong here with me!"

Her mother stood up from her chair as soon as Matias jerked Sadie.

The bodyguards appeared beside Sadie, one of them putting his hand on the gun holster on the side of his hip, the other folding his massive arms.

Matias looked from one to the other, taking notice of the gun, and then back to her.

"I'm speaking the *truth*. It's long past the time someone did," Sadie said. "And I will *not* come back." Unless she came to see her mother, but she didn't tell her father that.

Jasper appeared in the doorway, a breath of fresh air. The sight of him tickled her heart. The degree of joy startled her, although she gladly welcomed the feeling.

The guards and Matias turned to see him.

Jasper walked to Sadie, his gaze pinned on Matias and the guards as he came to stand beside her. He put his arm around Sadie. "Is everything all right?"

"Who are you?" Matias asked, noticing the way Jasper touched Sadie.

Ana Sophia appeared to Sadie's other side. "Jasper Roesch. He's from the investigative agency Sadie hired to get Darien off her back."

"You've taken up with a mere private investigator?" Matias sounded and looked appalled.

Of course, he'd consider any man not in an equal position as him inferior.

"He's much better than the one you lined up for her," Sadie's mother said.

Sadie shot a look her way. What was she saying?

"I'm sorry, Sadie. I was going to tell you, but he showed up before I could."

"What…?"

"He arranged for you to meet Darien."

Recalling how Darien had appeared when they'd first met, it made sense. Her father must have told him she'd be at that restaurant.

"How did you know Darien Jafari?" Jasper asked.

"He belonged to the same gentlemen's club."

"Were you aware of the full nature of his business?"

"Spacecraft type parts. Quite impressive."

"Were you also impressed with his drug dealing?" Jasper asked.

Matias's head moved back as though stunned. "I had a hard time believing he put a hand to my daughter, but drugs?" He shook his head. "Darien was a successful businessman. Are you sure you aren't mistaken?"

"Quite sure. He's also making illegal sales to prohibited countries," Jasper said.

"Why am I not surprised?" Sadie turned a deliberately reproachful look toward her father.

Chapter 13

Sadie didn't want to stop hugging her mother.

"It won't be as long this time," Ana Sophia comforted her.

Sadie took solace in that and leaned back, looking into her mother's dark eyes. Sadie hoped she'd be as lovely at her age.

With her hands on Sadie's upper arms, Ana Sophia moved away and then dropped her hands. "Call me when you can."

"I will." She stepped back, bumping into Jasper, who put his hand on her hip.

"Take care of my daughter," Ana Sophia said to him.

"I will." His deep, raspy voice sounded certain.

Her mother smiled fondly and Sadie would carry that image with her until she could see her again. With tears burning her eyes, she got into the sleek black sedan Jasper had arranged for them. The two guards would stay near her mother's house to be sure no one had seen Sadie.

Jasper kept her close when they reached the private airport, first checking their surroundings as they got out of the car. He looked back at the terminal building door.

"Do you see something?" She looked back and saw nothing that stood out.

"Come on. Let's hurry."

Someone was here. No one had waited for them outside her mother's house and no one had followed them, but somehow they'd learned she and Jasper planned to fly out of the private airport. They'd waited here for them.

Jasper looked back inside the small airport terminal. They hurried through the meager security and went outside onto the tarmac. As soon as they did, gunshots rang out inside the terminal. The few people inside screamed and Sadie saw them run for cover through the window.

Taking her hand, Jasper hauled her behind the wheel of a parked small plane, the one next to theirs. No sooner had they taken cover, bullets hit the plane and the other side of the wheel.

Drawing his gun, Jasper moved to get a look at the shooter and fired.

Sadie didn't see a clear path to their plane. It was beside this one but they would have to run out in the open to get there. But from the plane, the pilot began shooting back, as well. He stood just inside the open doorway with a high-powered rifle. Sadie should have expected that Jasper would plan ahead.

"He'll cover us."

"What?" He wanted her to make a run for it?

The shooter was inside the terminal door. Was there one or more? She heard more gunshots inside. He wasn't alone. There was more than one shooter.

"I'll cover you, too." Jasper faced her. "We have to get out of here."

"They're going to shoot at us."

"Not if we keep shooting at them."

The shooters joined together and fired at the pilot and then her and Jasper. Sadie ducked low behind the wheel. Did they mean to kill them both or just Jasper? Darien must have decided to just take her out instead of continuing to toy with her.

"What did you say to him when you were there?" she asked.

"Apparently, enough to bother him."

A man like Jasper could do that rather easily. His heroism was hard to hide or go up against.

He fired twice more, silencing the other shooters. "Now. Let's go!" He grabbed her hand and pulled her after him.

The pilot saw them and rained a shower of bullets at the shooters. Jasper fired with him. They made it to the stairs at the plane. Jasper pushed her to go first, turning to fire some more. She reached the top and saw Jasper duck as the shooters fired while the pilot took hold of Sadie and pulled her into the plane.

Bullets pinged against the plane.

"We have to go. Now." The pilot ran for the cockpit of the small jet.

Jasper took care of the steps and door. Then he peered through a window as the plane began to move. Sadie saw through her own window the shooters had run out onto the tarmac and continued shooting. But the pilot had the plane up to a decent speed and shortly thereafter the bullets stopped. Out of range.

Taking a seat before the plane took off, Sadie let her head fall back while she caught her breath. Jasper took the seat beside her, one of four on the plane. Their things had been brought ahead of them and Jasper leaned over to retrieve something from his laptop case.

Lowering a table tray in front of him, he put down a folder and opened it. "Steven gave me these when I was in Toronto."

Sadie examined some photos and had to move closer to be sure what she was looking at.

"I've already seen them."

Taking the photos from Jasper, she began to go through them. As she came to those of a wall with a collage of photos of her, she slowed. Some of them had writing in black marker with horrible words about her. The room must be somewhere in the castle-like home he'd built for her, but she'd never seen it. There were no windows so she assumed it was in the basement. A secret room?

She looked at Jasper.

"Yeah. Certifiable."

"Nuts," she said aloud.

"I think he had more plans for you than he was able to pull off. Just killing you doesn't seem like enough to satisfy this kind of craziness."

"No, it doesn't. He killed Bernie because he found out I cared about him."

"And when you went to DAI, he knew his toying had to stop. Then he just wanted you dead."

"But he still toyed. The dead animal?"

"Yes, but now he's desperate. He's afraid he'll get caught. A shoot-out at a private airport isn't exactly subtle. He's more dangerous than ever."

She thought of the innocent people at the airport who may have gotten killed. There hadn't been many at this hour, thankfully. She could only hope they had all gotten out of the way when the shooting had begun. The men hadn't come for them. All they would have wanted was to get past security to reach the tarmac.

Darien must realize what kind of man Sadie had protecting her. He'd stepped up his tactics…or stepped them down, operating like a terrorist.

Jasper leaned his head back, ready to get some sleep. "He'll start making mistakes now. Like he just did."

Starting a shoot-out at a small private airport was a mistake? She didn't see how. Because it was reckless?

She watched Jasper go to sleep, peaceful and unafraid. They'd be back in San Francisco in a several hours. She should try to get some sleep, as well. Except her mind was racing about Darien. She wished so deeply to be rid of him. Five years. She'd looked over her shoulder that long. So many times she'd broken down with a feeling of hopelessness that she'd never be free of him. The only thing that always got her through those moments was the reminder of what she'd built and the life she'd left behind.

But this man. Jasper was going to do that for her. When Bernie was murdered and his case went cold, she'd had no idea the case would lead back to Darien.

She hadn't seen that coming. She'd thought she was going to have to live in fear of Darien the rest of her life.

Jasper's calm demeanor tugged her heart, bringing her closer to him, a man so good and yet seemingly so unattainable.

"Why do you avoid relationships?" she asked.

He must not have fallen into deep sleep yet. His eyes popped open and he turned his head. "What?"

"The excitement. Why do you avoid relationships?" He felt guilty over Kaelyn's suicide, but his relations with Sadie were nothing like that. Sadie wasn't married. Their sex hadn't betrayed anyone else. Both of them were available.

"I don't avoid them." He didn't lift his head up or open his eyes.

She had a feeling there was more to his affair with Kaelyn than he'd told so far. "Okay, but I think you feel safer when you aren't in one."

Now his eyes opened. "Safer?"

"What are we?" she asked. "Are we a couple?" Did she even want to be a couple? With the baby they may not have a choice. "I guess I'm just trying to sort all of this out. Make sense of it." If that was even possible.

He didn't respond for a while and she could see him pondering the matter. "It doesn't have to make sense yet."

That kind of peeved her. "What is this, then? A meaningless encounter?"

"I wouldn't put it that way."

"Okay, then how about this—it's an encounter that doesn't mean anything…yet." And maybe never would. He would be safe looking at it that way. And so would she. Except something in her kept rebutting that analogy.

"I like that one a lot better."

She grew more annoyed and didn't understand why, which only intensified her angst. The baby tied them together. Sadie felt carried off on a small boat in a rolling sea with no motor or paddles. Where would the vessel take her?

When she and Darien had first moved in together, she used to fantasize about having a baby with him. She was such a different woman back then. She'd been independent but she'd also been naive when it came to men. She had a fairy-tale dream of how her love life would play out. True love with a handsome, successful, interesting man. The exhilaration of creating a new life from that wonderful love. Pure happiness. What a shock it had been that first time Darien had shown his evil side. She'd thought she'd given their relationship enough time to be sure he was the right man for her. Now she realized even if she'd given it more than a year, he would have behaved himself until he had her in his lair.

She rolled her head to look at Jasper again and saw him looking back at her.

"Are you who you seem?" she asked.

"What are you worried about, Sadie?"

She should be blatantly honest with him. That was something she'd never been with Darien. With Darien, she'd been satisfied with letting her dream of a perfect future take her on a journey. This time she wanted it to be real. No matter how ugly.

"I'm worried that I don't know enough about you to be having a baby with you."

"Getting to know someone takes time."

"Have you told me everything about you and Kae-lyn?" Aside from his affair that had split up a marriage and ended in the woman's suicide, Sadie had a feeling there was more to it than what he'd told her so far.

Judging by his prolonged silence, she began to grow uneasy.

After a few seconds more, he said, "She had a daughter. I didn't have many chances to get to know her, but I did have some, enough to get attached to her. I considered a future with her in it. Imaging that made me feel like I could be a good father."

Was he harboring a suppressed emotion about kids? How did he truly feel about them having a baby together? He was hard wired to do the right thing, but what did the baby really mean to him?

"Up until my uncle discovered the affair, I didn't recognize the wrongness in what I was doing. The people I would hurt. I caused that little girl to grow up without a mother, to grow up with an abusive father. He wasn't abusive to the girl, but he was to her mother. She must have seen things."

She understood how he would feel that way. She agreed getting involved with another person's spouse was wrong.

"Do you think you could have avoided the affair?"

He turned his head and took a while to respond. Then he shook his head. "It just happened. We started out as family. Then friends. Then close friends. She understood me. We had a lot in common. I can't tell you when it crossed the line. I only remember the first time I kissed her."

"And then there had been no turning back. Sounds

familiar." Maybe this is how he found himself involved with women. His heart sneaked up on him until he reached a point when it was too late. "You're a better detective than you are a lover." She smiled as she teased.

He didn't smile with her. "That's what worries me."

Every time he thought of Kaelyn and her daughter, he didn't feel like a hero, much less father material. He may even fear setting a bad example. Did he think he'd get involved in another affair? Maybe he feared he was susceptible. If he had no control once, he could lose control again. She had to ask a difficult question. The answer may not be what she wanted to hear.

"Everybody makes mistakes," she said. "The key is you learn from them. Do you think you've learned from your mistakes?"

"Yes, but at great cost to others."

Then he had hope not to repeat them. But for him to be sure he had to be deeply in love, and Sade was 100 percent certain he was not deeply in love with her. The next man she married wouldn't raise an alarm like that. Jasper raised a big alarm.

She rolled her head away. No more talking.

Back in Sadie's big house, Jasper noticed how she avoided him over the next few days. Today, he hadn't seen her at all and he found he missed her, even just seeing her. He sat in the library with his laptop, going over the latest surveillance of Darien. Outside, rain fell on the heavy side and dimmed the house enough to require lamps lit. It was after six so the sun would set soon.

He knew what Sadie was doing. She felt she needed

to protect herself. He might believe he had to be there for his child, but Sadie wouldn't ruin the rest of her life by marrying a man who didn't love her. That would be just as bad as marrying a man who deceived her. He wasn't sure how he felt about that. The fact that he'd allowed her to avoid him told him he agreed. He felt trapped into being with her, and that his regrets prevented him from considering going separate ways.

How could he have all these conflicting feelings when every time he looked at Sadie he felt anything but the desire to part ways? His passion for her seemed to grow rather than subside with the news of her pregnancy. Her absences only intensified that reaction.

After talking with Sadie, he realized his past had made him fear his ability to be a good father. Fear provoked him to run. Honor wouldn't allow him. But he wasn't gaining any confidence from Sadie. She'd had a rough experience herself. He wasn't the only one dealing with something like that. If only humans could see into the future and know which decisions to make.

His phone rang. Standing from the table when he saw the San Francisco detective's name, he answered as he moved to one of the windows facing the back of the house.

"We have another one," the detective said.

Jasper kept his curse to himself and listened to the man explain all they'd uncovered, which was a lot.

When he finished the call, he turned from the gloomy view through the window to see Sadie standing in the doorway. She held her hands in front of her and wore a worried look.

"I heard you talking," she said.

She must have heard enough to ascertain what had happened.

Jasper walked to her. "Another homeless man was shot." When he stopped, he put his hands on her upper arms in an attempt to steady her if she needed that, or just offer a comforting gesture. He knew this would be difficult for her. "Witnesses reported seeing Chad Long being forced into a car like the one we saw parked in front of the Revive Center."

Stumbling backward, Sadie put her hand over her mouth and tears came to her eyes. He let his hands fall. But when he saw her eyes tear up, he moved forward and took her into his arms, holding her while she cried. The desire to crush Darien had never been as strong as now.

"I'm sorry." He wished he could have done more sooner. But he and the team of detectives in San Francisco had made progress. "Because of our work, police were able to track down the men. Chad is in the hospital in critical condition. His attempted killers were arrested and their statements are being recorded now. They'll likely turn over information on Darien. And the evidence Steven gave me will probably be enough to have him extradited."

Sade kept her head against his shoulder until she regained control over her crying. Then she lifted her head.

Her teary eyes ripped at his soul, biting and tearing the gate of his primal being. The taste of vengeance gripped him. He'd have it. Oh, yes. He would.

"I don't understand why he's doing this," she said.

The time had come to tell her more. He'd held off until now to spare her. "I haven't told you yet, but two nights ago someone walked through the woods. We've stepped up patrols and a team chased the person away, but we think it was Darien testing our security. When he realized he couldn't breach the fence again, he must have decided to go after another homeless man." Tormenting her some more.

"That *bastard*!" she hissed.

"Yeah. If it wouldn't have been murder, I'd have killed him when I went to Toronto."

She reached up and put her hand on his face, affectionate and appreciative. "When will we know if Chad will be all right?"

"He's in surgery. It could be hours, maybe days."

"Oh," she breathed her distress. "I have to go there."

"I'll make arrangements. We'll fly there first thing in the morning." It was too late now and the storm would only delay them further.

Sadie stayed in his arms as she turned her head to look out the window. Even with the thick, sturdy construction the slap of rain was audible and the fog of heavy precipitation impaired visibility beneath bright exterior lighting. The faint rumble of wind told Jasper the gusts were much stronger than the cozy residents of Sadie's hideaway revealed. He'd made a good call delaying their departure until tomorrow.

He gently stepped back from her. "Give me a moment."

When she calmly moved away, hugging herself and walking in a daze to the big expanse of window, he quickly made a call on his cell to get a plane lined up for the morning, and then used the radio to contact the gatehouse to confirm inactivity.

Assured of their safety, he could give all his attention to Sadie and her emotional state after learning about Chad. He went to her.

"I'll start a bath for you." He placed his hand on her lower back to get her moving.

She didn't protest and walked ahead of him down the hall, leading him into her bedroom. When she vanished into her walk-in closet, he went into the spacious bathroom with cream-colored stone and dark wood floor. The oval Jacuzzi tub reminded him of the one in her pool room. He started that going and found some flowery smelling bubble bath and poured some in. By the time he lit two candles, he heard her behind him.

Turning, he saw she'd put on a robe, a satiny black thing that grabbed his attention. "I'll leave you to it." After shutting off the water, he started to step toward her and the door to the bathroom, but she put her hand on his chest.

"Would you stay?" she asked. "I don't want to be alone."

He couldn't stop a glance down to the V of her robe. Sadie seemed not to notice as she just leaned forward and put her hands and head on his chest. He wrapped his arms around her. She must need the comfort right now. He had not seen her this vulnerable before. The stress of Bernie's murder and all that had followed must have reached a threshold.

"It will be all right," he said. "I promise."

"Not if Chad dies. He can't die." She sounded on the verge of crying.

"We'll go see him tomorrow. By then he'll be out of surgery and in recovery."

If he survived...

And if he did, he'd likely be in Intensive Care.

Jasper wouldn't say that to Sadie.

He rubbed her back and held her until she moved back. When she looked up at him, her emotion had subsided, or warmed into something else.

"Will you get in the tub with me?"

Was she still vulnerable? He wouldn't take advantage of her. Just and right. He felt the best living to that code.

"I'm not sure that's such a good idea," he said.

"Screw good ideas," she purred. "All I need is to forget everything but whatever is in this moment… and every moment to come before morning. Are you with me?"

Then again, what difference would it make if they made love again? He'd already gotten her pregnant.

"Yes," he said.

"I need you close." She slipped off the robe.

Jasper found himself quite speechless and absorbed in her backside and slender, sexy legs as she stepped into the tub. She sat on the steeper-sloped side and looked at him, waiting.

A dream of a sexy woman waited for him in a tub of bubbly, warm water. He began removing his clothes, starting with his boots. Aware of how Sadie watched him pull off his shirt, he had serious reservations over where this would lead. But he did as she requested and stripped naked and stepped into the tub.

Resting back against the reclining side, he opened his arms. A soft, contented look came over her face and she moved to lean back against him. Her bare skin, slicked with water and bubble bath, enflamed him. She let her head fall back against his shoulder and closed her eyes.

Enjoying her profile, he wrapped his arms around her torso, avoiding contact with anything more female. But that put his hands on her stomach, which made him aware of what grew inside.

Sadie's eyes opened and she looked up at him.

Jasper shared his first sensation of awe with her. An inexplicable feeling expanded with the knowledge that he'd helped create a life. None of his initial panic intruded. He moved his hands over her skin. Her stomach was flat, of course, but soon she'd begin to show signs. Right now only the idea of the baby touched his imagination.

Sadie bent her head as she put her hand over his.

He shared another moment with her. Neither spoke. He just felt, as he was sure she did, too. Then after a while, she lifted her head.

Jasper moved his down and kissed her. The kiss was like no other. Intimate, and yet so profound his head spun. His heart hammered. He continued kissing her. She moved with him in such soft harmony he fell deeper into a dreamlike state.

She withdrew long enough to turn, water sloshing as she straddled him.

"Sadie." Did they want to do this?

"Shh. The damage is already done. How could this hurt anything?" She kissed him, much freer than the last time. While the first time they'd made love had been unexpected and full of urgency, this time he felt more of a connection. Finding out about Chad made this more personal.

Steam from the warm bath heated the bathroom. Cradling her rear, he lifted her and rose to sit on the corner curve of the tub. She straddled him and looped her arms around him. Without breaking their kiss, he ran his hands over her body and let her set the pace. Agonizing moments later, she satisfied his thirst for her but created an even more unbearable hunger as she slowly moved. Fevered heat nearly made him tremble just before he could hold back no longer.

Early the next morning, Jasper woke Sadie with soft kisses. She opened her eyes, drifting on the bliss of a light, airy dream. She lay in his arms, warm under the covers, his scent engulfing her and his sleepy eyes content and loving. This was much different than the last time they did this. Last time she woke alone in bed, now she never wanted to leave.

"Good morning," she said.

"Yes, it is." He rolled on top of her and resumed kissing her, taking the passion to the next level.

In the tub she thought she'd fly right out of her body on the hard, intense wave of sensation joining with him created. Again, he didn't hurry with the urgency of desire. She liked that he took control after letting her lead the way last night. But most of all, she liked waking up like this—in his arms.

He slowly pushed inside her, partially embedded and then sliding all the way. "Lift your knees."

She did, loving his commanding tone that sounded swept away with desire. He pulled his hips back and pushed into her again. Tingles showered her senses and drew a sound from her. Jasper touched the corner of her mouth and then the other, compelling Sadie to tip her head up to reach his lips for a real kiss. He pressed a soft kiss to her lips. She opened her mouth and he deepened the kiss.

When his lips left hers, she arched her neck to stay in contact, but he was out of reach.

"Do you want me?"

"Yes," she breathed.

"How much?" He moved slow and deep, knowing exactly where she needed him.

Sensation robbed her of coherent thought. "More."

His mouth found the swell of her breasts and he loved each nipple with his tongue. Then he rocked his hips against hers, creating sweet pressure that sent any lingering ability to think straight into oblivion. The sensations intensified, each movement was deliberate, practiced and sure.

"More," she urged him.

He gave her more, pushing harder into her. A deep coil of sensation began to unfurl. He held her gaze through her overwhelming orgasm. She cried out with the strength of it and heard him immediately follow her to that place of sheer ecstasy.

Coming back down to earth, she lay on her side with him behind her. He said nothing. She couldn't say a thing. She could only float in wonder over the way he made her feel. Except now apprehension began to encroach.

His forefinger traced patterns on her shoulder and arm. Goose bumps dotted her skin and he kissed them.

She felt a change in their relationship. That intimate moment when he'd had his hand on her stomach had triggered the shift, deepened their connection. For the better?

Would Jasper eventually grow tired of the monotony? He might stick around for the baby but would he distance himself? She might be overreacting but her experience with Darien made it difficult, if not impossible, for her to trust.

Chapter 14

Jasper sat with Sadie in the waiting room of the hospital. The doctors told them Chad hadn't awakened yet and if he didn't awaken soon they'd begin to get gravely concerned. Sadie hadn't taken that news well. She sat in the chair beside him, leaning her head on his shoulder.

He heard her stomach growl. "I'll go get us something to eat." He started to move.

She lifted her head. "No. Let me. I need to do something."

"I'll go with you."

"No." She shook her head. "I'll go."

She'd been behaving strangely ever since this morning. After making love, they'd taken a shower together, which had further cemented their bond. No negativity or weight of their circumstance intruded, not until they'd finished getting ready for the day, for the trip here. A gradual sobering had occurred. On the plane Sadie had fallen into silent withdrawal.

Jasper had to admit, the potency of their chemistry unsettled him. He knew it unsettled her. She didn't trust him. He had his own demons.

But he wouldn't leave her alone long. His phone rang and he saw it was Kadin.

He nodded to Sadie and she walked from the room. He'd let her get a head start, but after this call he'd have to make sure she was all right.

"Hey, Jasper. I have some more on Jafari."

As Jasper listened, he grew more and more stunned over the extent of criminal activities Darien had hidden from Sadie. And afraid that she might be more of a threat to him than she realized.

Sadie walked toward the elevator wishing she didn't feel so down in the dumps. Her night and morning with Jasper had been magical. Why couldn't she keep feeling that way? She already knew the answer, but that didn't stop her from wishing anyway. This was when clairvoyance would come in handy. If only she could see the future she'd feel safe.

Pressing the elevator down button, she stepped inside. A man entered just as she pressed the main level. With his head down, he reached over and pressed level two.

Something about him made her uneasy. A big man standing well over six feet, he had short, fine brown hair and a trimmed mustache. He looked at her and recognition slammed her. He was the man who'd killed Darien's supplier.

The elevator stopped at the second floor. Sadie moved quickly to the door as it began to open, but the man removed a gun from inside his jacket and pressed the barrel to her back.

"Walk off the elevator and go to the stairs," he said. "Make a sound and I'll kill you."

"Do that and you'll be caught."

"No. I'll be gone before anyone sees me."

His calmness frightened her. She walked off the elevator, searching for someone to help her. A nurse disappeared into a room and no one else was in the hall.

"Don't make a sound," he repeated. "My gun is silenced."

Nothing she said would persuade him. She had to do as he said. Her baby...

"Open the door," the man ordered.

Sadie had no choice. Just realizing that terrified her. She went into the stairwell.

He pushed her toward the descending stairs. Sadie went down, glancing back to see the man right behind her aiming the gun. He wouldn't kill her. If he intended that, he'd have done it already, wouldn't he? Especially here in the stairwell with no one around.

At the main level, she bolted for the door. If she could run into the hall and find help...

She had her hand on the doorknob when the man grabbed her long hair and yanked her backward. She collided with him and he then grabbed her arm, painfully keeping her from falling.

"Try that again and I'll kill you now," he said into her ear.

"Darien wants me alive," she said, not knowing if that was true but trying the scare tactic anyway.

"He's through with you after you sent your watch guard after him. He doesn't react well to anyone getting the best of him. He said if you gave me any trouble to not bother bringing you to him."

"I don't believe you."

"I don't care what you believe. Get moving." He pushed her toward the stairs.

She stepped down.

"Why is he doing this?" she asked.

"You don't know?" The man chuckled darkly. "That doesn't surprise me. He was a fool for using your computer in the first place. I kept telling him not to do that but he wouldn't listen."

Computer? What computer? Five years ago she'd had a laptop, the only computer she'd taken with her. She didn't use it anymore. She'd purchased an updated one last year. "Why was he using my computer?"

The man didn't appear to mind telling her, which probably meant he didn't consider her a threat. Which also meant he probably intended to kill her.

"To hide all his transactions."

Darien used her computer to conduct his drug dealings?

"After he was finished, he planned to destroy your laptop. In the meantime he wanted to make sure if anyone confiscated his computer they wouldn't find anything."

At the garage level, he forced her to open the door. But he took her arm again and stopped her long enough to check for other people.

"What's so important about my laptop?" she asked, stalling. "If police were to confiscate his computer, they'd likely take mine, too."

"Not if you weren't there. Darien planned to put you somewhere safe until the deal was done." He shook his head with a snide laugh. "He never imagined you'd get away on your own—and take the computer."

"Maybe he was too busy thinking of himself."

"He should have listened to me and killed you when he found you, instead of killing that bum."

Sadie closed her eyes briefly. Poor Bernie. He'd died for no reason, because of some sick man's need for revenge. Darien couldn't stand it that she'd left him, that she'd escaped him and he hadn't known.

"Get walking." He shoved her and she had to walk.

Sadie walked slowly. "How long have you been killing for Darien?" he asked.

"It's not always killing. I'm the other guy at his side. Steven was the public face. I'm the guy in the black market." He took her by her sleeve and yanked her in the direction of a parked van.

"How did Darien find me? How did he know Bernie and I were close?" she asked. That had always bothered her. Steven had always been careful when he'd come to see her so she still wasn't convinced Darien had learned from him.

"Your father told him where you were."

A shock wave made her stop walking as she gaped at the man. "What?"

"Darien and your father kept in contact after you disappeared. Your dad worked tirelessly to find you and Darien used that to his advantage." The big man narrowed his eyes as though in mock shrewdness. "Matias Loredo is a smart businessman but he has no instinct when it comes to people. People are only useful to serve as his pawns."

That definitely matched her father to a T. "How did my father find me?"

"He found out about your nonprofit. Saw a picture of you at one of your fund-raisers."

"I don't remember anyone taking a picture of me. I was careful about that. And I never agreed to do any news features."

"He had people all over the country keeping a watch out for you. Policemen. Reporters. Friends and business associates. One of them must have seen you at the fund-raiser and taken a picture." He grabbed her sleeve again and forced her onward. "Your father found you over a year ago. Darien took his time planning."

Darien had known for that long? As demented as he was, he likely enjoyed the planning.

"He didn't know where I lived, though."

"No, not until a few weeks before he asked me to kill Bernie."

He spoke as though killing was nothing, just another task. Sadie felt sick.

Shoving her between the van and the car next to it, he let go of her shirt. Sadie stumbled and kept her footing as she turned to face him.

"What are you going to do?" She didn't need to ask. He'd kill her, but maybe not here, in this public parking garage. She could see a car driving to a lower level, already having passed them.

She heard another's engine start.

"Darien can't risk you going to the police with what you know," the man said. He stood close to her, with the gun pressed to her stomach and his back to the garage. "Your dad thinks Darien will bring you home to him."

Would he just kill her right here? He'd shoot her and her body would fall onto the concrete? What about her baby? Would it make a difference if she told him she was pregnant? No hardened killer like him would care.

The car she'd heard backed out of its space. She saw it on the far side. The driver slowly pulled away from the space and would have to pass them to get to the exit.

"I wouldn't even consider trying to attract any attention," the man said.

She looked into his dark eyes as the car drove in a U-turn to head for the exit down the lane. The driver didn't glance her way, just kept going.

"Good girl."

"If you let me go, I'll pay you double what Darien offered."

"Get in the van." He leaned over and pulled the back door open.

In the few seconds it took for him to do that, Sadie decided to act. She grabbed his gun and stomped hard on his knee, bending it backward and hoping she broke or tore something. His hand loosened on the gun and she took it from him.

He retaliated too fast for her, hitting her face and grasping the gun over her hand, squeezing until pain bit her. Prying the gun from her, he would have aimed for her, but Sadie stepped back and bent so she could swing her leg. She clipped his wrist and the gun went flying.

Once she found her footing again, she bolted for the

front of the van, running around that and the next car before going between those parked vehicles. Out in the parking garage lane, she noticed a car approaching, coming in off the street.

She waved her hands above her head. "Help!"

The car stopped. Sadie ran to the passenger door.

As she put her hands on the handle, Bernie's killer fired at the driver. The driver ducked and started the car moving.

Bernie's killer jumped out of the way as the car passed and squealed tires into the turn to the lower levels.

Sadie turned and ran for the exit. She could see the opening, just fifty feet or so to go.

Bernie's killer gained on her. She heard his running feet on the concrete floor of the parking garage. He grabbed her hair first.

"No!" Sadie reached back and tried to pry his fingers from her hair. He yanked and made her lose her balance.

She stumbled as she attempted to correct her balance but then he tripped her. She twisted so she wouldn't land on her stomach, crashing painfully on the concrete on her side.

Bernie's killer had let go of her hair. Sadie rolled onto her back and would have jumped to her feet, but he had his gun aimed at her. He looked ahead toward the exit. No cars entered. He could shoot her right now and no one would see. No one in front of him…

Sadie heard another person running from behind Bernie's killer. As she looked there, she saw Jasper slow to a walk with a gun. He fired in the next instant.

Bernie's killer dropped, a hole in his head. He fell with staring eyes next to her.

"Ugh." She pushed his hand off her and scrambled to her feet.

Jasper ran to her. She threw her arms around him, *thank you for saving our baby* running through her mind but she didn't say the words aloud. She felt them, though. Jasper must, too, he held her tight from long seconds.

"Are you all right?" he asked.

"Yes. But for a few seconds I thought that was it," she said. "I thought I was dead."

"Not on my watch." He kissed her temple. "Let's go back up to the room. Chad woke up right after you left."

She made a sound of gladness and rushed off toward the elevator.

Jasper followed. On the ride up, he told her about Kadin's call.

"We already know he's from Iran," she said before he finished. What had Kadin found?

"Yes, but what Kadin discovered is he's receiving large payments from an Iranian company."

"Payments…" She stared at nothing as her mind raced with all her would-be killer had said. "He's selling equipment to Iran. That's what must be on my computer." She explained what the shooter had revealed in his overconfidence as he took her somewhere secluded to kill her.

"What's your computer got to do with anything?" Jasper asked as the elevator doors opened and they walked out.

"That big brute told me Darien has been after my computer ever since I went into hiding. He used it during his illegal transactions and planned to destroy it when he was finished."

"Protecting his own computer?"

"So it would seem."

"And now he's vulnerable."

"I don't think he's going to toy with me anymore. That man down in the parking garage was going to kill me."

"He won't get that close again."

"He also said my father told him where I was. He was trying to find me and someone recognized me at a fund-raiser. My father almost got me killed."

Jasper stopped at the hospital room door. "He wouldn't have told Darien to hurt you, would he?"

Sadie had no idea. "I suppose that depends on how angry he was over my leaving the way I did."

"He had to know you ran to protect yourself."

"He also knew I hated working for him."

Jasper looked at her while he seemed to think that over. "Without talking to him it's hard to tell."

The last thing she wanted to do was talk to her father again. "Fat chance of that ever happening."

Raising his hand, he touched her face, running his thumb over her lower lip as though he thought of kissing her. "Maybe you should forgive him."

"It's hard to forgive someone who isn't willing to change what caused the rift in the first place."

He leaned forward and did kiss her then. "Whatever you decide." Stepping back, he added, "I'll call the police while you go see Chad."

"Won't they ask too many questions?" This had graduated from a simple murder investigation to much more.

"It'll be an anonymous call. I checked and the big guy was smart enough to park somewhere out of view of cameras."

Of course he was…so he could kidnap her.

Back in Wyoming, Jasper helped Sadie look for suspicious files on her old computer. It didn't take long to find them. Darien hadn't even tried to conceal the folder, which he'd labeled SpaceTech, the name of his company. She hadn't gone to her documents folder after moving. Most of her computer use was online.

He was remarkably organized.

"He sure wasn't afraid to keep records," Jasper said. He sat beside her at the desk in the library.

"It was probably habit. He probably kept records like this for his legal transactions." He'd only separated these to make his legal dealings look buttoned up tight.

She opened the commercial invoice for one shipment. SpaceTech was listed as the consignee. The name of the shipper's point of contact made her go utterly still.

"That's the man I saw murdered." She pointed to the name, Henry Barnes.

"Not surprising. I didn't think he was killed over drugs."

"The drugs were planted to throw off authorities?"

"Darien went to great lengths to cover up his true dealings with this company."

Sadie opened another file, this one a shipping document where SpaceTech was the shipper.

"This one went to Dubai."

Jasper leaned closer. "It's the same component. Look at the part number."

The numbers matched on both invoices, but the descriptions differed. One read cryogenic accelerometers, and the other read aircraft parts.

"Bingo," Sadie said.

Henry must have discovered Darien was re-exporting the sensors.

"He must have diverted the shipment from Dubai," Jasper said. "Let's see if we can find anything showing the ultimate destination."

Sadie searched the rest of the files. She found a purchase order listing another company in Iran. Within that documentation her gaze caught on the name of that company, which showed it as a subsidiary of SpaceTech.

"Do you see that?" she asked Jasper, turning her head to find his warm and close to hers.

He met her eyes and a moment of intimacy passed between them. "Yes." Then he took over the mouse from her and opened another shipping document, this one from a courier out of Dubai. It showed the same part number.

Jasper straightened. "I'll make a call. We'll let officials bring him in for that. Then we can enlighten them on the murders."

Would he be charged in both countries? Would he serve out his time in the United States? Sadie didn't care as long as he was locked up for the rest of his life.

"Do you have a jump drive?" he asked.

She stood, opened a drawer and retrieved one.

"This one is empty." Figuring he needed all the files, she copied them and then handed him the USB device.

Jasper's radio went off and Sadie listened as the gatehouse guard announced the arrival of Matias Loredo.

Chapter 15

"I'm not going to see him." Sadie stormed from one end of the library to the other.

Jasper admired her butt before she pivoted and faced him for a trek back toward him. He could understand her tizzy, especially not now, after learning he betrayed her location and identity to Darien, but he had to talk to him.

"He couldn't have known what Darien was hiding," Jasper said.

"He knew about the murder."

That was significant. Matias knew what Sadie knew—that Darien had conspired to kill his supplier and she'd seen the murderer carry out the order. "Let him explain his side. If you don't then I will. It might reveal more information."

She looked at him as though silently asking, *Didn't*

they have enough? Sadie was obviously more than ready for this to be over, but it wasn't over until Darien was caught.

"Let him in," Jasper told the gatehouse guard.

Sadie gaped at him.

"You don't have to see him," he said.

Moving toward her, he slid his hand behind her head and kissed her.

Hearing Jasper talking in the waiting room off the front entry, Sadie stopped.

"I told you she doesn't want to see you."

"She let me in the gate."

"No, *I* let you in the gate."

"I came a long way. I dropped everything to make this trip. You can't stop me from seeing her. I need to talk to her. Now."

Oh, did that sound like her father. Sadie moved next to the door, staying out of sight.

"I'm not one of your employees," Jasper said. "If Sadie doesn't want to see you, you aren't going to see her. You'll have to go through me, and…" Jasper paused as though making an assessment. "Something tells me the only thing tough enough about you is your callous management style."

"So, she talked to you about me."

Sadie peeked around the edge of the door. Both men stood near a console table that ran behind a sofa, their sides to her.

Jasper didn't respond. He'd laid down his law. Enough said. He wouldn't let Matias have his way just because he made a demand. Love spilled over the core of her soul. Or affection. Or the buddings of real attraction. Whatever this thing inside her was that had manifested out of nowhere. Jasper would honor her wishes at all cost. No man would get past him, least of all her materialistic, overbearing father.

"Did she tell you the only time I communicated with her was when I had something disparaging to say about my workers? That I am a tyrant?" In one of his expensive silk suits, her father looked the same as she remembered. His silver hair was neatly trimmed and combed.

"That's close. She also said you were a supremacist and that she despises supremacists. Something along those lines." Jasper said that so casually that Sadie almost let loose a laugh.

She inched around the edge of the doorframe again and saw her father speechless—if only for a second— for the first time in her life.

"You called her Sadie," he said at last. "Her name is Catalina." His brittle tone sent her back in time, the sure indication of the onset of one of his domineering *talks*.

"Her name is Sadie now. If you knew anything about her, you'd know she isn't Catalina, especially not anymore."

"She's had five years to convince herself she doesn't belong at Loredo. She does. She's a great business-woman. My daughter has all of my most valuable traits. There's no one else I'd rather leave my dynasty to than her."

My daughter grated on Sadie. As if she belonged to him, as if only the fact that he'd created her, a near clone in his view, mattered beyond all else. While a small part of her argued it wasn't that simple, she closed herself off to any softening.

"Don't you get it?" Jasper had leaned toward Matias's face. "She doesn't want that for herself. And she *is* a great businesswoman. Look what she's done with the Revive Center. Or are you going to ignore what she's built because it doesn't follow *your* way?"

Sadie watched her father closely. He met Jasper's cool, righteous eyes and intruding proximity. She had never seen him hesitate like that before.

"I didn't come here to win her over," he finally said. "I know that won't happen overnight."

He planned to win her over? What did that mean? Would he try to charm her back to Loredo?

"Darien came to see me," he said.

Whoa. What? Sadie moved out from the protection of the wall. They saw her at the same time.

Her father turned and faced her. "Catalina..." He cleared his through and seemed to catch himself. "Sadie. You changed your mind." His eyes were different. Was that contrition she saw? Gladness. Triumph, yes, but not overpowering.

"No. Darien came to see you. Why?" She walked slowly into the room and stopped a few feet away from both men.

Jasper stood tall and alert without interfering. He'd shown her how much he understood and cared about her feelings regarding her father. And he supported her.

"He had all sorts of questions about you and a man named Jasper who confronted him in public." Matias turned to Jasper. "I assume that's you?"

"What did you tell him about me?"

"Just what Ana Sophia told me. You were from some type of cold case detective agency and were helping Sadie solve a murder of one of her homeless people." Matias was all business now. Matter-of-fact and seeming unaffected.

Didn't Jasper want Darien to know who he was? The element of surprise could sometimes work out favorably.

"Why did you tell him about me?" Sadie asked. "Why did you tell him where I was?"

"That's why I came here. Ana Sophia said you were attacked. I couldn't believe Darien would be behind such a thing, but then he came to see me and he was so angry. He turned into a completely different person."

Sadie folded her arms, not happy at all her father so easily took the man's side.

"One minute he exchanged pleasantries with me and the next he went off on a tangent about how you sent some sort of secret soldier after him. His animosity toward you shocked me. He didn't reveal that before then."

"Darien is an expert at fooling people, making them believe he's something he's not."

Her father moved toward her, stopping closer than she liked. "He fooled me. He told me it wasn't him at that bar. He said you were too far away to see clearly. He thought whoever you saw kill that man in Toronto must have also killed the detective."

"Of course he'd deny any involvement. The killer did murder the detective, but Darien directed him to do so." Seeing her father in this new light, where he'd become a victim of another person, changed her perception—some. That he had fallen so easily for

Darien's lies only convinced her more how little he actually knew her.

"Can you ever forgive me?" her father asked.

She couldn't respond.

"I would have never have told him where you were if you'd have come to me. If you'd have informed me of your plans."

So he could control her some more? "I needed to get away from you, too, Dad."

"I could have protected you."

Still, he ignored all she'd confessed to him, all her feelings. "I'm fine. And I will continue to be fine."

Matias glanced at Jasper, who'd stayed quiet through their talk. Then he returned his attention to Sadie. His usual stern face had softened. In his eyes she could see his regret, or regret for not recognizing a problem sooner so he could have fixed it sooner.

She waited for him to organize his words.

"I came here to apologize and to see what I can do to earn your forgiveness." He seemed genuinely sincere. "For both exposing you to Darien and for driving you away."

Sadie faltered. She could almost believe him. Could it be she'd broken through her father's stubborn drive to achieve?

"You need more time, I understand."

"Do you?" She had her doubts.

"I'd like you in my life." He smiled. "Your mother will have you in hers, so I can't fall behind her, right?"

If that was his attempt at humor, Sadie didn't laugh. He sounded too much like the father she despised. But he'd taken a step forward. She'd take that for now.

* * *

Jasper curbed his desire to follow where his male instinct led. Sadie had changed into something more comfortable after dinner, nothing sexy, just a simple white cotton gown that fell to her ankles. But it was so her. Few had glimpses of both sides of her, the sexy beauty and the mountain recluse. All in one fabulous body.

Taking a steaming cup of tea, she headed for the family room. Jasper followed, feeling tethered by her femininity. Sitting on the gray sectional, she started flipping channels. He sat beside her as she landed on a chick flick about an aspiring actress whose clumsy personality keeps the rejections coming.

Sadie glanced at him as though waiting for his protest.

He just grinned. "This is one of the better ones."

"You've seen it?"

"Parts. Once I went over to Kadin's house for a work party. We celebrated moving into the new building."

He watched her mull over what that could mean. More cases required more staff. The growth of DAI needed men like Jasper.

"He's talking about relocating to a bigger city," Jasper said.

She turned to him, wariness cooling her eyes. "Where?"

"Not New York. That's where his daughter was kidnapped and murdered. Maybe California or Texas. All the detectives are weighing in."

"His daughter was murdered?" No longer retreating behind her protective barrier, she seemed deeply moved.

Jasper nodded. "When she was a young girl. Kadin came from the New York PD. He was a good detective then. After his daughter was killed, he made it his life's mission to take down bad people. He's practically a celebrity. I'm surprised you haven't heard of him."

She faced the television, something taking her mood down. "I don't pay attention to crime on television or in the news. I avoid that whenever possible."

Ever since that Canadian detective had been murdered and up until Bernie.

"There were a lot of detectives at that party?" she asked.

Parties were much more palatable for her. Jasper liked that about her, but she should face the things that hurt her in her past. That's something he'd learned. Recently.

"Just about all of them. Kadin and his wife, Penny, Brycen Cage and his wife, Drury. They came down from Alaska. He's running a new division there now." He chuckled with a thought. "It took a woman like Drury to bring him back to his roots."

"He's from there?"

"Not born, but he worked there before he started his show. Still does them but not on the scale he used to." When she didn't ask any more questions, seeing how insight into his place of employment engaged her, he resumed the party attendees. "Rachel and Lucas Curran were there. They live in Bozeman. His father owns one of Montana's busiest private air transportation and tourism companies. He works remotely but travels a lot to the office and runs things for Kadin.

He's the business operations brain of the company. And then there's Reese and Jamie Knox."

"The security expert."

"The security expert." He smiled. "It took a lot for him to get her to leave her hometown in the southwestern mountains of Colorado. I'd say she's a lot like you but she was a sheriff's deputy."

"Not a rich heiress?" Although she smiled he sensed she may have taken some offense.

"I'm not saying you aren't tough."

"Maybe tough enough not to be swayed by a man who won't relocate."

Who said he wouldn't relocate? He didn't voice his thoughts. Why bother when he wasn't sure where he'd like to live? Close to DAI. He liked being in the thick of the action. Her curt declaration bit at him, though. Was she really that sure?

Rather than reveal his reaction, he leaned over and pressed a kiss to her mouth, then drew back to her dark, warming eyes. "We'll see about that."

His phone rang, interrupting what might have progressed into the bedroom. Seeing Kadin's name on the cell phone screen, he had to answer.

"Kadin."

"Jasper. How's Sadie holding up?"

"Better now that we know Chad will be all right." Jasper stood, feeling the need to move. Kadin didn't call unless he had something important to say.

Sadie followed his steps a few feet away with her eyes.

"Any news on Jafari?"

"Not yet. He's on the run, but he won't be able to

avoid detection for long, with both Canadian and US authorities looking for him."

"Good. I didn't call for that but I thought I'd get an update while I had the chance. Someone came to see you today. Someone who's been calling for days now even when told repeatedly you aren't here and we don't know when you will be. She won't say why she's calling so I haven't given her your number."

"Who is it?"

"Her name is Kendra Scott. She says she's not leaving until she talks to you."

"Why would I talk to her? Why is she insisting on me?" Most insisted on seeing Kadin.

"Get ready for this one," Kadin said. "She says it's related to her twin sister, and her twin sister was married to your uncle."

The floor may as well drop out from under his feet.

"I told her Kaelyn didn't have a twin sister," Kadin went on, "but she said they were both adopted by different parents."

Kadin must have learned all about Jasper's uncle and Kaelyn when he'd brought Jasper on as a DAI detective, but he must not have discovered the adoption piece.

"You're slipping if you missed that in my background check." He'd known Kaelyn had been adopted but she never told him about a twin.

"I didn't feel I needed to dig that deep. Still don't. You've never disappointed me."

Had any of his detectives? Kadin was good at picking the best.

Jasper saw Sadie watching him intently. She must

have sharpened her attention as soon as she heard Kaelyn's name.

"With things wrapping up there, when can you come back and meet her?" Kadin asked.

First Jasper felt a familiar bolt of excitement over starting a new case, which surprised him given this case would involve his uncle and revisiting Kaelyn's death. Just Kendra's association with Kaelyn would spur up ugly memories. But, also surprising, he didn't dread that. In fact, he thought it might be good for him.

Maybe not for his relationship with Sadie, however. The soon-to-be mother of his child.

"As soon as Jafari is captured."

"I can send two of our best to guard her. Nobody will get past them."

Kadin wanted him back as soon as possible. Jasper could tell. He also didn't doubt he'd send top guards with Special Forces experience.

"I'm surprised you haven't been back already. We know the killer is dead. All we need now is the man who conspired it all."

Normally he would have left by now. He looked at Sadie and saw her attentively watching and listening.

"You're a valuable asset here, Jasper. People need you here."

Working on-site gave him hands-on availability and he had quicker, more secure access to resources. Kadin didn't say, but he'd prefer Jasper didn't work remotely. The keen-minded man knew what Sadie was coming to mean to him.

"I understand," he said.

"Call me when you have a date."

"Will do." He ended the call and stood there look-

ing across the family room, old paintings tying colors
together with the rest of the room.

"Was that Kadin?" Sadie asked, jarring him from
his roaming thoughts.

"Yes."

"Someone is asking for you?"

"Kaelyn's twin sister." That she had a twin and that
twin had gone to DAI looking for him had him more
than curious. He could see it had triggered interest in
Sadie as well, but a different kind.

"What does she want?"

"I don't know. She refused to say. She'll only talk to
me. Kadin wants me back at DAI as soon as possible."

As she stared at him for long seconds, her expression blank but rigid, he sensed a storm brewing.

Standing, she faced him. "That's exciting." With
that she stepped out from the sectional and started
toward the stairs.

"Sadie." He went after her.

"I know where this is headed."

He caught her and turned her. "I can come back."

"When you're all finished with Kaelyn's twin sister?"

Not striking her as the jealous type, Jasper didn't
say anything. He let go of her arm.

"She probably has an interesting case for you,"
Sadie said.

"Sadie…"

"You'll have a bonus if she looks like Kaelyn, too.
Lucky you."

Were her hormones getting the better of her? No
matter, he had to set her straight. He stepped closer.
Tipping her chin up with his fingers, he said, "I won't

quit my job. I won't abandon you and our baby. And I sure as hell won't stray with a woman who looks like Kaelyn."

Her eyes softened, upper lids slipping lower. Her lips parted.

"But will you leave DAI to live here?" she asked, her voice low and shaky as though she struggled with passion.

He let her voice float through him and fed his eyes with the sight of hers meeting his growing hunger. Rather than answer, he lowered his head and kissed her, light and tender. He couldn't say he'd leave DAI.

She pushed his chest and stepped back. Building anger doused her passion. "You'll go back to work and visit when you can, won't you? Which won't be often. What's the point, Jasper? Why don't you just walk away and never look back? That's what you've done ever since Kaelyn committed suicide, isn't it?"

She spoke crass and blunt. Hearing *committed suicide* and directly linking it to his behavior hit him hard. He had avoided relationships but it wasn't fair for her to expect him to forget everything he'd built at DAI to come live here with her and the baby—just for the baby.

Or did this outburst of hers indicate a suppressed wish?

"I thought you didn't trust me," he said.

"I trust you."

"Not with your heart. I can keep Darien from killing you, but I can't make you open yourself to me."

"Is that really what you want?" she countered.

Again, she posed a question he couldn't answer. And also again, she wasn't playing fair.

"Is that what *you* really want, Sadie?" When she averted her head and said nothing, frustration billowed up. "Don't ask me questions you yourself can't even answer."

He strode out of the room, needing time away from her to gather his thoughts. One thing he knew for sure; he had to take a trip to DAI. He couldn't risk his job, or the meeting with Kendra. Sadie would just have to deal with his temporary absence. At least…he hoped it would only be temporary.

His gait slowed as he realized he wouldn't be happy leaving her, even temporarily.

The next morning, Sadie felt terrible. She'd accused Jasper of putting his job before her and the baby and hadn't considered his responsibility to DAI. He had a job he had to maintain. How could he do that if he was always with her? And they hadn't known each other long. The baby threw them together well beyond the natural progression of things.

After dressing in a blue-and-white college-style flannel over a white T-shirt and a pair of jeans, Sadie started downstairs and heard voices in the kitchen. Jasper and the new bodyguards from DAI. She descended the rest of the way quiet as a spider. Sneaking closer and staying out of sight, she went to the wall near the entrance. Peeking around the corner, she saw three men. Jasper laughed at something funny the tallest of them said. He was blond and the other was darker and much less animated. These must be Jasper's replacements. Handsome and strong…like Jasper.

"Seems we have an addition to our meeting," the

darker man said, moving his eyes toward the door where she stood.

So much for hiding. Smoothing her hair and tucking unruly strands behind her ear, she moved out from the wall as though she hadn't been standing there.

Jasper watched her with still-smiling eyes that warmed the nearer she came. She wondered if he covered the residual effects of their last exchange or if this maddening attraction brought on the natural reaction.

"Sadie," he greeted, "this is Dwayne and Hershel. They'll be watching you while I make my quick trip to DAI."

He must have added *quick* in deference to her.

She nodded to the darker man, Dwayne, and then the blond, Hershel. "Hello."

"A very nice hello to you." Hershel defied his wise name with a once-over that Jasper noticed with a slight scowl.

"I need to talk to you." Jasper gently took her arm and steered her away from the men.

In the living room, he let her go and she faced him.

"I'm going back to DAI in the morning," he said.

She figured he wouldn't wait long to go back. Holding on to her strength, she didn't allow herself to feel sad.

"I understand you have to work."

"Do you?" His brow rose as though skeptical.

"Yes. Come back when you can. I'll be all right." She always was. She had gotten good at making sure of that. But now she saw that her independence may have gone on too long, that maybe she should have at least tried to give other men a chance, give Jasper a chance.

He still seemed skeptical.

"My lack of trust in men…in you…made me say things yesterday that I shouldn't have," she said.

"I'm coming back, Sadie."

She really didn't want to hash this out again. "I believe you." She just didn't believe he'd stay. "I'd appreciate it if you slept in another room tonight."

By his lengthy silence she assumed he understood why. She might believe he'd come back but commitment was another issue. He'd be there for their baby, but how much? What would he consider *being there*?

"Sure. Okay." He nodded a few times awkwardly. "I'll call you when I get there."

Don't bother, she wanted to say. But her heart rejoiced with eager anticipation for that call.

Chapter 16

Jasper finished walking the perimeter and checking with the gatehouse and ops center guards. All was quiet, so he went inside the house and climbed the stairs to the library.

The soldiers Kadin had sent would stay close to Sadie once he left. Both had rooms next to hers. Jasper would take another down the hall. Her distance bothered him but he couldn't blame her. She didn't trust him to stick around and neither was sure they were right for each other. Even as the other voice in his head said that, his deeper self challenged, as though the statement didn't ring true.

The radio went live. "Mr. Roesch?"

It was the gatehouse guard.

"Yes?"

"Ms. Moreno is asking for you. She's waiting at the gate. She asked you to hurry."

Jasper left the library and ran down the stairs, pushing through the front door and jogging toward the entrance to the property. He could see the car, exhaust
fogging the chilly spring mountain air. The guard stood
inside the gatehouse, and the gate remained closed.

Slowing as he approached the driver, he bent and
saw Sadie in the back. He opened the door.

"Get in," she said. "We don't have much time."

"What happened?"

"Steven called. He said Darien had him and if I
didn't come alone he'd kill him. When Steven added
for me not to come no matter what Darien did to him,
I heard Darien beat him." She put her hand over her
mouth, as though reliving the horror.

Jasper got into the car. "It will be all right. Remember I said he's desperate. He's doing desperate things."

"Steven is my friend." Tears moistened her eyes.

Jasper slid closer and put his arm around her. When
she burrowed even closer, his heart surged with warm
affection.

"Did you talk to Darien?" he asked.

"Yes." Her lower lip trembled. "He will kill Steven
if I don't go alone."

Darien would kill Steven if he had the chance, but
Jasper could not put Sadie and the baby in a dangerous
situation. "You will, but you'll have plenty of backup."
He used his radio to call Dwayne and Hershel.

"Get out of this car, Sadie. We'll take one of the
SUVs."

Sniffling, she nodded with sad, worried eyes meeting his. She'd had all she could take of this and he'd
see to it she never had to be this stressed again.

Getting out with her, he told Sadie's driver to take the car back to the garage.

The soldiers drove up in a big black armored SUV. "What's the plan, boss?" the driver asked, the blond man.

"Which one of you is a good shot?" he asked.

"We're both top ranked," Hershel said from behind the driver's wheel. "We can take position with a clean shot through a window if we need to."

"We can get inside, too," Dwayne said from the passenger seat, the darker of the two. "Darien won't know we're there."

"He may not be alone."

"He's alone," Jasper said. "Nobody would follow him now. He's got too much heat on him. At most he'll have one or two."

"We can take two or three out," Hershel said.

Jasper hated the idea of Sadie going anywhere near Darien.

"It's the best way, Jasper," Sadie said.

"We won't send her in until we're sure we have the situation under control," Hershel said.

They might have control at first but things could go sour in a blink. But it was their best chance of saving Steven.

"All right." He looked at Sadie. "Get in."

Sadie climbed into the back and Jasper retrieved some weapons from the rear cargo area. Sitting next to her in the SUV, Hershel drove through the now-open gate while Jasper showed Sadie a handgun.

"This is a 9mm Glock. It's easy to use." He pressed the side button to release the magazine. "The bullets go in here. It's full now so you have fifteen." He put the magazine back in. "Pull the slide back and you now have a round chambered. Here's the safety. Turn that off when you see Darien. Don't worry about firing. I won't be far behind you."

"But if something goes wrong I'll be prepared."

"Have you ever shot a gun before?"

"Steven showed me a little."

Jasper didn't show his apprehension. He wouldn't let her out of his sight.

Sadie gave directions to the coffee shop where Darien had instructed her to meet. The public place had likely convinced her to go along with his demand to meet or he'd kill Steven. He must have some kind of plan to fool her.

"Park here," Jasper said to Hershel, who pulled to the side of the road, parallel parking under cover of trees a bit down from the coffee shop.

Jasper took Sadie's face between his hands. "I'll be watching you. Keep as much distance as you can from him. Don't get close enough for him to grab you. If he tries, run."

She nodded. "What if he has a gun?"

"He will. If he pulls it out, I'll kill him."

Not looking forward to witnessing that, Sadie bit her lip. Flashes of Henry came back to haunt her then, the way he looked at her with hope, and then that final fraction of a second when he knew his life would end. The gunshot. She'd shut her eyes but she'd seen the gory aftermath.

"I'll be with you, Sadie," Jasper said. "We all will."

Jasper's reassurance took away the ugliness of the memory. Realizing she'd shut her eyes just as she had in her mind, she turned to him. She pecked a quick kiss and would have gotten out of the car.

He stopped her. "He'll be expecting you and a driver. He'll be relieved when he doesn't see me."

"He'll suspect you're nearby," she said.

"He told you to come alone or he'd kill Steven. If he doesn't see me, he'll relax enough."

She nodded. "Okay."

To Dwayne he said, "You come with me." Then to Hershel he said, "After you drop Sadie off in front of the coffee shop, park as fast as you can and go around to the back. We'll radio you when we locate Darien."

"Roger that," the driver said.

Jasper kissed her this time, quick like she'd bestowed on him, but the brief heat fanned from the last and he remained close to her mouth, eyes absorbed with hers for just a moment before he left the car.

She watched him go to the sidewalk, Dwayne joining him, and then vanish into the trees as the driver pulled forward. Lights from several shops illuminated the street. The first in the line of brick and varying colored siding, the coffee shop teemed with activity. People filled most of the tables through the front windows. A man left and two women entered. A sidewalk chalkboard advertised a specialty scone, sold only on Wednesdays—today. A man stepped out from the narrow alley between the building and the trees. The alley led to the back of a house.

Darien stepped into the light and raised his hand, a friendly gesture, as though to ease her trepidation. Seeing him gave her a sick feeling, a wave of nausea rolling through her stomach and abdomen. All the old memories came forward, the shock of discovering his monstrous side, and the terror of being held captive in her own home, a beautiful home that had become so ugly. She'd loved the mansion he'd built for her. That's what had inspired her to build her castle in Wyoming, to bring back the beauty, the fairy tale.

Sadie's pulse kicked into high alert. But, oh, what a player. Tucking the pistol into her jacket pocket, she climbed out of the car. Although she wanted to, she didn't look toward the trees, fearing she'd give away Jasper's intent. Instead she looked toward the busy coffee shop. A couple exited, the man noticing her briefly before putting his arm around his girl and guiding her toward the small parking lot on the other side of the building.

Sadie walked toward Darien. He wore a long trench coat over his usual business attire, complete with a tie. Still the tall, dark and handsome man she'd met so long ago, his attractiveness did nothing for her now. He instilled only fear.

He smiled much in the way of a villain she'd seen in a movie, sly with a hint of craziness. "Catalina, so good to see you again." He outstretched his arms as though she'd go into them and greet a missed friend.

She stopped a good ten feet from him.

His smile flattened. "I suppose my method of getting you here is to blame for that."

"Where is Steven?"

"Ah, Steven. How long has he been communicating with you?"

Sadie didn't answer.

"Since you left? Did he help you?" When she again said nothing, he went on, "I always wondered how you got away. Steven wouldn't tell me anything."

"Where is he?" she demanded.

Darien leaned to one side, searching the street. "Did you come alone like I asked?"

"You didn't ask."

"Your driver left."

She waited for him to finish delaying. Was Steven already dead? A surge of rage gave her new strength. She'd kill him herself if he did.

"Right this way." Darien turned, outstretching his arm as though welcoming her into his lair. "I rented the house right here. I thought you'd feel more comfortable meeting me here, where you and Steven met."

Steven had told him that much. Harmless enough.

Sadie walked a good distance from him, stopping when Darien did to wait for her.

He smiled in that creepy way again and resumed his trek toward the dark house. He hadn't even left an outside light on. At the door, he opened it and moved aside to allow her to pass.

"You go ahead," she said.

"Afraid to get too close?"

When she didn't reply, he breathed a laugh and went inside. She slowly held the door open and entered.

"You know," Darien said, removing his coat, "there was a time when we were very close. You used to love me. We had a good, solid relationship."

She decided not to provoke him. "Where is Steven?"

His smile faded and several seconds passed.

Sadie slipped her hands into her jacket pockets, curling her right around the handle of the pistol. It was ready to fire.

Darien's gaze went down to the pockets and then rose. "He's in the basement." He gestured to the open stairway across from the back door.

She had a feeling he planned to lure her down there. "You first," she said.

With a sinister laugh, he did as she asked. Sadie followed him down the stairs. Stepping into an old, dimly lit basement with low ceilings, she searched for and found Steven. Tied to a chair at the far end, he lifted his battered head.

"Steven!" Sadie rushed to Steven, kneeling and checking the severity of his injuries. His left eye was red and swollen, his lip split.

She turned back to Darien. "What have you done to him?"

"Sadie," Steven said in a raspy, dry voice. "What are you doing here?"

"Are you all right?"

"Get out of here. He's lost his mind. He said he'd use me to bring you here and then he'd take you back to Toronto where he thinks you belong."

Hearing footfalls on the cracked, dirty cement floor, Sadie stood and withdrew her pistol, aiming it at Darien.

"That's far enough," she said.

Darien cocked his head as he looked at the weapon and then straightened, all very horror movie, insanity making him bolder than he should be. "You wouldn't shoot me." He chuckled. "You don't have the heart for it. You left your position with Loredo to help home-less people, people who can't make it on their own," he jeered.

She didn't expect him to understand. He was too

much like her father and she'd still been under her father's spell to see the signs. Only Darien had gone off the deep end, whereas her father showed promise to change his ways.

"I will shoot you if I have to," she said. "I'm not going anywhere with you. This ends now. After tonight, I will never have to fear you coming after me again."

"Coming after you," Darien continued to mock. "I'm merely bringing you home."

"My home is here now."

His sarcasm began to slip into anger, she could see. She'd quickly learned how to recognize when he'd change over into that horrible man.

"Your home is with *me*." He began to move toward her. "This is how things will go, Catalina. First, I'm going to take that gun from you, then I'm going to use it to kill Steven for double-crossing me—and to teach you a lesson never to leave me again—and then we are going to calmly walk out the front door, get into the car I have waiting and fly back to Toronto."

He actually thought he'd get through Customs?

"You're crazier than I thought," she said.

"Home is a little different now. We have to go somewhere safe for a while. Maybe for the rest of our lives. But I have it all set up. I had money stashed a long time ago in preparation for this sad turn of events. But don't think I'll go into hiding alone. No. I'll have my wife with me."

"We were never married."

"We will be." He moved closer still and Sadie began to wonder if he knew her better than she thought. Images of Henry in his last moments tormented her. She couldn't watch another life fade from eyes, even if those eyes belonged to a man as despicable as Darien.

She stepped away from Steven, attempting to draw Darien away from him. But that backfired when Darien removed his own gun and rushed to Steven's side, putting the gun against his temple.

"Darien, don't."

"Put your gun down and I won't."

Sadie looked at Steven, who watched her fearlessly through his one eye.

"Don't listen to him, Sadie," Steven said. "Shoot him."

"I'll kill him," Darien said.

Where was Jasper? Sadie adjusted her hold on the pistol and aimed for Darien's head. If she shot him he wouldn't be able to pull the trigger, right? She glanced at Steven, who nodded once, almost imperceptibly.

Just as Sadie fired, Jasper and Dwayne appeared in the basement and glass from a small basement window shattered.

Darien slumped to the floor, his gun going off but the bullet strayed far off course, hitting the wall to the right of the window. She'd shot him in the chest and another bullet had gone through his head, the one fired through the window.

Sadie rushed to Steven and untied his hands. Jasper appeared before him and untied his feet.

"He needs an ambulance," Sadie said.

"I'm all right," Steven protested.

"Already on the way," Dwayne said.

From the stairs, Hershel appeared.

"Nice shot," Dwayne said.

"Thanks." Hershel grinned as though he'd done nothing more than throw a football really far.

From outside, Sadie heard sirens grow louder.

Steven stood, rubbing his chafed wrists. Jasper pulled Sadie to him and held her in a tight embrace. "I'm so glad that's over."

Smiling, she leaned back and took in his worry. "It is over. Finally. Thank you." She never expected to solve Bernie's murder *and* be rid of Darien all at the same time. What a bonus. Except it was really finished. Jasper no longer had a reason to stay. He had to go back to Wyoming to investigate a new case. She had to say goodbye.

Chapter 17

"Welcome back."

Jasper looked up from his desktop computer at DAI. Kadin stood at the door of his office, dressed in black jeans and a vest with a tie over a white dress shirt, looking more like a father and a businessman than a cutthroat detective.

Up until now, Jasper had tried to weed through an overwhelming number of emails. He had so much catching up to do. But thoughts of Sadie kept interfering. He couldn't concentrate.

"Thanks."

"When are you meeting Kendra Scott?"

Jasper had to check the time, he'd drifted off about Sadie so often and so long he'd lost track. "Anytime now. She's late."

Kadin entered the office, closing the door behind him. "You seem different."

"Different?" Jasper leaned back in his chair, hoping he appeared nonchalant and his dilemma didn't show so much.

"Distracted. You're normally much more social. Everyone misses your wit around here."

Jasper wouldn't call himself witty, not all the time and certainly not as a trademark of his personality, but he had liked the social aspect of working for DAI. It made the grisly work of solving cold murder cases much easier and more like a job than something disturbing.

Kadin sat down on a chair before his desk and propped his ankle over his knee. "I'm starting to get pretty good at reading my detectives when they take cases that involve a beautiful woman."

Jasper could pick out which detectives Kadin referred to.

A knock on the office door interrupted. The receptionist opened the door a bit. "Ms. Scott is here."

Kadin stood. "Let's talk after you meet with her."

Why did Jasper get the feeling Kadin hoped Kendra's case would keep him here at DAI?

Kadin left and the receptionist opened the door wider to allow Kendra Scott to pass. A five-foot-seven redhead with bright green eyes stepped inside. She wore a sage-green dress with a brown leather jacket and boots. She removed her jacket as the receptionist closed the door.

"Mr. Roesch. I'm so glad to finally meet you."

Jasper stood and moved out from behind his desk to shake her hand, more than idly curious why this woman had insisted on seeing him.

"Kadin said you've been trying to reach me."

"Yes." She glanced around the office. "Maybe we should sit for this."

He obliged her and followed her to the small conference table he had in his office, sitting across from her.

She placed her hands on the table and looked down at them awhile. Then she finally lifted her eyes. "There is no easy way to say this so I'm just going to come out and say it."

Jasper rarely waited on pins and needles but he did now.

"Kaelyn Johnston is…was…my twin sister."

Well, her news could have been worse. And then he wondered how he'd never known.

"We were both adopted by different parents when we were very young," Kendra said.

"I'm sorry for your loss." What else could he say? And why had she singled him out to tell him?

"That's only part of the reason I came here," she said. "The main reason I'm here is my sister didn't commit suicide. She was murdered."

Jasper didn't give in to shock. Too many family members jumped to that conclusion when someone close took their own life. "I saw the police report. None of the details of her death point to foul play."

"Then her killer covered his tracks really well. He must have known the cops would look hard at her death, especially you."

Jasper went over all the facts in his mind and still wasn't convinced. "I would have caught something like that."

"Maybe you're being overconfident."

"I doubt it. Kaelyn was extremely important to me. I would have caught any sign of foul play."

"Not if there wasn't any sign of it. Not if the killer left no trace."

"Kaelyn found me and we started writing and talking before she died. We even met once. We had plans to see each other regularly."

"She made plans to go see you?"

"Yes, and she was excited and happy."

That differed from the Kaelyn he remembered toward the end. Could it be she hadn't committed suicide? If she'd made plans to be with her twin sister, why would she? Kaelyn must have been glad to reunite with her lost twin sister, and she had to know Jasper could have gotten her there safely—and undetected.

Jasper felt released from years of guilt. He also felt compelled to look into this new information. It would have changed the way he'd investigated her death to begin with.

But Sadie tugged him another direction. In fact, his feelings for her and the future he could have with her far outweighed his ambition to further embroil himself in Kaelyn. Kaelyn had caused him trouble from the moment he'd met her. She'd been beautiful and smart and charming and he'd definitely been attracted, but his relationship with her had been too complicated. Too difficult. With Sadie, everything seemed to fall into place on its own.

"I'd like to hire you to look into her death," Kendra said.

"Of course. I'll see to it that one of DAI's best is assigned."

Kendra seemed crestfallen. "But… I was hoping you'd take the case. After all, you knew her. You *loved* her."

"Kaelyn was a wonderful person. I loved spending time with her, and for a long time I grieved her death. But I didn't love her the way you might think. I don't regret what happened between us. In fact, I'll always have good memories of our time together. But I have someone else in my life now, and my priorities have to lie with her."

Further disappointment pulled her face down. "I understand. I'm disappointed, but I do understand."

"I'll make sure you get a good detective. He'll be unbiased and experienced."

Kendra stood, picking up her purse. "She's a lucky lady."

He smiled slightly. He'd be a lucky man if she took him back.

After Kendra left, Jasper walked to Kadin's office, his steps faster than usual. An eagerness to be back with Sadie drowned out any other purpose. A weight had been lifted off him. He was going back to her. Sadie. His Sadie.

And their baby…

Even that didn't take the spring out of his step.

He reached Kadin's open door. Kadin stood at his whiteboard and put the marker down when he saw him.

"Sadie is pregnant," he blurted.

Kadin seemed at first disappointed and then accepting. "That's a doozy."

Jasper entered the office. "We didn't plan on it, but it just…seemed to happen. I want to do the right thing but I also don't want to lose what I have going for me here."

Stuffing his hands into his pockets, Kadin faced him. "That's nature's way of making you grow. Do the right thing. You'll find out it's what you want anyway."

How could he be so sure?

"Hey, it happens. Happened to me. Love hits you when you aren't prepared for the blow."

He felt like this is what he wanted. To be with Sadie and raise a child. Maybe more than one. Settle down. Nothing he'd done professionally had ever felt so exhilarating.

"I keep losing good detectives this way," Kadin said, and then after a lengthy pause where he must be thinking, he added, "This won't be the first time I've allowed one of you to work remotely. I guess I'm lucky that at least you're not leaving Wyoming."

"It's not a bad drive here," Jasper said.

"For now anyway. I get a lot of complaints about this location. Living in a small town like this doesn't appeal to everyone. I'll probably have to relocate, or at least set up headquarters in a bigger city."

"You've given it some thought?"

"I've had to."

"What city?"

"I'm not sure yet. California. Texas. Not New York, that's all I know at this point."

Jasper nodded.

"Can you travel when you need to?" Kadin asked.

"Yes, as long as I don't miss the birth of my child."

"Then take some time off until after that. Let me know when you're ready to get back to work."

Sadie galloped back to the stable on a big white horse, feeling freer than she had since she'd left To-

ronto. She'd just taken a ride all by herself and didn't
have to worry about anyone attacking. Yesterday, she'd
taken her Ferrari for a spin and gone to Jackson Hole
for a day of shopping.

She'd reduced security and had made plans to travel
regularly to the Revive Center, all locations. The activity at her house had reduced significantly. She had
much more time alone. That both satisfied her and
gave her too much time to think about Jasper. His
goodbye had been sweet and full of promises to return when he could. Sadie didn't like how she perked
up every time the phone rang or the gatehouse guard
called to announce an arrival. Usually the arrivals
were deliveries.

Dismounting, she made herself take in the crisp
blue sky and smell the forest as she led the beautiful
mare to the stable and a waiting groom. Before Jasper
she didn't have to try to appreciate the splendor of her
home and the wilderness surrounding her.

Before Jasper...

What about before Darien?

Before Darien she hadn't been afraid of men. Was
she afraid of men? She handed the reins to the groom
and thanked him, petting the mare's soft white nose
before heading for the house. She'd gotten so con-
ditioned to be on guard with Darien that she transferred that to any other man. Add to that her lack of
dating since escaping. How long would she have gone
on that way? Sure, she'd joined a dating site, but she
hadn't joined with any serious intent. She'd joined for
the social interaction. The anonymity had appealed
to her. Then Jasper had popped into her life. From

the moment she'd seen him in front of DAI he'd captivated her.

Sadie remembered smiling at him when she'd walked back into her house after finishing with police at the coffee shop. Steven and the DAI soldiers had gone their own ways. Jasper had smiled back. Peace, at last. They'd stayed up awhile, munching on junk food, drinking soda and watching *The Magic of Belle Isle* until the sun began to rise. Happiness completed her.

The time had come to sleep, and she couldn't share her bed. Not with him leaving the next day. Happiness dimmed with encroaching reality. They'd embraced, kissed softly but briefly and went to separate bedrooms.

He had already left by the time she woke early in the afternoon, starving and craving fried chicken.

Inside her house, she closed the door. Expecting silence, the sound of the television in the family room surprised her. Finley had gone to town for the day and no other house staff was scheduled until dinnertime. Who was here?

She walked slowly to the threshold of the family room.

Jasper stood beside a console table behind the couch. A big vase of red roses, a box of chocolates and a wrapped gift weren't there the last time she'd been in here.

"Finley let me in," Jasper said.

He must have arrived just after she'd gone to the stable. Finley had left after her.

"What are you doing here?"

"What do you think I'm doing here?"

Sadie walked farther into the room, inspecting the

chocolates in a heart-shaped box. So traditional for such an untraditional man. Apprehension tamed her enthusiasm over seeing him.

She stopped at the console to admire the beautiful roses. "Is this an apology?"

"No, but it could be a peace offering."

Opening the box of chocolates, she lifted one and put it into her mouth. Caramel and chocolate tickled her taste buds.

"I came to my senses after Kaelyn's twin sister came to see me."

Sadie turned to him, pausing with another piece of chocolate in her hand. Kaelyn had a twin? How had he come to his senses?

"When Kendra told me she was Kaelyn's twin sister and presented evidence that Kaelyn might have been killed by another man she was seeing, everything became so clear."

"What became clear?"

He moved toward her. "You. Me." He stopped right before her. "The baby."

"Kaelyn was murdered?"

"She was sleeping with another man the same time she carried on with me," he said. "She loved me but now I see she didn't love me the way two people should. I also see I didn't love her. I loved the excitement, and so did she. Except her playing around may have gotten her into some trouble. I don't know if she was murdered or not. I put Kendra in touch with another detective. I'm through with that part of my life. I don't blame myself for Kaelyn's death anymore. Kendra gave me that when she came to see me. I can finally put that behind me. I can stop chasing excitement to take the place of a real relationship."

He put his hands on her upper arms.

Sadie's head reeled with what he declared. And then she realized she'd done her own soul-searching while he was away.

"I've come to some conclusions myself," she said.

"Yeah?" He grinned.

"I can stop running now. I don't have to be afraid anymore. Darien is gone. He will never be able to hurt me again. And just because he did doesn't mean I have to let that get in the way of something good… of someone good."

Him.

"That's fantastic news because I have something I need to ask you." Moving back, he reached into his pant pocket and retrieved something he had in his hand. "Now, I took your personality into consideration when I went looking for this."

Sadie let her held breath go. He didn't…

"I found a special store that makes one-of-a-kind jewelry." As he said the last he opened his palm to reveal the most stunning ring she'd ever seen. Perched on a white gold band, a sunburst halo made of blue sapphires surrounded a big center diamond.

"It's beautiful."

She felt like a princess in her own timeless fairy tale as he lifted her left hand and slid the ring onto her ring finger. It fit perfectly. How did he know?

"Must be meant to be," he said.

With her heart bursting with love and joy, she threw her arms around him and kissed his mouth.

"When do you want to get married?" he asked between smooches.

"As soon as we can plan it. Before I get huge." She kissed him longer this time, then followed that with more quick ones.

"Are you going to invite your dad?" he asked.

She stopped kissing him. She didn't want to invite him, but he had seemed to try to improve their relationship the last time she'd seen him.

"I think you should. Being a grandfather might mellow him out."

"Maybe." She'd talk to her mother.

Her life seemed so different now. It was different. Change for the better. She'd dreamed of a life like this before she'd met Darien. Now she felt she had a real shot at the dream. She intended to live this gift to the fullest. And be thankful every day for Jasper. He brought her this joy.

* * * * *

If you loved this novel, don't miss other suspenseful titles by Jennifer Morey:

TAMING DEPUTY HARLOW
COLD CASE RECRUIT
JUSTICE HUNTER
A WANTED MAN

Available now from Harlequin Romantic Suspense!

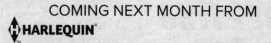

SPECIAL EXCERPT FROM

H HARLEQUIN®

ROMANTIC suspense

*After giving up her son as a surrogate,
PI Adeline Winters must work with Jeremy Kincaid, her
baby's father, to save their son from a vengeful kidnapper—
who might be Livia Colton herself!*

Read on for a sneak preview of
MISSION: COLTON JUSTICE
by **Jennifer Morey**, *the next book in*
THE COLTONS OF SHADOW CREEK *continuity.*

"So, why you? Why Jamie?"

"Not everyone is rich like me," he said. "That would narrow down her options."

"You suspect Livia because she had a reason to despise Tess, but other than her nefarious character, I don't see enough to suspect her."

"If Livia survived that accident, she's desperate. Desperate people do desperate things."

Adeline nodded, folding her arms. "Desperation is valid." All this depended on Livia having survived the accident.

She went to the bookshelf along a side wall of the family room, where an electronic frame switched through several photos. Most included Jamie. His adorable, smiling face and bright blue eyes spoke of a happy boy. The pictures of Tess haunted her. She felt at odds falling for Tess's husband, especially knowing how much Tess had loved him. Although now Adeline questioned that love. If Tess had approached

Oscar with a proposal to start up their affair again, could she have loved Jeremy as much as she'd claimed?

Jeremy reached to the photo frame and pressed a button to stop its cycling. Adeline didn't realize he'd followed her across the room until then. He'd moved closer and she felt his warmth. She also sensed his absorption with one photo, in which Jamie must have been about two. He sat at a picnic table with a cake before him, and what looked like half his piece covering his face around his mouth. He smiled big.

"That was the first time he was really happy."

After Tess died.

"He had all his friends over. I set up an inflatable bounce house in the backyard and gave him his first tricycle for his present."

Adeline stared at Jamie's playful face and felt a surge of love. She'd helped to create such an angel. Now that angel was in the hands of someone evil, and they might not ever get him back. He could be killed. He could be dead already.

Unable to suppress the sting of tears, she turned to Jeremy for comfort. "Oh, Jeremy."

Jeremy took her into his arms. His hands rubbed her back, slow, sensual and firm. Then he pressed a kiss on her head. She felt his warm breath on her hair and scalp. With her arms under his and hands on his back, she snuggled closer, resting the side of her head on his chest.

"We'll find him," he said.

Don't miss
MISSION: COLTON JUSTICE by Jennifer Morey,
available October 2017 wherever
Harlequin® Romantic Suspense books
and ebooks are sold.

www.Harlequin.com

Love the Harlequin book you just read?

Your opinion matters.

Review this book on your favorite
book site, review site, blog or your own
social media properties and share
your opinion with other readers!

Be sure to connect with us at:
Harlequin.com/Newsletters
Facebook.com/HarlequinBooks
Twitter.com/HarlequinBooks

LOVE
Harlequin
romance?

Join our Harlequin community to share your thoughts and connect with other romance readers!

Be the first to find out about promotions, news, and exclusive content!

Sign up for the Harlequin e-newsletter and download a free book from any series at

www.TryHarlequin.com

CONNECT WITH US AT:

Harlequin.com/Community

Facebook.com/HarlequinBooks

Twitter.com/HarlequinBooks

Instagram.com/HarlequinBooks

Pinterest.com/HarlequinBooks

ReaderService.com

**ROMANCE WHEN
YOU NEED IT**

HSOCIAL2017

THE WORLD IS BETTER WITH

Romance

Harlequin has everything from contemporary, passionate and heartwarming to suspenseful and inspirational stories.

Whatever your mood, we have a romance just for you!

Connect with us to find your next great read, special offers and more.

f /HarlequinBooks

@HarlequinBooks

www.HarlequinBlog.com

www.Harlequin.com/Newsletters

HARLEQUIN®

A *Romance* FOR EVERY MOOD™

www.Harlequin.com